SANDOKAN

The Pirates of Malaysia

SANDOKAN

The Pirates of Malaysia

Emilio Salgari

Translated by Nico Lorenzutti

ROH
PRESS

Sandokan: The Pirates of Malaysia
By Emilio Salgari
Original Title: *I pirati della Malesia*
First published in Italian in 1896
Translated from the Italian by Nico Lorenzutti

ROH Press
First paperback edition
Copyright © 2007 by Nico Lorenzutti

For information address:
info@rohpress.com

Visit our website at
www.rohpress.com

Cover design: Nico Lorenzutti

Special thanks to Felice Pozzo and Hanna Ahtonen for their invaluable advice.

ISBN: 978-0-9782707-3-5

Printed in the United States of America

Contents

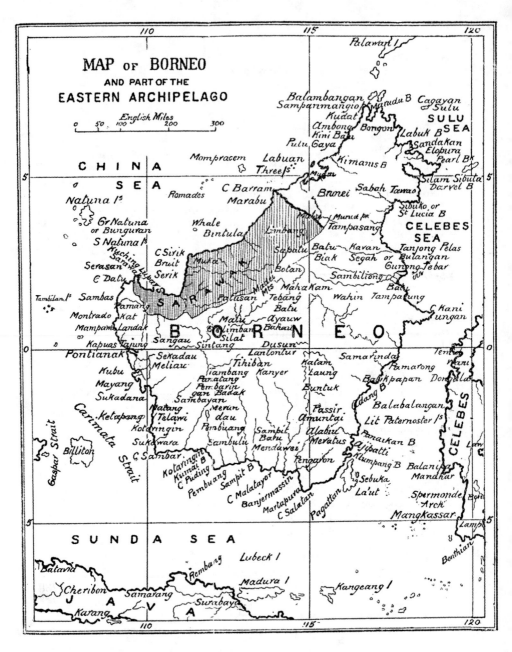

Map adapted from:

The Expedition to Borneo of H.M. Dido for the Suppression of Piracy: With Extracts from the Journal of James Brooke, Esq., of Sarawak

by Admiral of the Fleet Henry Keppel, GCB, OM

Part I

The Tiger of Malaysia

Chapter 1
The *Young India*

"Mister Williams, where are we?"

"In the heart of Malaysia, my dear Kammamuri."

"How much longer before we reach our destination?"

"Bored, are you?"

"No, just in a great hurry; the *Young India*'s barely moving."

Mister Williams, a forty-year-old American sailor, just over five feet tall, looked at his companion in dismay. The man in question was a tall, dark Indian about twenty-four or twenty-five years of age, with noble, almost refined features, naked to the waist, save for his earrings and several gold neck-rings that rested gracefully above his broad chest.

"What!?!" the American cried out indignantly. "Barely moving? That's an insult, my good Maratha."

"For those in a hurry, Mister Williams, a cruiser flying at fifteen knots would be advancing at a crawl."

"By the devil, why such haste?" asked the quartermaster, scratching his head. "Off to collect an inheritance?"

"Hardly! If you knew..."

"Well then, don't keep me in the dark, young man..."

"Pardon? The wind makes it hard for me to hear..."

"Ah, playing deaf now, are we? You're hiding something that much is obvious! That young woman with you... "

"Back to my original question, Mister Williams. When are we going to reach port!?"

"Which port, my friend?"

"Sarawak."

1

"It's up to Fate. You never know what can happen at sea. A typhoon could come bearing down upon us at any moment; or a gang of pirates could board our ship and send us to the devil with a kris between our ribs and two lengths of rope round our necks."

"There be pirates in these waters?" smirked the Indian.

"You'd best believe it. And they're every bit as dangerous as those stranglers you have in India."

"Really?"

"Look over there, towards the bowsprit. What do you see?"

"An island."

"It's teeming with pirates. That's Mompracem, my friend. Makes me shiver just saying the name."

"Why's that?"

"That little patch of land is home to a man that's bloodied the waters of Malaysia. Have you ever heard speak of Sandokan?"

"No."

"Sandokan, the Tiger of Malaysia, and the name isn't given lightly. He's ferocious, merciless! If we fell into his hands, he'd slay us without a second thought."

"And the British haven't moved to crush him?" asked the Indian, surprised.

"Destroying the Tigers of Mompracem is no easy feat," replied the sailor. "Back in 1850, the British assembled a powerful fleet and stormed the island. They captured the Tiger after a tremendous battle, but before they could reach Labuan, the pirate mysteriously escaped."

"And returned to Mompracem?"

"No. For two years there wasn't so much as a peep out of him, he'd vanished from these waters, but then a few months ago he reappeared at the head of a new band of pirates, Malays and Dyaks, fearless to a man. After slaughtering the handful of British colonists fool enough to settle in his former lair, he retook his island and began to rove the sea once more."

A whistle sounded from the bridge, as a gust of wind rattled the masts.

2

"Uh oh!" said Mister Williams, quickly raising his head. "Looks like things are about to take a turn for the worse."

"What do you mean?" the Indian asked nervously.

"See those dark clouds? They sure don't mean clear sailing."

"Are we in danger?"

"The *Young India*'s a solid ship; she's weathered many a storm. Now, to work, the sea's getting restless."

Mister Williams had not been mistaken. The water had turned leaden and the sea, until then as smooth as glass, had begun to toss and roll.

In the east, towards the large island of Borneo, an enormous cloud as black as tar slowly shrouded the setting sun. Albatross cried out nervously as they flitted about the climbing waves.

A dead calm followed that first gust of wind; claps of thunder rumbled in the east, filling the sailors with apprehension.

"Clear the deck!" bellowed Captain MacClintock, gesturing for the passengers to be taken below.

Everyone reluctantly obeyed, going down through the hatches along the bow and stern. One man, however, had remained behind, the Indian Kammamuri.

"I said clear the deck!" thundered the captain.

"Captain," said the Maratha, advancing determinedly, "Are we in danger?"

"You'll know once the storm has passed."

"I have to get to Sarawak, Captain."

"And you will, provided we don't sink."

"I have to get to Sarawak! It's important!"

"Mister Williams, get this man out of here! I have no time for this."

The Indian was dragged away and forced down the nearest hatch. A strong wind blew from the east, roaring through the ship's rigging. Thunder rumbled incessantly as the black cloud stretched across the sky.

The *Young India* was a magnificent three-masted schooner that bore her fifteen years well. Her light but solid construction, her enormous sails, her strong keel, reminded one of those daring blockade runners that were to play an almost legendary role in the American Civil War.

She had set sail from Calcutta on the 26th of August 1852, bearing a cargo of iron rails for Sarawak. She carried fourteen sailors, two officers and six passengers; blessed by favourable winds she had arrived in Malay waters in less than thirteen days, or more precisely, she had arrived within sight of the dreaded island of Mompracem, home to the fiercest pirates in the South China Sea.

By eight, they were in almost total darkness. The sun had disappeared behind the clouds, and the wind roared with ever-increasing intensity. The sea raged about them; mammoth swells collided and disappeared in a spray of foam as enormous waves broke against the shores of Mompracem, its sinister mass looming menacingly before them.

The *Young India* raced forward, pitching over the waves, hurtling into troughs and climbing mountains of water, her masts tearing at the clouds.

Barefoot, faces drawn, their hair whipped by the wind, the sailors grumbled as they went about their tasks. The scuppers could not keep pace, and the decks streamed with water, making each manoeuvre more difficult. Commands and curses mixed with the cries of the storm.

By nine, the three-master, tossed about like a toy, had arrived in the waters off Mompracem.

Mister Williams held the wheel with all his strength, but despite his efforts, the *Young India* was dragged so close to the reefs and shoals ringing the island, the crew feared she would be dashed to pieces.

Much to his horror, Captain MacClintock sighted several fires burning along the shore. A flash of lightning illuminated a tall man standing at the edge of an immense cliff that towered over the sea. Arms crossed, he stood motionless as the elements swirled violently about him.

The man's eyes flared like burning coals and were fixed upon him strangely. For a moment it appeared to the captain that the man had waved in friendship, but he could not tell for certain, for darkness returned within seconds, and a gust of wind quickly tore the *Young India* away.

"May the Good Lord save us!" exclaimed Mister Williams, who had also sighted the man. "That was the Tiger of Malaysia."

His voice was stifled by a powerful clap of thunder, the start of a deafening symphony. The heavens erupted in flames, bathing the storm-tossed sea in a sinister light. Lightning streaked the air in a thousand patterns, tearing through the sky, darting about the ship and slicing beneath the waves, as frightening roars filled the air.

The sea, as if not to be outdone, swelled to enormous heights. Waves grew into mountains, sparkling gold in the light, as they climbed towards the heavens. The wind, too, added its voice, roaring furiously as it drove clouds of warm rain across the sky.

Pitching wildly, the *Young India* battled fiercely to stay ahead of the elements. She groaned beneath the onslaught of waves; she climbed, she dove, thrashing the waters with her bowsprit, as she was dragged north, then south, against her helmsman's will.

There were times when the crew thought the ship had began to sink, so large were the waves rushing over the decimated bulwarks. Then, without warning, the harsh north wind shifted and began to blow her towards the east.

The ship could resist no longer. To sail against the typhoon was sure death. Though the crew had not sighted so much as a trace of land in the west, except for the dreaded shores of Mompracem, Captain Mac-Clintock had to acknowledge defeat and attempt to escape with all the speed the *Young India* could muster from her few remaining sails.

Two hours had passed since the ship had tacked about; however, the waves had not relented, as if determined to sink her.

The lightning storm had almost passed, only a few flashes appeared from time to time; the darkness had grown so thick the crew could see no more than two hundred paces before them. Suddenly, a menacing roar reached the captain's ear.

"Look off the bow!" he thundered, his voice booming over the wind and waves.

"Reefs!" yelled a voice.

Captain MacClintock rushed towards the bow, grabbed onto the fore-stay and climbed up onto what remained of the bulwarks.

Though all was dark and the wind howled about him, the roar of the backwash was unmistakable. There could be no doubt. A chain of rocks stood a few cable lengths from his ship, perhaps an extension of the reefs that defended Mompracem.

"Ready to tack!" he cried.

Mister Williams gathered his strength and pulled mightily on the wheel. Almost simultaneously, the ship struck something hard.

The collision, however, had little effect. Only a small part of the false keel had been torn away by the reef. The wind continued to blow them east as waves pushed the vessel forward.

Despite the danger, the crew managed to maintain an extraordinary sangfroid and perform the manoeuvre. The *Young India* came about, tacked two hundred meters and escaped from the perilous waters. For a moment it appeared all would end well. The sounding line had been cast immediately and measured a depth of fourteen fathoms off the bow.

Thoughts of salvation had begun to spread among the crew, when, suddenly, the sound of backwash thundered before the boom.

The sea swelled with even greater violence, signalling a new danger.

"Helm hard up, Bill!" thundered Captain MacClintock.

"Reef below bow!" yelled a sailor that had gone down to the bowsprit.

His warning did not reach the stern. A mountain of water thundered down upon the starboard side of the three-masted vessel, knocking her violently to port, dragging down the crewmen that had been clinging to the braces and smashing the lifeboats against the winch.

There was a formidable roar followed by the sound of splintering wood as a sudden collision shook the masts from bow to stern.

Crashing against the reef, the *Young India* had been gutted with one blow; six sailors, torn from the ship by the waves, had been tossed against the rocks.

Chapter 2
The Pirates of Malaysia

The final hour had sounded for the unfortunate *Young India*. Wedged between two rocks, her frame torn, her keel shattered, she was little more than wreckage soon to be scattered by the waves.

Rumbling incessantly, the sea bubbled furiously about the ship, smashing her repeatedly against the reef, dragging away lifeboats and sections of the bulwarks, frame, and deck, tossing them about with a loud roar.

Aboard her, the survivors, mad with terror, ran from bow to stern, looking for shelter, yelling, cursing, and praying for help. One sailor scrambled up the ratlines, another attempted to reach the crow's nest, while a third sought refuge upon the crosslets. Some raced about haphazardly, praying to the lord and the Madonna, as others tried to don the nearest life preserver, or grab hold of anything that could float, as they prepared for the vessel to wrench apart.

Captain MacClintock and Mister Williams, who had been through worse, were the only two that managed to retain their composure. Realizing that the three-master would not break free, they rushed below deck. Any last hope of setting sail was quickly dashed; the hold was full of water.

"Poor darlin'," said Mister Williams, moved by the scene before him, "she's breathed her last!"

"I'm afraid so, Bill," replied the captain, even more shaken than his quartermaster. "This'll be the *Young India's* final resting place."

"What'll we do?"

"We'll have to wait 'til dawn."

"Think she'll weather the storm?"

"We can only hope. The reef cut through her frame like an axe. I doubt she'll come free."

"We should inform the crew. They're scared half to death."

The two old salts went back up on deck. The sailors and the passengers, their faces twisted in terror, rushed upon them; anxiously showering them with questions.

"Is it over?" asked some.

"Are we sinking?" asked others.

"Are we going to survive?"

"Where are we?"

"First, we must remain calm," said the captain. "There's nothing to fear."

Kammamuri immediately stepped forward.

"Captain," he asked calmly, "Can we still make it to Sarawak?"

"I'm afraid that's impossible, Kammamuri. The *Young India* will never leave this reef."

"My master is there, Captain."

"He'll have to wait."

The Indian's face grew sullen.

"May Kali protect him," he murmured.

"All is not yet lost, Kammamuri," said the captain.

"We're not going to sink?"

"Not as long as we keep our heads. Come dawn, we'll get our bearings and assess our situation."

The captain's words appeared to sooth the troubled spirits of the crew, and they began to hope in the possibility of rescue. Those that had begun making rafts abandoned their work; those that had climbed up the masts, after a brief hesitation, slid back down. Order soon returned to the deck of the shipwrecked vessel.

The sea continued to rage. Giant waves attacked the reefs, crashing down upon them with frightening noise. Pounded from bow to stern, the *Young India* groaned helplessly as the remains of her bulwarks and shattered keel were swept away. Sometimes she would shake so strongly the crew feared she would be torn from the reef and dragged in among the waves. Fortunately, she held fast, and the crew, despite the imminent danger, managed to grab a few hours sleep.

At four in the morning, the sky began to clear in the east. The sun rose with the rapidity common to the tropics, its arrival heralded by a magnificent red sky. The captain, standing in the crow's nest on the mainmast, Mister Williams at his side, kept his eyes fixed northwards, where he had sighted a dark mass less than two miles away.

"Well, Captain," said the quartermaster, angrily chewing some tobacco, "Recognize that bit of land?"

"I believe so. It's still dark, but... see those reefs?... There's no mistaking it, that's Mompracem."

"Great God!" murmured the American, grimacing. "What a bad place for a wreck."

"Looks like it, Bill."

"Call it what it is, Captain; a pirates' lair. The Tiger of Malaysia has returned."

"What!?!" exclaimed MacClintock, starting slightly. "The Tiger of Malaysia is back on Mompracem?"

"Yes."

"That's impossible, Bill! It's been almost two years since that scoundrel disappeared."

"He's back, I tell you. Four months ago, he attacked the _Arghadah_, and she just barely escaped after a gruelling battle. A sailor that had fought against the bloody pirate once before, told me he had spotted him on the bow of a prahu."

"Then we're done for. He'll attack us."

"By God!" yelled the master, suddenly turning pale.

"What's the matter?"

"Look, Captain! Look over there!"

"Prahus, prahus!" yelled a voice from the bridge.

Having turned as pale his quartermaster, the captain cast his eyes towards the island and sighted four large Malay prahus rounding a cape just three miles from them. Light, trim, and low keeled, the ships flew over the waters with surprising speed, their large sails bulging with wind.

9

The captain immediately recognized them for what they were: pirates! With a few words, he quickly informed the crew of the new danger; stubborn resistance was their only hope.

Unfortunately, the ship's armoury was not well stocked. There were no cannons, and though they carried enough rifles to arm the crew, most were in disrepair. There were, however, several boarding sabres, slightly rusted, but still serviceable, a few carbines, a few revolvers and a good number of axes.

Having armed themselves as best they could, the sailors and the passengers rushed towards the stern, which now, underwater, would likely be the boarding point. The American flag rose majestically to the peak of the mainsail, and Mister Williams nailed it in place. They would fight to the death.

The four Malay prahus continued to advance rapidly. Now no more than seven or eight hundred paces away, they prepared to attack the poor three-master with all their might.

The sun was rising on the horizon, allowing those aboard the *Young India* to clearly make out their attackers.

There were eighty or ninety of them, bold, well-built men, naked to the waist and drawn from the various tribes of Asia: Bugis, Macassars and Javanese, olive skinned Malays, handsome Dyaks with copper bracelets adorning their limbs, and several Chinese, their shaven heads distinguishing them even from that distance.

They were armed with stupendous silver carbines inlaid with mother-of-pearl, large parangs, scimitars, poisoned krises, and kampilangs, huge cudgels they wielded like sticks. Weapons waving menacingly, that vast legion of men kept their eyes fixed upon the *Young India*, filling the air with ferocious cries to frighten those aboard her.

When the vessels were four hundred meters away, a cannon blast thundered from the first prahu. A cannonball smashed the bowsprit, splitting it in half and plunging its tip into the sea.

"Take heart, men," thundered Captain MacClintock. "Fire a broadside!"

Several rifle blasts followed that command. Ferocious cries emanated from aboard the prahus, a sure sign the lead had not gone to waste.

"Well done!" yelled Mister Williams. "Those wretches won't have the courage to attack us. Ready! Fire!"

His voice was stifled by a series of formidable discharges. The pirates had begun their attack.

The four prahus began to smoulder as they unleashed a relentless rain of iron. Cannons, firelocks, and carbines fired in unison, smashing, felling, and destroying everything in their path with mathematical precision.

In less than an instant, four castaways lay lifelessly on deck. The foremast, severed beneath the crow's nest, came crashing down, dragging yardarms, sails and cables along with it. Triumphant cheers gave way to groans of agony and cries of fear. Retaliation was impossible; that hurricane of steel was destroying the ship with frightening speed.

Realizing that all was lost, the castaways emptied their muskets and fled towards starboard, attempting to take shelter behind what was left of the lifeboats. Many had been hit, and cries of agony filled the air as blood poured from their wounds.

Less than fifteen minutes later, with cannon fire covering their advance, the pirates arrived beneath the vessel's stern and prepared to board it.

Captain MacClintock and three other men immediately rushed to repel the attack, but a volley of grapeshot stopped them in their tracks.

A terrible cry filled the air, "Hurrah for the Tiger of Malaysia!"

The pirates threw down their carbines, picked up their scimitars, axes, clubs and krises and began to board, grabbing onto the bulwarks, backstays and ratlines. Several had rushed to the peak of the prahus' masts, running along the yardarms before diving onto the rigging of the threemaster and sliding down onto her deck. In an instant, the few remaining defenders, now outnumbered, fell along the bow, stern, quarterdeck and forecastle.

Only one man remained alive, standing by the mainmast, armed with a heavy, wide-bladed boarding sabre. Defending himself with the courage of a lion, the Indian Kammamuri hacked away at the onslaught of enemy weapons, striking blows in all directions.

"Help! Help!" the poor man howled hoarsely as he fell to the ground.

"Stop!" thundered a voice. "Quarter to the brave. That Indian is a warrior."

Chapter 3
The Tiger of Malaysia

The man that had shouted those life-saving words appeared to be between 32 and 35 years of age. He was tall, with white skin, fine aristocratic features, and light blue eyes. A black moustache lined his smiling lips. He was dressed with extreme elegance: a large hat of Manila hemp, a brown velvet jacket with gold buttons, brocaded pants, and long boots of red leather. A large sash of blue silk was wrapped about his waist. A magnificent Indian carbine was slung over his shoulder, and a scimitar with a hilt of gold, inlaid with a diamond as large as a walnut, hung from his side.

He gestured for the pirates to make way then advanced towards the Indian, who had not yet even thought of standing up, such was his surprise at finding himself still alive. He looked the man over for several minutes, carefully taking in every detail.

"So, what do you have to say for yourself, young man?" he asked happily.

"What?..." exclaimed Kammamuri, surprised at finding a European in command of those ruthless pirates.

"Surprised to be alive?"

"It seems like a miracle."

"There's no doubt of that, young man."

"Why did you spare me?" the Indian asked.

"Well, you aren't white for starters."

"You hate whites?"

"Yes."

"Aren't you white?"

"Good Lord, I'm pure-blooded Portuguese!"

13

"I don't understand, then why do you..."

"Stop there, young man; don't ask for an explanation."

"So be it. Well then, why did you spare me?"

"Because you're a warrior, and, I admire warriors."

"I'm a Maratha," said the Indian proudly.

"A noble race. I have an offer for you: care to join us?"

"Me? A pirate!"

"Why not? By Jupiter! You'd be great."

"If I were to refuse?"

"I'd no longer be responsible for your head."

"Well then, consider me part of your crew."

"Good man. Hey, Kotta, see if you can find a bottle of whiskey. Americans always keep a good supply on board."

A Malay, about five feet tall, with strong, powerful arms, went down into the cabin of the late Captain MacClintock and returned minutes later with a couple of glasses and a dust covered bottle.

"Whiskey," said Yanez, reading the label. "These Americans are truly men of taste."

He poured two glasses, offered one to the Indian and asked, "What's your name?"

"Kammamuri."

"To your health, Kammamuri."

"To yours, Mr. ..."

"Yanez."

They gulped down the drinks in one shot.

"Now, young man," said Yanez, always in good cheer, "time to pay a visit to Captain Sandokan."

"Who?"

"Good Lord! The Tiger of Malaysia."

"You're going to take me to him?"

"Certainly, my friend, he'll be more than happy to receive a Maratha. Let's go, Kammamuri."

The Indian did not move. He appeared slightly embarrassed. He cast his eyes upon the pirates then focused them upon the stern.

"What's the matter?" asked Yanez.

"Sir..." said the Maratha uncertainly. "I have a favour to ask."

"Ask away, my friend."

"There's a woman with me."

"A woman! White or Indian?"

"White."

"Where is she?"

"Hiding below in the hold."

"Bring her up on deck."

"You promise no harm will come to her?"

"You have my word."

"Thank you, sir," said the Maratha, deeply moved.

He ran to the stern and disappeared through the hatch. A few minutes later, he was back on the bridge.

"Where is she?" asked Yanez.

"She'll be here shortly. Do not speak to her, sir; she's mad."

"Mad! Who is she?"

"Here she is!" exclaimed Kammamuri.

The Portuguese turned towards the stern.

Wrapped in a large white silk cape, a woman of exquisite beauty had suddenly emerged from the hold and halted near the base of the mizzenmast.

She was around fifteen years old, elegant, attractive and graceful with delicate, rosy skin, large black eyes, and a small thin nose. Her lips were as red as coral and bore a charming smile that revealed small white teeth. Her hair was parted in the front by a clip studded with large diamonds and fell to her shoulders in a shower of midnight curls that reached all the way to her waist. Her eyes swept over those armed men and the bodies strewn among the wreckage, but not a trace of fear upset her gentle features.

"Who is she?" asked Yanez, clutching Kammamuri by the arm, his voice a hoarse whisper.

"My mistress," replied the Maratha. "The Guardian of the Temple of the East."

The young woman did not move. Yanez took several steps towards her and studied her fixedly.

"What a resemblance!" he exclaimed, turning pale.

He quickly returned towards Kammamuri, grabbed his arm once again and whispered, "Is she English?"

"She was born in India to English parents."

"How did she get like that?"

"It's a long story."

"You'll tell it to the Tiger of Malaysia. Time to set sail, my good Maratha. Men, strip this vessel of her valuables then set her ablaze."

Kammamuri approached the madwoman, took her by the hand and led her into the Portuguese man's prahu; she did not offer the least bit of resistance, nor did she utter a single word.

"Let's go," said Yanez, as he took hold of the rudder.

The waters had calmed, but at times a few large waves still broke upon the reef. Guided by those skilled, intrepid sailors, the prahu sailed past the rocks, bouncing about the swells like a rubber ball, sailing off with fantastic speed, her bright wake lighting the playground of several enormous sharks.

In less than ten minutes, she had reached the furthest point of the island, rounded it without reducing speed then headed towards a large bay. Twenty sturdy longhouses lined the shore, protected by tall palisades, deep moats bristling with spears, and a triple line of trenches equipped with large cannons and numerous firelocks.

A hundred and fifty Malays, naked to the waist and armed to the teeth, came out of the trenches and rushed towards the shore, filling the air with savage cries as they waved their axes, pikes, krises, scimitars, carbines and pistols.

"Where are we?" asked Kammamuri uneasily.

"This is our village," replied the Portuguese.

"Is this where the Tiger of Malaysia lives?"

"See that red flag? He lives up there."

The Maratha raised his head. Atop a giant cliff that towered over the sea, stood a large hut defended by thick, sturdy walls. A large red flag emblazoned with the head of a tiger fluttered majestically from its rooftop.

"Are we going up there?" he asked nervously.

"Yes, my friend," replied Yanez.

"How will he receive me?"

"In the manner becoming a warrior."

"Will my mistress be accompanying us?"

"Not just yet."

"Why not?"

"Because she resembles..."

He fell silent. A strong emotion had suddenly altered his features, and his eyes had grown damp. Kammamuri noticed the change.

"You seem upset, Señor Yanez," he said.

"You're mistaken," replied the Portuguese, pulling the rudder towards him to avoid the reef. "We're here, Kammamuri."

The prahu dropped anchor, her bow pointing towards the shore.

The Portuguese, Kammamuri, the madwoman and the pirates disembarked.

"Take this woman to the most beautiful hut in the village," said Yanez, assigning the Guardian to the pirates.

"They won't harm her, will they?" asked Kammamuri.

"No one would dare touch her," said Yanez. "On this island, women are respected far more than they are in India, perhaps even more so than in Europe. Come, my friend."

They headed towards the immense cliff and went up narrow steps cut into the rock, passing sentries armed with carbines and scimitars.

"Why so many precautions?" asked Kammamuri.

"The Tiger of Malaysia has a hundred thousand enemies."

"Do the men not love their captain?"

"We idolize him, but others... if you knew how the British hate him, Kammamuri. Here we are. Do not show fear."

They had arrived before the great hut, an imposing structure defended by numerous moats, trenches, gabions, cannons, mortars and firelocks. The Portuguese cautiously pushed against a large door of teak wood strong enough to withstand a cannon blast, and lead Kammamuri into a room carpeted with red silk, cluttered with axes, daggers, European carbines, Malay krises, Turkish jatangs, lace, cloth, bottles, majolicas from China and Japan, bars of silver, piles of gold, and vases overflowing with pearls and diamonds.

In the midst of all that chaos, Kammamuri spotted a man dressed in sumptuous robes of silk and gold, lying on a rich Persian rug in the centre of the room.

He could not have been more than thirty-two or thirty-three years of age. He was tall, well built, with a handsome bronzed face and thick black wavy hair that fell freely about his strong shoulders. He had a high forehead, sparkling eyes, and thin lips that bore an indefinable smile. A magnificent beard gave his features a proud look that inspired fear and respect. One could tell at first glance that he possessed the ferocity of a tiger and the strength of a giant.

When the two men entered the hut, he sat up and fixed a piercing look upon them.

"What news do you bring me?" he asked a slight quiver in his metallic voice.

"Victory," replied the Portuguese, "and a captive."

The pirate's brow darkened, and he fell silent.

"Is this the man you spared?" he asked after a few minutes had passed.

"Yes, Sandokan. Does it displease you?"

"You know I have the greatest respect for your whims, my friend."

"I know, Tiger of Malaysia. This man wishes to join us. I saw him fight, he's a warrior."

The Tiger's eyes flashed as the wrinkles vanished from his brow.

"Approach," he said, addressing the Indian.

Kammamuri, still shocked to be standing before the legendary pirate that had bloodied the waters of Malaysia for so many years, stepped forward.

"Your name?" asked the Tiger.

"Kammamuri."

"And you are?"

"A Maratha."

"A warrior."

"Yes, Tiger of Malaysia," said the Indian proudly.

"Why did you leave your country?"

"I have to get to Sarawak."

"The land of that dog, James Brooke?" asked the Tiger, not hiding his hatred.

"I do not know this James Brooke."

"So much the better. What takes you to Sarawak then?"

"My master."

"And what does he do? Is he one of the rajah's soldiers?"

"No, he's the rajah's prisoner."

"Prisoner? Why?"

The Indian did not reply.

"Tell me your story," said the pirate. "There are no secrets among my men."

"It will require some time, it's a long story."

"So much the better, sit down and tell your tale."

Chapter 4
Kammamuri's Tale

Kammamuri did not wait to be asked a second time. He sat down upon a pile of velvet cushions, collected his thoughts and asked, "Tiger of Malaysia, have you ever heard speak of the Sundarbans?"

"An area along the delta of the Ganges," replied the pirate, "I've never been there, but I can imagine what it's like."

"It's a vast place, crisscrossed by rivers, teeming with swamps, islands, and sandbanks. Ferocious animals lurk behind every tree. My master was born there, in an area known as the Black Jungle. Strong and handsome, he was the bravest man I'd ever known. He feared nothing, not the poison of a hooded cobra, not the prodigious strength of a python or the claws of the great Bengal Tiger, not even the nooses of his enemies."

"His name?" asked the pirate.

"Tremal-Naik, hunter of tigers and serpents in the Black Jungle."

The Tiger of Malaysia jumped to his feet and fixed his eyes upon the Maratha.

"A Tiger hunter?" he asked. "It takes great courage to face a tiger. I like this man already. Continue."

"One night, Tremal-Naik was returning from the jungle. It was a magnificent evening, a true Bengali evening; the air was sweet, the sun had set and stars had just begun to appear in the sky. He had walked a long way without encountering a soul, when suddenly a vision of incredible beauty appeared in a mussenda bush less than twenty paces before him."

"A vision?"

"A young woman with dark black hair, pale skin, and lovely eyes. She gave him a melancholy look then disappeared. Though she had appeared for only an instant, Tremal-Naik was thunderstruck; it was love at first sight. A few days later one of our men was murdered on Rajmangal, an island not too far from our hut. He had tracked a tiger to its shores and was found dead with dark marks around his neck."

"Oh!" exclaimed the pirate, surprised. "Who could have strangled a tiger hunter?"

"Patience, sir, all will be revealed. As I've said, Tremal-Naik was a brave man. We went to investigate and landed on Rajmangal at midnight, determined to avenge our unlucky companion. At first all was quiet, but then mysterious sounds began to emanate from underground, and suddenly, several men emerged from the trunk of an immense banyan tree, their chests marked by bizarre tattoos. We soon discovered they were our poor friend's assassins."

"Well?" asked the pirate, his eyes shining joyfully.

"Tremal-Naik did not hesitate. A blast from his carbine felled their leader and covered our escape."

"Well done, Tremal-Naik!" the Tiger exclaimed enthusiastically. "Continue. What a great story! It's more entertaining than a boarding raid."

"My master decided it best to separate to confuse our pursuers. He took refuge in a large pagoda where he found... any guesses?"

"The young woman?"

"Yes, the young woman. Those men had been keeping her prisoner."

"Did you find out who they were?"

"Thugs, Indian stranglers that worship the Goddess Kali. They honour her with constant human sacrifice."

"Fearless men. I know them well," said the pirate. "I had a few among my men."

"Thugs among your men?" exclaimed the Maratha, shuddering. "I'm done for."

"Do not fear, Kammamuri, that was long ago. Continue your tale."

"The young woman had fallen in love with my master, and aware of the danger he ran, she urged him to take flight, but he was not a man that frightened easily. He remained there and awaited the Thugs, determined to fight them, and, if possible, escape with the prisoner. But alas...

he had placed too much confidence in his own strength. It was not long before twelve stranglers entered the pagoda and attacked. Despite his stubborn resistance, he was captured, thrown to the ground, tied up and stabbed by their leader, the merciless Suyodhana."

"And he did not die?" asked Sandokan, his interest increasing with every word.

"No," continued Kammamuri, "He did not die. A short while later I found him in the middle of the jungle, bleeding, the dagger still embedded in his chest, but very much alive."

"Why had they tossed him in the jungle?" asked Yanez.

"So the tigers could dispose of his body. I brought him back to our hut and after a great deal of care, he managed to heal, but his heart remained wounded by that young woman's eyes... Once he regained his strength, we embarked for Rajmangal, determined to free his beloved. We waited for darkness, sailed down the Mangal and landed on the island. The banyan tree was unguarded; we found the secret entrance and descended into their lair, making our way forward through dark tunnels. We had learned that the Thugs, having failed to quell the love the young woman had for Tremal-Naik, had decided to burn her alive, to appease the ire of their deity. We ran to her rescue."

"Why was she forbidden to fall in love?" asked Yanez.

"As Guardian of Kali's Sacred Temple she had to remain pure."

"What scoundrels!"

"Having made our way through long tunnels and slain whatever sentries appeared before us, we arrived in a vast cavern filled with a hundred columns, lit by infinite lamps. Two hundred Indians sat quietly in that ghostly light. A statue of Kali filled the centre, before it, a basin containing a tiny red fish believed to house the spirit of the goddess; a great pyre had been built off to one side.

"At midnight, Suyodhana appeared with his priests, dragging forth the unhappy young woman, drugged with opium and who knows what other kinds of mysterious concoctions. She was not putting up the least bit of resistance. A man lit a torch, and the Thugs began their death chant. When she had almost reached the blazing pyre, Tremal-Naik and

22

I pounced like lions, firing our weapons in all directions. Within minutes we had smashed through that sea of men, grabbed the young woman and headed back into the tunnels.

"Where were we heading? No one knew. There was no time to stop and think. We ran blindly, striving to put as much distance between the Thugs and ourselves as possible. Once they had recovered form their initial shock, they immediately came after us! We ran for a good hour, heading further below ground, until finally we came upon a well. We climbed down into it and found ourselves in a cavern. Unfortunately, it was a dead end. We tried to climb back out, but it was too late, the Thugs had sealed us in!"

"Damn!" exclaimed Sandokan. "Maratha, your story is riveting! How did you escape?"

"We didn't."

"Great thunders!"

"They laid siege to us immediately, lighting fires around the cavern. The heat was unbearable. Just as we thought we were going to be roasted alive, they unleashed a gusher of water into the well. We rushed to quench our thirst, drank our fill, and fell to the ground unconscious. It was only after we awoke that we realized they had mixed in some kind of narcotic.

"Knowing the Thugs to be merciless, we resigned ourselves to death, but to our surprise we were spared. It was not an act of kindness. Unbeknownst to us, Suyodhana had hatched an infernal plan that would destroy the young woman's love for Tremal-Naik and dispose of him once and for all.

"At that time, an Englishman, calling himself Captain Macpherson, a bold determined man, whose daughter had been kidnapped by the Thugs, was waging a merciless war against Suyodhana and his men. Hundreds upon hundreds of stranglers had fallen into his hands; he fought without quarter, determined to destroy them, assisted by the full might of the British government. Thugs were sent to kill him, but he always managed to escape. Suyodhana feared him greatly; he pitted Tremal-Naik against him, promising in reward the hand of the Guardian of the Temple of the East, the dark haired young woman my master loved so. The captain's head was to have been her wedding present!"

"And Tremal-Naik accepted?" asked the Tiger anxiously.

"He had no choice. He loved the Guardian immensely, and he was at Suyodhana's mercy. I won't relate all the dangers he faced to fulfill that horrible pact. A lucky combination of events put him in the captain's employ, but one day, he was found out and imprisoned. He did not, however, abandon his mission. Once he escaped, he learned that Captain Macpherson was planning to attack the Thugs in their lair. A ship had been prepared for the expedition, and Tremal-Naik managed to sneak aboard. That same night, with the aid of several accomplices, he made his way into the captain's cabin. The moment of truth had arrived. With a swipe of his blade, Tremal-Naik would finally have the captain's head. His blood was racing, his conscience rebelled, screaming at him not to commit that act, but my master would not yield. Unaware of Suyodhana's infernal treachery, he believed it was the only way to free his fiancée."

"Did he kill him?" Sandokan and Yanez asked anxiously.

"No," said Kammamuri. "Just as he was about to strike, his beloved's name escaped his lips. The captain awoke. That one word prevented a heinous crime, for the captain was the Guardian's father."

"Good Lord!" exclaimed Yanez. "What an incredible story!"

"All true, Señor Yanez."

"Wait, your master surely must have known his fiancée's name. He shouldn't have been surprised when..."

"Yes, of course, but her father had taken the name Macpherson to hide his identity from the Thugs. He feared they would kill his daughter if they suspected he was attempting to rescue her."

"Continue," said Sandokan.

"You can imagine what happened next. Finally aware of Suyodhana's fiendish scheme, my master confessed everything. He offered to lead the captain into the Thug's lair. When they landed on Rajmangal, my master descended into the underground temple, pretending to bear the captain's head. Once he was reunited with his beloved, he gave the signal and the British attacked. Suyodhana, however, managed to escape, and as my master, the captain, his fiancée and the soldiers left the caves to return to the ship, they heard him yell menacingly, 'We'll meet again in the jungle!' That sinister man kept his word.

"Several hundred stranglers had gathered on Rajmangal, having been informed of Captain Macpherson's expedition. Led by Suyodhana, they outnumbered the British twenty to one. The ship's crew rushed to aid their captain, but their efforts were in vain. All fell, overpowered by the sheer number of their enemies, the captain was the first to die. The ship was captured and torched, its remains set adrift down the river. Only Tremal-Naik and the Guardian were spared.

"Three days later, the British authorities in Fort William arrested my master. He had been driven insane by some mysterious liquid Suyodhana's men had forced down his throat and denounced as a Thug. There were no lack of witnesses; Kali has numerous followers even in Calcutta. Because of his insanity, he was spared and condemned to eternal exile on Norfolk, an island to the south of Australia."

"What a terrible ordeal!" exclaimed the Tiger after a brief silence. "Suyodhana hated Tremal-Naik that intensely?"

"Yes. And he could not allow the Guardian's love. So he hatched a plan that would rid him of both his enemies and forever destroy the young woman's heart. She could never have loved her father's murderer."

"Suyodhana is a monster."

"Is your master still insane?" asked Yanez.

"No, the doctors cured him."

"Didn't he attempt to defend himself? Didn't he tell his story?"

"He tried to, but no one believed him."

"Why is he in Rajah Brooke's custody?"

"The ship transporting him to Norfolk sank off the coast of Sarawak. Unfortunately, he won't remain in the rajah's custody for long."

"Why not?"

"A ship headed for Norfolk has recently set sail from India; if my calculations are correct, she'll reach Sarawak in six or seven days."

"What's the name of that ship?"

"The *Helgoland*."

"Did you see her?"

"Yes, before we set sail."

"Where was the *Young India* heading?"

"To Sarawak, I planned to rescue my master," Kammamuri said firmly.

"Alone?"

"Alone."

"You're a bold young man, my good Maratha," said the Tiger of Malaysia. "What became of the Guardian of the Temple of the East?"

"Suyodhana held her prisoner in the caverns of Rajmangal. She had gone mad after the slaughter in the jungle."

"How did she escape?" asked Yanez.

"She escaped?" asked Sandokan.

"Yes, little brother."

"Where is she now?"

"You'll know soon enough. Tell us everything, Kammamuri. How did she escape?" asked Yanez.

"While my master had gone off to kill Captain Macpherson, I pretended to let myself be persuaded to join the cult. I remained with the Thugs even after Suyodhana's atrocious vendetta, keeping close watch upon the Guardian of the Temple. Knowing for some time that my master had been condemned to the Isle of Norfolk and that the ship carrying him had been wrecked off the coast of Sarawak, I made plans to escape. I bought a rowboat, hid it in the middle of the jungle, and then on a night of drunken celebration, while the Thugs were in a state of intoxication, I went to the Sacred Pagoda, stabbed the guards, freed the Guardian, and escaped. I reached Calcutta the next day and boarded the *Young India* four days later."

"And the Guardian?" asked Sandokan.

"She's in Calcutta," said Yanez hurriedly.

"Is she beautiful?"

"Very," said Kammamuri. "She has dark hair and lovely dark eyes."

"And her name?"

"I've already told you, the Guardian of the Temple of the East."

"Yes, but that can't be her real name."

"No... of course not... It's Ada Corishant."

The Tiger of Malaysia jumped forward.

"Corishant!... Corishant!..." he howled. "The same as my poor Marianna's mother! Good Lord! Good Lord!..."

He fell to the ground, face twisted in pain, hands clutching his heart, heavy sobs roaring from his chest.

Frightened and surprised, Kammamuri had gotten up to rush to the pirate's aid, but two powerful arms held him back.

"A word," said the Portuguese, tightly clutching the Indian by the shoulders. "What was the name of the young woman's father?"

"Harry Corishant," replied the Maratha.

"Great God! Was he a captain of the sepoys?"

"Yes, sir. How did you know?"

"Quick, get out of here!"

"Why? What happened?"

"Silence! Go!"

He grabbed the Maratha by the shoulders, pushed him out the door and barred it shut behind him.

Chapter 5
In pursuit of the *Helgoland*

The Tiger of Malaysia had immediately recovered from that terrible outburst. Though still shaken, his face once again bore the proud expression that inspired respect and instilled terror in the bravest of men, and his lips, though slightly discoloured, bore a melancholy smile. Sweat lined his brow, as a fierce light blazed in his eyes.

"Has the storm settled?" asked Yanez, sitting down beside him.

"Yes," said the Tiger hoarsely.

"You get upset every time something reminds you of Marianna."

"I loved her intensely, Yanez. That unexpected memory was like a bullet in the heart... Marianna, my poor Marianna!"

A second sob erupted from the tiger's chest.

"Take heart, little brother," said Yanez, also moved by the memory. "Do not forget that you are the Tiger of Malaysia."

"Certain memories are too overwhelming, even for the Tiger."

"Do you have the strength to talk about Ada Corishant?"

"Yes, Yanez."

"Do you believe the Maratha's story?"

"He has no reason to lie."

"So, what are you going to do about it?"

"Yanez," Sandokan replied sadly, "do you remember a conversation we had with Marianna one night as we sat beneath the cool shade of a durian tree?"

"Almost word for word. 'Sandokan, my love,' she said, 'I have a cousin in India, daughter of my mother's brother, she is very dear to me.'"

"Continue, Yanez."

28

"'She's disappeared. It's rumoured she's been kidnapped by Indian Thugs. Her father has searched for her desperately but without success. Sandokan, my love, rescue her, and return her to him.'"

"Enough, Yanez, enough!" howled the Tiger, "Those memories are tearing at my heart. I can't believe I'll never see that sweet woman again! Marianna, my poor Marianna!"

The pirate's hands went to his face as sobs erupted from his powerful chest.

"Sandokan," said Yanez, "You have to control yourself."

The pirate raised his head.

"You are right, my friend," he replied.

"Shall we continue then?"

"Yes."

"You have to remain calm."

"I will."

"What are you going to do about Ada Corishant?"

"What am I going to do? Need you ask? We'll rescue her, then set off for Sarawak and liberate her fiancé."

"Ada Corishant is safe, Sandokan," said Yanez.

"Safe!... Safe!..." exclaimed the pirate, jumping to his feet. "Where is she?"

"Here."

"Here!... Why didn't you tell me sooner?"

"Despite the dark hair, she bears a strong resemblance to Marianna. I was afraid you'd collapse at the sight of her."

"I want to see her, Yanez, I want to see her!"

"Very well then, you'll see her immediately."

He went and opened the door. Kammamuri, visibly anxious, was seated upon the remnants of a gabion, waiting to be summoned.

"Señor Yanez!" he exclaimed, his voice trembling slightly as he rushed towards the Portuguese.

"Calm yourself, Kammamuri."

"Are you going to rescue my master?"

"We'll try," said Yanez.

"Thank you, sir, thank you!"

"You can thank me once we've rescued him. Now go down to the village and bring your mistress up here."

The Maratha rushed down the narrow steps, howling with joy.

"A good man," murmured the Portuguese.

He went back into the hut and approached Sandokan. The Tiger had sat down once again and buried his face in his hands.

"What are you thinking about, little brother?" he asked soothingly.

"The past, Yanez," replied the pirate.

"Never dwell on the past, Sandokan. It only makes you suffer. When are we going to set sail?"

"Immediately."

"For Sarawak?"

"For Sarawak."

"It won't be easy. Rajah Brooke is a powerful man."

"I know, but our men are the pirates of Mompracem and I am the Tiger of Malaysia."

"Are we going directly to Sarawak or are we going to scout the coast first?"

"We'll patrol the bay. We must sink the *Helgoland* before we set foot ashore."

"A wise precaution."

"So you approve?"

"Yes, Sandokan, and..."

He fell silent. The door had swung open and there on the threshold stood Ada Corishant, the Guardian of the Temple of the East.

"Here she is, Sandokan!" exclaimed the Portuguese.

The pirate turned about. When his eyes fell upon the woman in the doorway, he let out a cry and retreated a few steps, reeling slightly, coming to a halt only when his back struck against the wall.

"What a resemblance!" he exclaimed. "What a resemblance!"

The madwoman had not moved. She stood motionless, her eyes fixed on the pirate. Then, without warning, she took two steps forward and whispered, "Thugs?"

"No," said Kammamuri, appearing behind her. "No, mistress, they are not Thugs."

She shook her head and made her way towards Sandokan, who appeared fixed to the wall. She put a hand to his chest and rubbed it lightly, as if searching for something.

"Thugs?" she repeated.

"No, mistress, no," said the Maratha.

Ada drew back her large white silk cape, revealing a gold breastplate inlaid with large diamonds, and adorned with a relief of a Nagi, a snake woman with a coiled serpentine body. She studied that mysterious symbol, the mark of the Indian stranglers, at great length, then looked at Sandokan's chest.

"Where is Kali's mark?" she asked, her voice changing tone.

"These men are not Thugs," said Kammamuri.

The madwoman's eyes flashed for an instant. Had she understood the Maratha's words?

"Kammamuri," whispered Yanez. "What happens if you utter her fiancé's name?"

"No! No!" exclaimed the Maratha as a look of terror spread across his face. "She'd faint."

"Is she always this serene?"

"Always, provided she doesn't see a noose or a statue of the Goddess Kali, or hear the sound of a tarè or a ramsinga."

"What happens then?"

"She becomes delirious for several days and often attempts to run away."

The madwoman turned about and slowly headed towards the door. Kammamuri, Yanez, and Sandokan, who had overcome his initial shock, quickly followed her.

"Where is she going?" asked Yanez.

"I don't know," replied the Maratha.

The madwoman had come to a stop just outside the hut. She cast a curious glance upon the trenches and paling then walked towards the edge of the cliff, her eyes fixed upon the sea, watching the waves as they

31

crashed against the reefs ringing the island. At one point, she turned, laughed, and said: "The Mangal!"

"What?" asked Sandokan and Yanez in unison.

"The Mangal. It's the river about the Thugs' island. She thinks she's still in India."

"The poor woman!" sighed Sandokan.

"Do you think we'll be able to help her regain her reason?" asked Yanez.

"I hope so," replied Sandokan.

"Is she going to accompany us?"

"Yes, Yanez. The British could attack Mompracem during our absence."

"When are you planning to set sail?" asked Kammamuri.

"Immediately," said Sandokan.

Kammamuri took Ada by the hand and made his way down the steps. Yanez and the Tiger of Malaysia followed close behind.

"What kind of impression did that poor woman make on you?" the Portuguese asked Sandokan.

"A painful one, Yanez," said the pirate. "I hope I can restore her happiness!"

"She does resemble Marianna, doesn't she?"

"Yes, yes, Yanez!" exclaimed Sandokan, his voice filling with emotion. "She has the same features. My sweet Marianna! Enough talk, Yanez, the suffering is unbearable!"

They reached the first longhouses in the village, just as the prahus carrying the plunder from the *Young India* were entering the bay. Sighting their captain, the crews greeted him with an enthusiastic cheer, drew their weapons and waved them frantically.

"Long live the invincible Tiger of Malaysia!" they howled.

"Long live our brave captain!" replied the pirates in the village.

With a single gesture, Sandokan summoned them all before him. There were about two hundred in total, mostly Malays and Dyaks from Borneo, men as courageous as lions, as ferocious as tigers, each one prepared to die for the captain they idolized.

"Tigers of Mompracem," he said. "The Tiger of Malaysia is about to undertake an expedition that may cost the lives of a great many of us. An Englishman, son of a race that has done us great evil, is holding one of my friends captive, the fiancé of this poor madwoman who is the cousin of our beloved Queen of Mompracem."

A cry of anger filled the air.

"Tigers of Mompracem, I want to rescue this poor woman's fiancé."

"We'll rescue him, Tiger of Malaysia, we'll rescue him!" yelled a voice. "Who holds him captive?"

"Rajah James Brooke, 'the Exterminator'."

The pirates roared with rage.

"Death to James Brooke!"

"Death to the Exterminator!"

"To Sarawak! To Sarawak!"

"Vengeance, Tiger of Malaysia!"

"Silence!" thundered Sandokan. "Karà-Olò, come forward."

A giant man with yellowish skin, limbs heavy with copper bracelets and chest adorned with necklaces of pearls and tiger teeth, stepped toward the pirate, clutching a large sabre.

"How many men in your band?" asked the Tiger of Malaysia.

"Eighty," replied the pirate.

"Are you afraid of James Brooke?"

"I fear no one. When the Tiger of Malaysia gives the order to attack Sarawak, my men and I will follow."

"You and your men will board the *Pearl of Labuan*. Make sure the prahu is well supplied with gunpowder and cannonballs."

"It shall be done, Captain."

"What about me, Captain?" asked an old Malay pirate, whose face and chest bore the scars of many a battle.

"You, Mayala, will remain on Mompracem with the rest of the men; let the young embark for Sarawak!"

"Yes, sir! I'll defend our island for as long as there's blood in my veins."

After having spoken with the leaders of the various bands and issuing their final orders, Sandokan and Yanez returned to the great hut and quickly made their preparations.

They selected carbines, pistols, scimitars and sharp poisoned krises, hid several pouches containing millions in diamonds beneath their clothes, and went back towards the shore.

The *Pearl of Labuan*, her sails raised, rolled among the waves, impatient to set out to sea. Karà-Olò's eighty men stood on deck, awaiting their orders.

"My Tigers," said Sandokan, turning to address the pirates that had gathered along the shore, "Defend my island."

There was a roar of assent as the Tigers of Mompracem drew their weapons and waved them in the air.

Sandokan, Yanez, Kammamuri and the Guardian got into a longboat and quickly made off towards the ship. Once they were aboard, the prahu raised anchor and headed out towards the open sea, sailing away to the cries of, "Hurrah for the Pearl of Labuan! Long live the Tiger of Malaysia! Long live the Tigers of Mompracem!"

Chapter 6
From Mompracem to Sarawak

The *Pearl of Labuan*, the ship with which the leader of the pirates of Mompracem was about to undertake his daring expedition, was one of the largest, most beautiful prahus to ever sail upon the vast seas of Malaysia.

She weighed a hundred and sixty tons; triple the weight of an ordinary prahu. Her keel was narrow, her lines quick, her bow was tall and of solid construction; her masts were strong and fitted with large sails, the yards measured no less than 60 meters across. At full sail, she flew like a bird and could outrun the fastest steamers and sailing vessels of Asia and Australia.

Nothing about her indicated she was a pirate ship. No cannons were visible, nor did she have gun ports or a large crew. At first glance, she appeared to be an elegant merchant prahu, transporting precious cargo in her hold, sailing off to do business in China or India.

However, had anyone descended into her hold they would have quickly discovered just what kind of merchandise the prahu bore. Instead of carpets, gold, spices, and tea, she was filled with bombs, rifles, daggers, boarding sabres and enough gunpowder to destroy two tall ships.

Anyone venturing below deck would have found six long-range cannons resting upon their carriages, ready to unleash barrages of grapeshot and cannonballs, as well as two large mortars, grappling hooks, axes, sabres and parangs, the preferred weapons of the Dyaks of Borneo.

Having sailed past the numerous rocks and reefs that guarded the bay, the quick *Pearl of Labuan* pointed her bow towards the coast of Borneo, or, more precisely, towards Cape Sirik on the western tip of the vast Bay of Sarawak.

The weather was splendid, the waters calm, a few fiery red cirrus clouds in the sky overhead. The sea remained clear: not a wave, not a sail, not a trace of smoke to announce the presence of a steamboat on the horizon. Despite the light breeze, not a ripple marred that vast expanse of lead grey water.

Having settled Ada in the largest cabin on the stern, Yanez and Kammamuri had come back up on deck. They found Sandokan pacing back and forth, arms crossed, his head lowered in contemplation.

"What do you think of our ship?" Yanez asked the Maratha, who had leaned against the stern railing, his eyes fixed upon the steep cliffs of Mompracem disappearing in the distance.

"I've never sailed on anything this fast, Señor Yanez," replied the Maratha. "Pirates choose their vessels well."

"You're right, my friend. There's not a steamship that can keep pace with the *Pearl of Labuan*. If this wind holds, we'll be within sight of Sarawak in a few days."

"Do you foresee any trouble?"

"That's hard to predict. The *Pearl of Labuan* is well known in these waters, and there are many cruisers out patrolling the shores of Borneo. Some reckless fool may decide to measure himself against the Tiger of Malaysia."

"And if that were to happen?"

"Good heavens, we'd accept the challenge. Sandokan never runs from a fight."

"I'd hate to come up against a warship."

"They do not frighten us. We have enough sabres and rifles in the hold to arm a city, enough bombs to sink a fleet and enough powder to raze an entire village."

"But only eighty men!"

"Do you know what kind of men they are?"

"I know they're brave, but…"

"They're Dyaks, my friend."

"So?"

"They're headhunters, fearless warriors."

"Headhunters?"

"Yes, my friend. Dyaks. They live in the vast jungles of Borneo and are renowned for their fighting skills. They're formidable."

"And dangerous as well. What if one night they decided to turn on you and take your head?"

"There's no need to be afraid, young man. They respect and fear us more than they do their gods. The Tiger needs but utter a word, just give them a glance, and they become as docile as little lambs."

"When do you think we'll reach Sarawak?"

"In five days, barring no surprises."

"Storms?"

The Portuguese shrugged.

"With Sandokan at the wheel, the *Pearl of Labuan* could challenge a cyclone. Our only real annoyance would be the sudden appearance of a cruiser."

"Are there many?"

"They sprout up all over like poisonous weeds. The Portuguese, British, Dutch and Spanish have all pledged war against piracy. A war they'll fight to the death."

"And so one day the pirates will disappear from these waters."

"Oh not at all!" exclaimed Yanez, with deep conviction. "Piracy will last for as long as there are Malays on Earth."

"Why's that?"

"The people of Malaysia don't have the slightest inclination to accept 'the blessings' of European civilization. Malay pirates have been around for several centuries and will exist for many more. It's a bloody trade, passed on from father to son. They're expert in theft, battle, pillaging and assassination, terrible means to be sure, but means that allow them to survive."

"But surely the constant battles must affect their numbers?"

"Not much, Kammamuri, not much! Malays multiply like insects. When one dies, another is born and the son is no less brave nor less bloodthirsty than the father."

"Is the Tiger of Malaysia a Malay?"

"No, a Bornean of high caste."

"Señor Yanez, why has such a formidable man so generously offered to rescue my master? He's never even met him."

"Because your master is Ada Corishant's fiancé."

"Has he met Ada Corishant before?" asked Kammamuri, surprised.

"No, never."

"I don't understand..."

"Let me explain, Kammamuri. Three years ago, in 1849, the Tiger of Malaysia had reached the zenith of his power. He possessed numerous prahus, several cannons and commanded legions of ferocious Tigers. With but a word, he could make all of Malaysia tremble."

"Were you with the Tiger then?"

"Yes, for several years by that point. One day, Sandokan learned of a beautiful, charming young woman living in Labuan. Overcome by a desire to see her, he set off for Labuan, was attacked by a cruiser, beaten and wounded. His ship and crew lost, he struggled to reach the shore and the shelter of the forest, where, after a dizzying run, he lost consciousness. He awoke... can you guess?"

"I can't even imagine."

"In the home of the very woman he had set out to see."

"Oh! What an extraordinary coincidence!"

"Up until that day, the Tiger of Malaysia had been driven by vengeance. He lived for battle. But at the sight of that young woman, he fell madly in love."

"Who? The Tiger? Impossible!" exclaimed Kammamuri.

"It's the truth," said Yanez. "He loved the young woman, she returned his love, and the two planned to run off together."

"Run off? Why?"

"The young woman's uncle was a captain in the British navy, a harsh man, violent, and one of the Tiger of Malaysia's most merciless enemies.

I'll skip over the battles we fought against the British, the Tiger's misfortunes, the bombing of Mompracem, the narrow escape. In the end, Sandokan married the young woman, and the two retired to Batavia, accompanied by thirty Tigers and myself."

"And the others?"

"Dead. Killed in battle."

"Why did the Tiger return to Mompracem?"

Yanez did not reply and the Maratha, surprised by that sudden silence, turned his head and saw the Portuguese quickly wipe away a tear.

"You're crying!" he exclaimed.

"Don't be silly," said Yanez.

"Why deny it?"

"You're right, Kammamuri. I've seen the Tiger of Malaysia, who had never so much as shed a tear, cry uncontrollably. My heart breaks every time I think of Marianna Guillonk."

"Marianna Guillonk!" exclaimed the Maratha. "Who's she?"

"The young woman that escaped with the Tiger of Malaysia."

"One of Ada Corishant's relatives?"

"A cousin, Kammamuri."

"So that's why the Tiger has promised to save my master and his fiancée. What happened to Marianna Guillonk?"

"She was laid to rest 10 months ago," Yanez said sadly.

"She's dead?!"

"Yes..."

"And her uncle?"

"Oh, he's very much alive and still hunting for Sandokan. Lord James Guillonk has sworn to hang the two of us side by side."

"Where is he now?"

"We don't know. However, I have this feeling of foreboding... bah, it's foolish really; I stopped believing in premonitions long ago."

He lit a cigarette and began to pace the deck. The Maratha noticed that Yanez, usually so jovial, had suddenly become quite sombre. Realizing he had drawn up painful memories, Kammamuri tactfully withdrew and headed off towards his mistress' cabin.

The wind remained favourable, growing in strength and increasing the *Pearl of Labuan*'s speed. She was soon advancing at seven knots per hour, and if she maintained that pace, it would not be long before she reached Cape Sirik.

At midday, the Romades appeared off the port side, a group of islands about forty miles from the coast of Borneo. They were inhabited mostly by pirates, ready allies with Mompracem. Several prahus reached the *Pearl of Labuan*'s side, their crews filling the air with cheers as they wished the Tiger and his crew good hunting.

Throughout the day, a brigantine and several Chinese junks were sighted off in the distance, but the Tiger of Malaysia, not wanting to risk his men in unnecessary battle and fearing that he would arrive too late to capture the *Helgoland*, did not give those ships a second thought.

The next day, as dawn was breaking, the crew sighted the isle of Whale, a fairly large landmass ringed by numerous reefs about a hundred and ten miles from Mompracem. A gunboat flying a Dutch flag was exploring the shore, undoubtedly searching for some pirate ship, but as soon as she spied the *Pearl of Labuan*, she sailed off at full speed. Instantly, sailors with long-range carbines covered her deck, as gunners rushed to man a large cannon on her starboard side.

"Little brother!" exclaimed Yanez, approaching Sandokan who was calmly studying the gunboat. "Those scoundrels have smelled something, looks as though they're getting ready for battle."

"You shouldn't jump to conclusions," replied the Tiger, "they'll probably just follow us for awhile."

"I don't relish the idea of being followed by a gunboat."

"You're not afraid, are you?"

"No, little brother. But what if she follows us all the way to Sarawak?"

"They won't hold their fire that long. If they suspect something, they'll attack and we'll sink them."

"Best we keep our guard up, Sandokan. We both know James Brooke has an excellent fleet, and often has his ships fly foreign flags or change their appearance when hunting for pirates."

"Yes, I know that old wolf's tricks. To lure out pirates, he dismasts his own ship, the *Royalist*, then once his enemy is within range, he sprays them with volleys of grapeshot."

"His tactics work, that devil of a man has exterminated all the pirates that used to beat the coast of Sarawak."

"It's true, Yanez. The *Royalist* has purged half the coasts of Borneo; she's sunk enemy prahus, torched villages, and destroyed forts with her cannons. There's no question the rajah is a brave, resourceful man, but he's no match for the pirates of Mompracem. Our Tigers will give him the fight of his life."

"You plan to challenge him?"

"Oh, yes. His days are numbered."

"Look, Sandokan. The gunboat's requesting we show our flag."

"Well, we'll be happy to oblige. Kai-Malù, show those curious wretches a British, Dutch or Portuguese flag."

Minutes later, a Portuguese flag fluttered from the prahu's stern.

Her curiosity satisfied, the gunboat immediately sailed off, but instead of returning to the Isle of Whale still visible on the horizon, she tacked and headed south. Sandokan and Yanez frowned.

"Hmm!" said the Portuguese. "Something's up."

"I know, brother."

"She's heading towards Sarawak, no question about it. Once she's out of sight, she'll change course, guaranteed."

"She has a clever crew. They immediately realized we were pirates."

"What are you going to do?"

"Nothing, for now. She's moving faster than we are."

"Do you think she'll be waiting for us in Sarawak?"

"I'd wager on it."

"Her captain may alert Brooke's fleet and lay a trap for us at the mouth of the river."

"We'll fight."

"We only have eight cannons, Sandokan."

"Yes, but the *Helgoland* will have several more. We'll amuse ourselves, my good friend, you'll see."

For two days, the *Pearl of Labuan* sailed at a distance of thirty miles from the coast of Borneo, at all times within sight of the shore marked by the peak of Mount Patau, a giant covered by a magnificent forest, towering 1,880 feet above the sea.

On the morning of the third day, she rounded Cape Sirik, a rocky promontory at the north end of the vast Bay of Sarawak.

Fearing he would be forced to face James Brooke's fleet at any moment, Sandokan raised the Dutch flag, ordered the cannons loaded and had two-thirds of the crew hide below deck. He pointed the ship's bow towards Cape Tanjong-Datu, the westernmost point of the bay; the *Helgoland*, coming from India, would pass close to it. Towards noon, much to the general surprise, the *Pearl of Labuan* sighted the Dutch gunboat she had run across three days earlier near the Isle of Whale. Recognizing her instantly, Sandokan smashed his fist upon the bulwark.

"That gunboat again!" he exclaimed with a frown, baring teeth as sharp as a tiger's.

"She's spying on us, Sandokan," said Yanez.

"Then we'll sink her."

"We'll do no such thing, Sandokan. Cannon blasts could attract Brooke's fleet."

"The rajah's fleet does not frighten me."

"We've got to be cautious, Sandokan."

"Fine, as you wish. We'll be cautious, but mark my words, that gunboat will be waiting for us at the mouth of the Sarawak."

"Aren't you the Tiger of Malaysia?"

"Yes, but we have the Guardian of the Temple of the East aboard. She could be hit by a cannonball."

"We'll shield her with our chests."

The Dutch gunboat arrived to within two hundred meters of the *Pearl of Labuan*. They could make out the captain standing on deck, spyglass in hand, and around thirty sailors armed with carbines, crowding about the bow. Several gunners stood by a large cannon on the stern. She sailed past the prahu, then tacked and pointed her bow south towards Sarawak. Three-quarters of an hour later, a tuft of smoke was all that remained visible.

"Damn!" exclaimed Sandokan. "If she gets within range of my ship again, I'll sink her with a broadside."

"We'll meet up with her in Sarawak," said Yanez.

"I hope so, but..."

A cry from above interrupted his words.

"Steamer on the horizon!" yelled a pirate, sitting astraddle the large yardarm on the mainmast.

"Could be a cruiser!" exclaimed Sandokan, his eyes brightening. "Where is she coming from?"

"The north," replied the topman.

"Can you make her out?"

"No, just her smoke and the tip of her masts."

"The *Helgoland*?!?" exclaimed Yanez.

"Unlikely! She'd be coming from the west, not from the north."

"She could have docked in Labuan."

"Kammamuri!" yelled the Tiger.

The Maratha, who had climbed up onto the stern railing, jumped down and rushed towards the pirate.

"Would you recognize the *Helgoland*?" asked the Tiger.

"Yes, sir."

"Follow me!"

The two men rushed towards the backstays, climbed up to the tip of the mainmast and fixed their eyes upon the emerald surface of the sea.

Chapter 7
The *Helgoland*

A three-masted vessel had suddenly appeared on the horizon, where the sky blended into the sea, and though she was still far off, it was obvious she was a ship of enormous dimensions. Her smokestack spewed black torrents into the air; her bulk, her masts and her shape, left no doubt in anyone's mind; she was a warship.

"See her, Kammamuri?" asked Sandokan, who was studying the on-coming vessel with the utmost attention, trying to make out the flag flying from the peak of her mainsail.

"Yes," replied the Maratha.

"Do you recognize her?"

"Wait... it's... the *Helgoland!*"

"Are you certain?"

"Yes, sir. Look, she has a straight bow, three identical masts, and twelve gun ports. There's no mistake, that's the *Helgoland!*"

A sinister light flashed in the Tiger of Malaysia's eyes.

"She's large enough to keep us busy for a while!" exclaimed the pirate.

He grabbed onto a shroud and slid to the deck below. The pirates gathered their weapons and flocked about him, each man awaiting the order to spring into action.

"Yanez!" yelled Sandokan.

"Coming, little brother," replied the Portuguese, rushing from the stern.

"Take six men down into the hold and smash in the prahu's sides."

"What? Smash in the prahu's sides? Are you crazy?"

44

"I have a plan. The crew aboard that ship will hear our cries for help and rush to assist us. You'll pretend to be a Portuguese ambassador en route for Sarawak and we'll be your escort."

"And then?"

"Once we're aboard, it won't be difficult to take possession of her. Hurry, the *Helgoland*'s approaching."

"Little brother, you're truly a great man!" exclaimed the Portuguese.

Yanez chose ten men and went below. They made their way through the vast stores of weapons, cannonballs, and barrels of powder, past the old cannons used as ballast, and took their positions. Five men to port, five to starboard, clutching axes, awaiting final instructions.

"We've got to act quickly," said the Portuguese. "Strike with all your might, but don't make the holes too large. We've got to sink slowly if we want to avoid the sharks."

The men began to hack away. The boards were as solid as steel, but in less than ten minutes, two enormous jets of water had erupted into the hold and rushed towards the stern. The Portuguese and the ten pirates rushed up on deck.

"We're sinking," said Yanez. "Steady now, men, hide your pistols and your krises. We'll need them tomorrow."

"Kammamuri," yelled Sandokan, "Bring your mistress up on deck."

"Are we jumping ship, Captain?" asked the Maratha.

"No, there's no need for that just yet. But if we do, I'll take care of the young woman personally."

The Maratha rushed below deck, gathered his mistress in his strong arms, and, without meeting any resistance, carried her up to the bridge.

The steamboat was still a good mile away, but if she kept advancing at fifteen knots per hour, she would reach the prahu's waters within minutes.

The Tiger of Malaysia manned a cannon and fired. Carried by the wind, the sound of the explosion reached the vessel, which immediately pointed her bow towards the prahu.

"Help! Help!" howled the Tiger.

"Help! Help!"

"We're sinking!"

"Help! Help!" yelled the pirates.

Listing to starboard, the prahu was slowly sinking, tottering like a drunken sailor. The dull roar of water rushing through the two openings emanated from the hold, at times punctuated by the sound of the powder barrels smashing against the cannons. The mainmast, sawed off at the base, swayed for a few minutes, then fell into the sea, dragging the great sail and the shrouds along with it.

"Throw the artillery overboard," commanded Sandokan, feeling the prahu giving way beneath his feet.

The cannons were thrown into the water, followed by barrels of gunpowder, cannonballs, rigging and all the spare masts.

Grabbing buckets, six men rushed into the hold to slow the damage of the incoming waters.

The *Helgoland* had come to a stop three hundred meters away. Six longboats were immediately lowered into the water and set off towards the sinking prahu at full speed.

"Help! Help!" yelled Yanez, standing on the port bulwark, surrounded by his men.

"Hold on," yelled a voice from the nearest launch.

The boats advanced furiously, noisily slashing through the waters. The helmsmen, sitting at the stern, tiller in hand, encouraged the sailors as they rowed at full strength, in perfect unison, without missing a single stroke.

A short time later, the prahu was boarded from both sides.

The officer in command of that small squadron, a good-hearted young man of native descent, jumped upon the deck which now rested just above the waterline. Spotting the madwoman, he courteously removed his hat.

"Please hurry," he said, "First the lady, then the others. Is there anything you wish to save?"

"No, commander," said Yanez. "We've thrown everything overboard."

"Everyone into the boats!"

The Guardian, Yanez, Sandokan and several Malays and Dyaks boarded the officer's launch, while the rest of the crew settled in the remaining boats.

The small squadron quickly rowed off and headed towards the ship, which now advanced at reduced speed. The water had just reached the prahu's bridge, and the *Pearl of Labuan* rolled from bow to stern, her unsteady foremast shaking dangerously.

The ship folded to one side, rolled and disappeared beneath the waves, creating a small whirlpool that drew the launches back twenty meters. A large wave dragged off what remained of her.

"The poor *Pearl!*" exclaimed Yanez, his heart filling with pain.

"Where did you set sail from?" asked the officer, having remained silent until then.

"Varauni," replied Yanez.

"What happened?"

"We ran against a reef near the Isle of Whale."

"Who are those natives aboard your vessel?"

"Dyaks and Malays. An honour guard assigned to me by the Sultan of Borneo."

"So you are...?"

"Yanez de Gomera y Marhanhao, a captain in the service of His Majesty the King of Portugal, and ambassador to the Court of the Sultan of Varauni."

The officer removed his hat.

"It was an honour to rescue you, sir," he said, bowing.

"The pleasure was mine, sir. You have my deepest gratitude," said Yanez, bowing in reply. "Without your help, none of us would have survived."

The launches had drawn up beside the ship. The ladder was lowered then the officer, Yanez, Ada, Sandokan and the others climbed up on deck where the captain and crew anxiously awaited them.

The officer introduced Yanez to the captain, a handsome man in his forties with a large moustache and a face deeply bronzed by the tropical sun.

"A bit of good fortune, sir, we arrived just in time," said the captain, vigorously shaking the hand the Portuguese had proffered.

"Absolutely, my good Captain. My sister would surely have died."

"Your sister, Mr. Ambassador?" asked the captain, studying the young woman who had not yet uttered a word.

"Yes, Captain, the poor woman is mad."

"Mad?"

"Yes, sir."

"So young and beautiful!" exclaimed the captain, fixing a compassionate look upon the Guardian of the Temple of the East. "She must be tired."

"Yes, I believe so, Captain."

"Mister Strafford, take the young lady down to the best cabin on the stern."

"Thank you. That is most kind. It would be best if her servant went as well," said Yanez. "Kammamuri, accompany Miss Ada."

The Maratha took the young woman by the hand and followed the officer to the stern.

"You must be tired and hungry, sir," said the captain, turning towards Yanez.

"We haven't slept for two long nights and it's been two days since we last ate."

"Where were you headed?"

"Sarawak. Captain, allow me to introduce you to the Sultan of Varauni's brother, S. A. R. Orang Kahaian," said Yanez, presenting Sandokan.

The captain enthusiastically shook the Tiger of Malaysia's hand.

"Great Heavens!" he exclaimed. "An ambassador and a prince aboard my ship? This is indeed a special event. Gentleman, my ship is at your disposal."

"Thank you, Captain," replied Yanez. "Are you headed for Sarawak as well?"

"Yes, sir, we'll make the trip together."

"What a bit of luck!"

"Are you by chance going to see Rajah James Brooke?"

"Yes, Captain, I have to sign an important treaty."

"Do you know the rajah?"

"No, Captain."

"Then I'll introduce you, Ambassador. Mister Strafford, take the ambassador and his Highness below and serve them lunch."

"What about our men, Captain?" asked Yanez.

"We'll put them up in steerage, if it's alright with you."

"That'll be fine, Captain. Much appreciated."

Yanez and Sandokan followed the officer into a large cabin furnished with great elegance. Two large windows, covered by silk curtains, looked out onto the stern.

"Mister Strafford," said Yanez, "who are our neighbours?"

"The captain is on your right and your sister is on your left."

"Excellent, we can tap on the walls for a little conversation."

Having assured them that lunch would soon be served, the officer bowed and left.

"Well, little brother, what do you think?" asked Yanez once they were alone.

"Everything is going according to plan," replied Sandokan. "Those poor devils have mistaken us for true gentlemen."

"What do you think of the ship?"

"She's a first class vessel and she'll cut quite a figure in Sarawak."

"Have you counted the number of men aboard?"

"Yes, I'd say about forty or so."

"Good Lord!" exclaimed the Portuguese, grimacing.

"You're not afraid of forty men?"

"That's no small number."

"There are a good many of us, and we're all excellent warriors, Yanez."

"Yes, but the British have excellent cannons at their disposal."

"I've ordered Hirundo to scout the vessel and take note of the ship's armaments. He's a clever young man; he'll bring us all the information we need."

"When are we going to strike?"

"Tonight. We'll be at the mouth of the river by noon tomorrow."

"Shh, here comes our lunch."

A young man, assisted by two cabin boys, brought in a magnificent meal, two medium-rare steaks, a colossal pudding, and some select bottles of gin and French wine. The two pirates, on the verge of starvation, sat at the table and efficiently attacked the food before them. They had just begun to make a dent in the pudding, when they heard a faint step and a soft hiss outside their cabin door.

"Come in, Hirundo," said Sandokan.

A handsome, well-built young man, with lively features and bronze skin entered the room, closing the door behind him.

"Sit down and tell us all you've learned, Hirundo," said Yanez. "Where are our men?"

"In steerage," replied the young Dyak.

"What are they doing?"

"Checking their weapons."

"How many cannons are there in the battery?" asked Sandokan.

"Twelve, Tiger."

"These British are well armed. James Brooke will have his work cut out for him if he attempts to board us. We'll sink the *Royalist* with a broadside. Now listen, Hirundo, I have a plan."

"I'm all ears."

"No one is to make a move just yet. Once the moon sets, go disable the cannons in the battery then have everyone rush onto the deck yelling, Fire! Fire! The crew, the officers and the captain will come out of their quarters. Only attack if they refuse to surrender. Do you understand?"

"Perfectly, Tiger of Malaysia."

"Now go next door to the Guardian's cabin, tell Kammamuri to barricade the door and not to come out until the battle is over."

"It shall be done, Tiger of Malaysia."

"Excellent, dismissed."

Hirundo quickly set off to carry out his orders.

"We'll force them to surrender. I'd regret having to kill these men after they've shown us such generous hospitality," said Sandokan.

The two pirates calmly finished their meal, drained several bottles, took a few sips of tea then stretched out on their beds and patiently awaited the signal to rush on deck. Towards eight, the sun disappeared beneath the horizon and darkness began to descend upon the sea.

Sandokan peered out a porthole. He sighted a dark mass rearing towards the clouds off the port side and a white sail cutting across the horizon off the stern.

"We're within sight of Mount Matang," he murmured. "Tomorrow we'll be in Sarawak."

He approached the cabin door and rested an ear against it.

He heard two people come down the stairs, a whisper, then two doors open and close, one to the right, one to the left.

"Excellent," he murmured. "The captain and the lieutenant are in their cabins. All is going to plan."

A short while later, he heard the captain's clock chime nine, then ten. When it struck eleven, he jumped out of bed.

"Yanez," he exclaimed.

"Yes, little brother," replied the Portuguese.

The Tiger of Malaysia took two steps towards the door, his right hand on the hilt of his scimitar. A loud cry thundered from the ship's waist and echoed over the sea.

"Fire! Fire!"

"It's time!" exclaimed Sandokan.

Having opened the door, the two pirates sprang onto the bridge like tigers.

Chapter 8
The Bay of Sarawak

At the sound of that terrible cry, the engineer had immediately cut the engines, but the *Helgoland* continued to advance beneath the last turns of her propeller.

An indescribable confusion reigned over the deck by the time the two pirates had arrived. Sailors tumbled out of the bow forecastle, half-naked and half-asleep, colliding into one another, as they groggily rushed to their posts. The watchmen, no less terrified, believing that the fire had already grown to alarming proportions, quickly gathered the buckets scattered about the deck. The Tigers of Mompracem emerged from the hatches like a rising tide, pistols in hand, krises between their teeth, ready for battle. Cries, shouts, curses, commands and questions flew from all directions.

"Where's the fire?" asked one.

"In the battery," replied another.

"To the magazine! To the magazine!"

"Form a chain."

"To the pumps!"

"The captain! Where's the captain?"

"Man your posts!" thundered an officer. "Remain calm! Man the pumps! Man your posts!"

Suddenly, a voice thundered from the middle of the deck.

"It's time, my Tigers!"

The Tiger of Malaysia rushed in among his men. He had drawn his scimitar and its blade sparkled in the dim lantern light.

A ferocious cry filled the air, "Hurrah for the Tiger of Malaysia!"

The ship's crew, surprised and frightened at the sight of all those armed men ready to attack, rushed confusedly to the bow and stern, grabbing axes, sabres, planks and anything else they could use to defend themselves.

"Traitors! Traitors!" they cried.

Krises drawn, the pirates were about to smash through those walls of humanity, when the Tiger of Malaysia stayed them with a gesture. The captain had appeared on deck and was bravely heading towards them, clutching his revolver.

"What's happening?" he asked imperiously.

Sandokan left the group and headed towards him.

"It should be obvious, Captain," he said, "My men are about to attack your crew."

"Who are you?"

"The Tiger of Malaysia, my good captain."

"What!... Where's the ambassador?"

"There at the centre of the action, pistol drawn, ready to fire upon you, if you do not surrender immediately."

"Wretches!"

"Steady, Captain. The pirates of Mompracem rarely allow an insult to go unpunished."

The captain took three steps back.

"Pirates!" he exclaimed. "You're pirates!"

"There are none more dangerous."

"Back!" he thundered, raising his revolver. "Back or I'll kill you!"

"Captain," continued Sandokan, moving towards him, "There are eighty of us, armed and ready for battle, you have only forty men and most are unarmed. You are not my enemy and I do not wish to take your lives needlessly; surrender, and I swear no harm will come to you."

"What exactly do you want then?"

"Your ship."

"So you can rove the seas?"

"No. To do a good deed, to right an injustice."

"And if I were to refuse?"

"I'd unleash my Tigers against you and your crew."

"This is robbery!"

Sandokan drew a large pouch from beneath his shirt, showed it to the captain and said, "Here's a million in diamonds, take it!"

The captain froze, stunned.

"I do not understand," he said. "You have enough men to take possession of this ship, but you're offering me a million pounds instead! Who are you?"

"I am the Tiger of Malaysia," replied Sandokan. "Do you surrender or do I unleash my men?"

"What are you going to do with us?"

"We'll put you in a launch and allow you to go on your way."

"Where?"

"You're not too far from the coast of Borneo. Now make your decision."

The captain was hesitant. Perhaps he feared that once his men had laid down their weapons, the pirates would rush to butcher them. Yanez immediately guessed what was passing through the man's mind and came forward.

"Captain," he said, "there's no need to doubt the Tiger of Malaysia's word. He's never broken a promise."

"You're right," said the commander. "Men, lower your weapons; any resistance would be in vain."

The sailors, who only moments ago had foreseen a terrible future, threw down their knives and axes without hesitation.

"Excellent," said Sandokan.

At his signal, two whalers and three launches were stocked with provisions and lowered into the water. Unarmed, the sailors filed past the pirates and took their seats in the awaiting boats. The captain was the last to leave.

"Sir," he said, halting before the Tiger of Malaysia, "we don't have so much as a weapon to defend ourselves, or a compass to guide us."

Sandokan removed a gold compass from a chain hanging from his shirt and handed it to the officer.

"This will guide you," he replied.

He drew two pistols from his belt, removed a magnificent ring adorned with a diamond as large as a walnut from one of his fingers, and offered them to the captain along with the large pouch.

"These weapons are for your defence, this ring is a souvenir, and the purse of diamonds is to reimburse you for the ship," said Sandokan.

"You're the strangest man I've ever met," observed the captain, receiving the three objects. "Haven't you stopped to think that I could fire these weapons at you?"

"You'll do no such thing."

"What makes you say that?"

"You're an honourable man. Now go!"

The captain gave a quick salute and went down into the launch. It immediately rowed off, heading west, followed by the others.

Twenty minutes later, the *Helgoland* sailed swiftly towards the coast of Sarawak, which was then no more than a hundred miles away.

"Now let's go pay a visit to Kammamuri and his mistress," said Sandokan, after having set the course.

"Let's hope nothing has happened to poor Ada," added Yanez.

The two pirate leaders went below and knocked upon the Guardian's cabin door.

"Who is it?" asked Kammamuri.

"Sandokan."

"Did we win, Captain?"

"Yes, my friend."

"Long live the Tiger of Malaysia!" howled the Maratha.

He quickly pushed away the furniture he had piled up behind the door and opened it. Yanez and Sandokan entered.

The Maratha was armed to the teeth. He was still clutching his scimitar, and his belt was heavy with daggers and pistols. The madwoman lay upon a small divan, nervously plucking the petals of a Chinese rose she had taken a short while earlier from a vase full of flowers.

Seeing Sandokan and Yanez, she shot to her feet, terror reflected in her eyes.

"The Thugs!... The Thugs!..." she exclaimed.

"They are our friends, mistress," said the Maratha.

She looked at Kammamuri for a moment, then sat back down upon the couch and returned to her flower.

"Did the battle cries have any effect upon her?" Sandokan asked the Maratha.

"Yes," he replied. "She began to tremble, stood up, and yelled, 'The Thugs! The Thugs!', then sat back down and fell silent."

"Nothing else?"

"Nothing else, Captain."

"Keep a close eye on her, Kammamuri."

"I won't leave her side."

Yanez and Sandokan went back up on deck, arriving just as the watchmen sighted a red light far off to the south. It appeared to be moving quickly; the two rushed to the bow and carefully scanned the waters.

"A ship's lantern," said the Portuguese.

"Undoubtedly. And that makes me nervous," replied Sandokan.

"Why is that, little brother?"

"That ship could encounter the launches."

"By the devil! That's all we need!"

"There's no need to fear, Yanez. The *Helgoland* is armed with several excellent cannons. Wait... that's a steamship. Look, you can just see the smoke."

"Good Lord! You're right!"

"Man the cannons! Man the cannons!" thundered the Tiger of Malaysia.

"What are you doing?" asked Yanez, grabbing him by an arm.

"It's the gunboat, Yanez."

"Are you sure?"

"Positive! This time we'll sink her."

"If we fire at her, they'll start shelling us as soon as we get within sight of Sarawak. If we don't sink her with our first broadside, she'll rush off to that scoundrel Brooke and report us."

"By Allah!" exclaimed Sandokan, struck by that reasoning.

"Now let's remain calm, little brother," said Yanez.

"What if she picks up those launches?"

"It's unlikely, Sandokan. It's dark, the launches are flying towards the west, and, if I am not mistaken, the gunboat's bow is pointing north. They won't cross paths. Do you think otherwise?"

"No, but spotting that damned gunboat again..."

"There's no need to trouble yourself, little brother. Let her head north in peace."

The gunboat that had been so stubbornly, but most likely unknowingly, following the pirates of Mompracem was by then only a short distance away. Red and green lanterns shone from her port and starboard sides, a white light from the peak of her foremast. They could make out the helmsman standing at the stern, next to the wheel.

She sailed past the *Helgoland,* tacked, then headed north and disappeared, a bright, phosphorescent wake marking her path. Less than ten minutes later, they heard a distant voice cry out, "Ahoy there in the gunboat!"

At the sound of that cry, Sandokan and Yanez rushed towards the quarterdeck and cast their eyes north.

"The launches?" Sandokan asked uneasily.

"I don't see anything but the gunboat," observed Yanez.

"Advance cautiously and prepare for battle."

Sandokan remained on deck for several hours, hoping to pick up another cry, but heard nothing other than the sound of the wind whistling through the rigging and the clatter of waves breaking against the side of the ship.

At midnight, deep in thought, he descended into the captain's cabin and found Yanez resting on one of the beds. The *Helgoland* sailed throughout the night, traversing the Bay of Sarawak, which grew narrower with each passing meter. The watchmen had not seen anything unusual, except once. At two in the morning, a dark shadow had been sighted about 500 meters off the starboard side. It sailed past at great speed and quickly disappeared. They had thought it a prahu sailing with her lanterns extinguished.

At dawn, the vessel lay forty miles from the mouth of the Sarawak River. The city was only a few hours march from the shore.

The sea and the wind were favourable. Several prahus and a few jong rested at anchor; the lush green slopes of Mount Matang towered faintly in the west.

Sandokan, ill at ease in that stretch of water patrolled by James Brooke's ships, the self-proclaimed 'Exterminator of Pirates', ordered the British flag hoisted up the gaff as a large red banner unfurled from the peak of the mainmast. He had the cannons loaded, the battery stocked with bombs, and ordered his men to draw arms from the magazine.

At eleven that morning, the coast was just seven miles away. It was covered by a stupendous forest and protected by numerous reefs. By noon, the *Helgoland* was rounding the peninsula and heading determinedly into the bay; a short while later she dropped anchor at the mouth of the river, across from Point Montabas.

Chapter 9
The Battle

The mouth of the river formed a kind of natural harbour sheltered from the fury of the sea by a series of reefs and sandbanks. Sago trees, mango trees and groves of pisang laden with golden fruit lined the shore; beyond them, chattering bands of toucans and howling troops of Langur monkeys abounded among the gambir, betel and camphor trees.

Numerous vessels populated the river, Malay, Bugi, Bornean, and Macassar prahus, large Javanese jongs with painted sails, heavy Chinese junks, as well as small Dutch and British ships. Some unloaded cargo while others awaited a favourable wind to raise anchor.

Dyaks lined the reefs and sandbanks, fishing for their next meal, as flocks of albatross and frigate birds wheeled over the bay.

As soon as the *Helgoland* had dropped anchor in the middle of the river, Sandokan quickly scanned the surrounding ships. His eyes immediately fell upon a small, well-armed schooner three hundred meters up the river, strategically anchored to block the path of any approaching vessel.

Upon closer scrutiny, he frowned and cursed beneath his breath.

"Yanez," he said to his friend, who was standing nearby, "Can you make out the name of that ship?"

"Sense trouble?" asked the Portuguese, raising his spyglass.

"I'm not sure. Any luck?"

"Yes. We're looking at the *Royalist*."

"James Brooke's ship. I thought as much."

"Good Lord!" exclaimed the Portuguese. "A formidable neighbour."

"That I'd gladly sink to avenge our brethren."

"You'll do no such thing, unless she attacks us first. We must be cautious, little brother, extremely cautious, if we wish to free poor Tremal-Naik."

"You're right, Yanez."

"Look, there's a boat approaching. Now who do you suppose that could be?"

Sandokan leaned over the bulwark and turned his eyes to where Yanez had pointed. A small canoe was making its way towards the ship. It was manned by a native dressed in a red chawat[1] and a headdress adorned with feathers and a large toucan beak. Copper rings ornamented his arms and legs.

"It's a bazir," said Sandokan.

"A what?"

"A holy man that reveres Dinata or Giuwata, the two gods of the Dyaks."

"What would he want with us?"

"Probably wants to tell our fortunes."

"We have no use for his predictions."

"On the contrary; we'll receive him, Yanez, and obtain information on James Brooke and his fleet."

The small boat drew up beside the ship; Sandokan ordered a rope lowered and the bazir climbed up on deck with surprising agility.

"What brings you here?" asked Sandokan, speaking in the language of the Dyaks.

"I've come to sell my knowledge of the future," replied the bazir, his many bracelets jingling softly.

"Spare me your predictions. I have need of information."

"What kind?"

"Listen closely, my friend. I wish to learn a great many things, if you can answer my questions, you'll be rewarded with a splendid kris and enough tuwak to last you a month."

The Dyak's eyes sparkled greedily.

"Ask away," he said.

---

[1] Loincloth

"Where are you from?"

"Sarawak."

"What is Rajah Brooke up to?"

"He's bolstering his defences!"

"Does he fear a revolt?"

"Yes, it's rumoured our former sultan's nephew has allied himself with the Chinese."

"Have you been in Sarawak this last month?"

"Yes."

"Did you see a prisoner, the color of bronze, arrive in Sarawak?"

The bazir fell silent.

"A tall, handsome man?" he asked after several minutes.

"Yes, strong and handsome," said Sandokan.

"An Indian?"

"Yes."

"He was brought here a few months ago."

"Where was he taken?"

"I do not know, but the fisherman that lives down there could tell you," said the Dyak, pointing to a small hut on the left bank. "He accompanied the prisoner."

"Can I meet this fisherman?"

"He's off fishing now, but he'll return to his hut tonight."

"Excellent. Hirundo, give this man your kris and find him a small barrel of gin."

The pirate did not wait to be told twice. He ordered some men to place a small barrel of alcohol in the canoe and gave his kris to the bazir, who went off as happily as if he had just been awarded an entire province.

"What are you up to, little brother?" asked Yanez, once the Dyak had rowed off.

"We'll strike immediately," replied Sandokan. "It'll be dark in an hour and we'll send for the fisherman."

"And then?"

"Once we learn where they're keeping Tremal-Naik, we'll go to Sarawak and pay a visit to James Brooke."

"James Brooke?"

"We won't go as pirates. You'll pose as a Dutch ambassador."

"We'll run a terrible risk, Sandokan. If Brooke discovers who we are, he'll hang us both."

"There's no need to worry, Yanez. The rope that'll hang the Tiger hasn't been woven yet."

"Captain," said Hirundo, "Some ships are approaching."

The Tiger of Malaysia and Yanez turned towards the mouth of the river and sighted two heavily armed brigantines flying the British flag, attempting to round Point Montabas.

"Great!" said Yanez. "More warships!"

"Surprised?" asked the Tiger of Malaysia.

"I would not underestimate Brooke's resources, little brother. This may not be a chance arrival."

"There's nothing unusual in this, Yanez. There are always a good number of British ships docked here."

After having tacked for a half our, the two brigantines made their way up the river, towed by a half dozen vessels. They saluted the rajah's flag with two cannon blasts, sailed past the *Helgoland* and dropped anchor on either side of the *Royalist*. Night fell quickly after their arrival, blanketing the forests, reefs, boats, junks, and prahus in total darkness.

The time had come to send for the fisherman. A launch was lowered into the water; Hirundo and three pirates quickly climbed aboard and set off for the shore. The Tiger of Malaysia was watching the boat row off, when suddenly the Portuguese rushed towards him, visibly shaken.

"Sandokan!" he exclaimed.

"What's the matter?" asked the pirate "You look terrified!"

"They're planning to attack us!"

"Impossible!" exclaimed the Tiger, looking about menacingly.

"It's true I tell you! Look towards the sea."

Sandokan, suddenly feeling uneasy, cast his eyes towards the mouth of the river. His hands ran instinctively to the hilts of his kris and scimitar.

A soft roar escaped his lips. A large, menacing, dark mass lay anchored near the reef, blocking their path to the bay. It was a ship of immense proportions and she was showing the *Helgoland* her side.

"Damn!" he murmured, not concealing his rage. "How can this be happening? It's impossible."

"She's pointing her cannons at us!" said Yanez.

"Who could have betrayed us?"

"I'd wager on the gunboat."

"Impossible. The gunboat was heading north."

"But at two this morning the watchmen sighted a dark mass flying toward Sarawak."

"And you think...?"

"The gunboat has sounded the alarm," concluded Yanez. "It may have rescued the British in those launches. Who knows? The man that yelled out 'Ahoy there in the gunboat!' could have been a British sailor that had jumped overboard during the battle."

Sandokan turned about and cast his eyes upon the *Royalist.* James Brooke's ship had not moved, but the two British vessels had advanced a considerable distance towards the *Helgoland,* and the Tiger of Malaysia's ship would now be caught in a crossfire.

"Ahh!" exclaimed Sandokan, "They want a fight? Well then, so be it! My cannons will show them who I am!"

He had just uttered those words when a sharp cry rang out from the left bank towards where Hirundo had taken his men.

"Help! Help!" came the cry.

Sandokan, Yanez and the pirates rushed to starboard and fixed their eyes on the dark forest.

"Who was that?" exclaimed a pirate.

"May Dinata make me take my own head if that wasn't Hirundo's voice," said a well-built Dyak.

"Hey! Hirundo!" yelled Yanez.

Two rifle blasts sounded from beneath the trees, followed by four splashes. Despite the profound darkness, the pirates sighted four men swimming desperately towards the ship.

"It's Hirundo!" exclaimed the pirate.

"This is getting serious!" exclaimed another.

"Could this be a joke?" asked a third.

"Silence," said the Tiger. "Throw them a rope."

The four men reached the vessel within minutes. It took them mere seconds to grab onto the rope and climb up onto the bulwark.

"Hirundo!" said Sandokan, recognizing the four pirates he had sent off in search of the fishermen.

"Captain," yelled the Dyak, shaking off the water, "We're surrounded."

"Damn!" thundered the Tiger. "What did you see?"

"The forest is teeming with the rajah's soldiers. They're armed with rifles, hiding behind trees and lying among the bushes. It looks as if they're awaiting the signal to fire."

"You're sure you're not mistaken?"

"There are more than two hundred men; I saw them all with my very eyes. Didn't you hear the two rifle blasts they fired at us?"

"Yes, I heard them."

"What are we going to do, little brother?" asked Yanez.

"We're trapped hear; we'll prepare for an attack. We'll let them fire the first shot. Tigers! To arms!!"

The pirates, who had been standing a respectful distance away, came forward at the Tiger's command. Their eyes sparkled, their hands rested upon the hilts of their krises. Battle was imminent and they were impatient for it to begin.

"Tigers of Mompracem," said Sandokan, "James Brooke, the Exterminator, is preparing to attack us. He has murdered thousands of men, thousands of Malays and Dyaks; their souls ask you, their brethren, for vengeance. Swear before me now that you will avenge them."

"We swear!" replied the pirates in unison, as a wave of frightening enthusiasm rippled through them.

"Tigers of Mompracem," continued Sandokan, "There are four of them for every one of us. We'll shower them with fire and steel for as long as we have powder and cannonballs, then we'll set fire to the ship.

Tonight, we'll show those dogs what the Tigers of Mompracem can do. Man your stations! Fire upon my command!"

A hushed cry was the only response to those rousing words uttered by the Tiger of Malaysia. The pirates, with Yanez at their head, rushed into the battery and pointed the black throats of their cannons towards the enemy ships. Two pirates remained on the bridge, standing near the wheel, while Sandokan carefully observed enemy movements from the forecastle.

At first glance, the four ships preparing to shell the *Helgoland* with their forty cannons appeared to be in a state of deep slumber. Not a single sound emanated from them; however, a careful eye could spot shadows flitting about their decks.

It won't be long now, thought Sandokan. In ten minutes, fifty cannons will light the bay, filling the air with the roar of artillery, the howls of the wounded, and the cries of the victors! What a magnificent sight it will be!

Suddenly a frown appeared upon his brow.

"Ada!" he murmured, "What if she were to be struck by a bullet? Sambigliong! Sambigliong!"

A Dyak quickly rushed to the Tiger's side.

"Yes, Captain," he replied.

"Where's Kammamuri?" asked Sandokan.

"In the Guardian's cabin."

"Go there immediately. Take some men and start piling as many barrels, mattresses and as much scrap metal as you can find along the walls of the cabin."

"To secure it from cannon fire?"

"Yes, Sambigliong."

"Leave it to me, Captain. Not a scrap of iron will get in."

"Go, my friend!"

"Should I remain in the cabin once the fortifications are complete?"

"Yes, if we're forced to abandon ship, it'll fall to you to save the Guardian. You're the best swimmer in Malaysia. Hurry, Sambigliong! The enemy is preparing to attack."

The Dyak rushed towards the stern. Sandokan returned to the bow and carefully scanned the waters. A flare shot up from the vessel blocking the mouth of the river. Instantly, a light flashed from the *Royalist's* bridge, followed by a formidable discharge.

The Tiger of Malaysia jumped as the tip of the mainmast, blunted by an eight-calibre cannon ball, crashed to the deck.

"Tigers!" he howled. "Return fire!"

Tremendous cries filled the air, "Long live the Tiger of Malaysia! Long live Mompracem!"

A brief, menacing silence ensued then the small waterway lit up from end to end.

Flashes of fire, smoke and cannonballs erupted from the four enemy vessels, tearing at the darkness and shattering the silence; a blaze of musket fire flashed from the forest and spread with inconceivable speed along the shore.

The battle had started. The five vessels fought with overwhelming anger, flashing and thundering, as a hurricane of iron tore through the air.

The *Helgoland*, anchored in the middle of the bay, furiously defended herself from her giant attackers. She fired from her port side, she fired from her starboard side, without missing a single shot, returning a volley for each volley received, bomb for bomb, knocking down masts, shredding rigging, toppling cannons, smashing in batteries, ramming through hulls, bombarding the very forests that concealed James Brooke's men. She looked like a ship of steel defended by an army of titans.

Her masts shook, her yardarms fell, enemy fire gutted her launches, demolished her bulwarks, smashed through her sides and killed her crew, but what did it matter? There was enough gunpowder and cannonballs for all, and the men aboard the *Helgoland* gave no quarter, determined to perish rather than surrender. Every blast, every discharge, was accompanied by the battle cry of the Tigers of Mompracem, "Vengeance! Long live Mompracem!"

The Tiger of Malaysia stood at the centre of the ship, contemplating the horrible spectacle before him.

That formidable man stood motionless upon the bridge as it trembled beneath his feet, among the flashes of fifty cannons, eyes blazing, hair blowing in the wind, lips parted in a frightful smile, clutching a scimitar. Masts fell before him, grapeshot roared past angrily as it smashed through the deck plates, bombs exploded in a shower of burning shrapnel, but the pirate merely smiled as death rained down about him. His enemies, spotting him on that heroic vessel, standing firm, among that hurricane of steel, could not hide their admiration.

The battle lasted for half an hour, growing ever fiercer, ever more ruthless. The *Helgoland*, riddled with holes from the grapeshot, and torn to pieces by the relentless barrage from no less than fifty cannons, was now no more than a smoking hulk.

Masts, rigging, bulwarks, and deck plates lay in ruins. The ship was little more then a sponge; the river rushing into every hole. She was still firing, continuing to reply to those four enemies that had sworn to sink her, but she could not sustain the battle for much longer. Ten pirates lay dead in the battery; two cannons had been destroyed, smashed to pieces by enemy fire; cannonballs were in short supply, and the stern was filling with water. Ten, perhaps fifteen minutes more, and the heroic *Helgoland* would have sunk beneath the waves.

Bravely firing one of the largest cannons, Yanez quickly realized the gravity of the situation. At the risk of being shot, he rushed to the Tiger of Malaysia's side.

"Little brother!" he yelled.

"Fire, Yanez! Fire!" thundered Sandokan. "They're moving to board us."

"We can't keep this up any more, little brother! The ship is sinking!"

A formidable crash followed those words. Struck by a broadside of grenades, the forecastle had fallen, smashing in the crew's quarters and part of the deck. The Tiger of Malaysia roared in anger.

"It's over! Tigers, it's over!"

He rushed into the battery from where the Tigers of Mompracem continued to bombard the enemy vessels. Kammamuri quickly appeared before him.

"Captain," he said, "water's gushing into the Guardian's cabin."

"Where's Sambigliong?" asked the Tiger.

"In the cabin with my mistress."

"Is she still alive?"

"Yes, Captain."

"Bring her on deck and stand ready to jump into the river. Tigers, everyone on deck!"

The pirates fired their cannons one last time then rushed onto the deck, making their way through the wreckage.

Towed by several launches, the enemy ships were approaching, planning to board the *Helgoland* at their first opportunity.

"Sandokan!" yelled Yanez, unable to find his formidable friend. "Sandokan!"

His only reply was the victorious cries of the enemy crews and the blasts form the pirates' carbines.

"Sandokan!" he repeated, "Sandokan!"

"Here I am, brother," replied a voice.

The Tiger of Malaysia rushed onto the deck, clutching a scimitar in his right hand and a torch in his left, followed by Sambigliong and Kammamuri carrying the Guardian of the Temple of the East.

"Tigers of Mompracem!" thundered Sandokan. "Fire one last volley!"

"Long live the Tiger!" howled the pirates as they emptied their carbines at the four vessels.

The *Helgoland* rocked like a drunkard as she rapidly gave way beneath the continual barrage of enemy fire. Water roared through every tear in her sides, quickly pulling her down into the river. Thick clouds of smoke spewed from the bow, the stern, hatches, gun ports and batteries. The Tiger of Malaysia's voice rang out one last time among the roar of cannons.

"Abandon ship! Sambigliong, take the Guardian and jump into the river!"

The Dyak and Kammamuri jumped into the water, carrying the young woman. The others followed quickly, swimming among the enemy vessels that had drawn up alongside the sinking ship. One man alone had remained aboard, the Tiger of Malaysia, scimitar drawn, the torch burning brightly. A sinister smile spread across his lips, as a ferocious light flashed from his eyes.

"Long live Mompracem!" he yelled.

A formidable hurrah echoed through the air. Twenty, forty, one hundred men rushed onto the *Helgoland*'s shaking deck, weapons at the ready. The Tiger of Malaysia waited no longer. With one quick move he leaped over the bulwark and disappeared into the water.

Almost at the same instant, a horrendous explosion tore the ship in two; a giant flame shot towards the sky, lighting the river, the enemy ships, the forest and the mountains, as a shower of flaming wreckage rained down from the heavens. The enemy vessels and their crews had disappeared among the smoke and flames; the *Helgoland*'s powder magazine had caught fire and destroyed them all.

Part II

The Rajah of Sarawak

Chapter 1
The Chinese Tavern

"Hey! Good man!"

"Milord!"

"To hell with your *Milords*."

"Sir!"

"To hell with your *Sirs*."

"Monsieur? Señor!"

"Go hang yourself. What kind of lunch is this?"

"Chinese, Señor, this is a Chinese tavern."

"What makes you think I want to eat Chinese food?! What are these bugs moving about my plate?"

"*Chooi Har*. Drunken shrimp from Sarawak."

"You'd have me eat live shrimp? Hell!"

"It's Chinese cuisine, monsieur."

"And this roast?"

"Young dog, Señor."

"What?"

"Young dog."

"Hell! Eat a puppy? And this?"

"Cat, Señor."

"Thunder and lightning! Cat!"

"A meal fit for a king, sir."

"And this fried stuff?"

"Mice fried in butter."

"Dog of a Chinaman! Are you trying to poison me!?!"

"Chinese cuisine, Señor."

"The Devil's cuisine, you mean. Hell! Drunken shrimp, fried mice, roast dog and cats for lunch! If my brother were here, he'd die laughing. But, I guess there's no need to be fussy. If the Chinese can eat this stuff, I guess Europeans can as well. Best just to dig in!"

Speaking in such a way the man made himself comfortable in the bamboo chair, drew a magnificent kris with a diamond-studded, gold hilt from his belt, and encouraged by the appetizing aroma, began to carve the roast dog into small pieces.

Between mouthfuls, he studied his surroundings.

The room had a low ceiling; paintings of dragons, exotic flowers, crescent moons, and mystical animals covered the walls. Beneath them, Chinese men with long *bianzi*[2] and drooping moustaches snored upon benches and mats. Several tables of varying size were scattered about randomly, occupied by rough-looking, black-toothed, olive-skinned Malays and various semi-clad Dyaks armed with parangs, heavy knives more than a half meter in length. Many consumed jars of arak or tuwak or smoked long opium pipes; others chewed *siri*, a mixture of betel leaves and areca nuts, at times spitting dark red blobs of saliva onto the floor.

"What a band of ruffians!" muttered the man as he tore into the cat meat. "I wonder how that scoundrel James Brooke manages to keep the wretches in line. He must be as sly as a fox and..."

A sharp whistle from outside the tavern interrupted his thoughts.

"Oh!" he exclaimed.

He placed his fingers to his lips and replied in kind.

"Yes, Señor!" yelled the tavern keeper, skinning a large dog whose throat he had just slit.

"May Confucius hang you!"

"Did you call, monsieur?"

"Quiet. Skin your dog and leave me be."

A tall, well-built, bare-chested Indian with a silk kerchief fastened about his waist and a kris dangling against his right hip, entered the

---

[2] A long plait of hair or ponytail traditionally worn by Chinese men. Also know as the Manchu queue.

room, his large dark eyes scanning the interior. Upon spotting the new arrival, the European who had been gnawing at a fried cat leg, stood up and murmured, "Kammamuri!"

He was about to leave the table, but a rapid gesture from the Indian warned him not to move.

"Understood. There's danger in the air," he murmured. "Best keep your guard up, my friend."

After a brief hesitation, the Indian sat down at an empty table next to him. The tavern keeper immediately rushed to take his order.

"A glass of tuwak!" said the new arrival.

The Chinese turned about and had a glass and a jar of tuwak brought to the table.

"Are they spying on us?" the European whispered to Kammamuri, as he continued to devour his meal.

The Indian nodded affirmatively.

"What an appetite you have, sir!" he exclaimed loudly.

"I haven't eaten anything in over twenty-four hours, my friend," replied the man who, as the reader may have already imagined, was the good Yanez, the Tiger of Malaysia's ever-loyal friend.

"Have you come from very far?"

"From Europe. Hey! Wretched barkeep, some tuwak!"

"Take some of mine, sir." said Kammamuri.

"I accept, young man. Won't you join me? Try a bit of all this stuff they brought me."

The Maratha did not wait to be begged; he sat down beside the Portuguese and began to eat.

"We may speak freely," said Yanez. "No one will suspect we're friends. Is everyone alright?"

"Yes, Señor Yanez," replied Kammamuri. "Shortly before dawn we left the forest and hid in a large swamp. The rajah sent soldiers to search along the mouth of the river, but they did not find our tracks."

"We were lucky, Kammamuri."

"I know. If we'd stayed aboard thirty more seconds, we would've blown up along with the ship. Fortunately, it was too dark for the soldiers to spot us swimming ashore."

"What about Ada?"

"She came through it unscathed, Señor Yanez. Sambigliong and I brought her ashore."

"Where's Sandokan now?"

"Deep in the forest, about eight miles from here."

"Safe then."

"I hope. I spotted some of the rajah's guards patrolling the forest."

"Damn!"

"What about you, aren't you running any danger?"

"What kind of crazy fool would mistake me for a pirate? Me, a white man, a civilized son of Europe?"

"Keep your guard up, Señor Yanez. The rajah's a very cunning man."

"I know, but we're just as cunning, even more so."

"Any news on Tremal-Naik?"

"I've asked several people, but no one has seen or heard anything."

"Poor master," murmured Kammamuri.

"We'll rescue him, you have my word," said Yanez. "It begins tonight."

"What are you going to do?"

"Try to get close to the rajah and become his friend."

"How?"

"I have an idea; it's simple but effective. I'll start a fight, make a lot of noise, threaten to kill someone and have myself arrested by the rajah's guards."

"And then?"

"After they've arrested me, I'll invent some kind of fabulous tale and try to pass myself off as a noble lord, perhaps a baron..."

"What should I do?"

"Nothing, my good Maratha. Go back to Sandokan and inform him that all is proceeding according to plan. Come buzz about the rajah's palace tomorrow. I may need you."

Kammamuri stood up.

"Just a moment," said Yanez, drawing a heavy purse from his pocket and offering it to Indian.

"What's that for?"

"For my plan to work, I can't have so much as penny in my pocket. Give me your kris; it isn't worth much, now take mine, the gold and diamonds could purchase this tavern let alone the meal. Hey! Infernal barkeep, six bottles of Spanish wine."

"You plan to get drunk?" asked Kammamuri.

"Leave it to me; I'll give them quite a show. Goodbye, my friend."

The Indian tossed a shilling onto the table and left as the Portuguese began to uncork the expensive bottles. He gulped down two or three glasses and gave the remainder to the Malays sitting nearby, who, though quick to accept, were stunned at finding such a generous European.

"Barkeep!" the Portuguese yelled again, "Bring me some more wine and one of your best dishes."

The Chinese tavern keeper, ecstatic at doing such great business and in his heart begging the Great Buddha to send him a dozen such clients every day, brought forth more bottles and terra-cotta pots filled with delicate birds' nests seasoned with salt and vinegar, a dish only wealthy men could afford.

Despite having eaten enough for two, the Portuguese dug in once again, drinking heartily and offering wine to all those seated about him.

His exotic banquet finally came to an end a half hour after sunset; large talc lanterns had been lit in the tavern, bathing the drinkers in the soft light dear to the sons of the Celestial Empire.

He lit a cigarette, examined his pistol then stood up, murmuring, "Time for the show, Yanez."

It was simple; he would leave without paying. The tavern keeper would make an infernal racket, he would be even louder, the rajah's guards would rush in to quell the disturbance and he'd be arrested. Sandokan himself could not have come up with a better plan. He blew out three puffs of smoke and headed calmly towards the door. He was about to cross the threshold, when he felt a hand upon his jacket.

"Monsieur!" said a voice.

Yanez turned with a frown and found the tavern keeper standing before him.

"What can I do for you, you scoundrel?" he asked, feigning offence.

"Your bill, Señor."

"For what?"

"You have not paid me. You owe me three pounds, seven shillings and four pence."

"Go to hell. I haven't so much as a penny in any of my ten pockets."

The Chinese tavern keeper's face grew ashen.

"You will pay me," he yelled, grabbing the Portuguese.

"Unhand me you scoundrel!" howled Yanez.

"You owe me three pounds, seven shillings and..."

"Four pence, I know, but I'm not going to pay you, you wretch... go skin your dog and leave me be."

"Then you're a thief, sir! I'll have you arrested!"

"Try it!"

"Help! Arrest this thief!" howled the furious tavern keeper.

Four scullery boys armed with saucepans, pots and skimming spoons rushed in to help their boss. Things were unfolding as planned. The Portuguese could not have asked for a better reaction.

With a firm hand he grabbed the tavern keeper by the throat, picked him up and threw him out the door, smashing his nose against the boulders lining the path. Then he turned and made short work of the four scullery boys; a series of kicks enough to send them flying to their master's side.

A torrent of devilish cries filled the air.

"Help!" howled the tavern keeper.

"Thief! Assassin! Kill him! Murder him!" howled the scullery boys.

Chapter 2
A Night in Prison

Such cries emitted by Chinese men in the Chinese quarter, had the same effect as a gong sounding in a street in Canton or Peking. In less than two minutes, about two hundred of the tavern keeper's countrymen, armed with bamboo sticks, knives, rocks and umbrellas, had gathered in front of the tavern door, howling and shouting at the top of their lungs.

"Get the thief!" yelled some, waving their clubs and umbrellas menacingly.

"Hang the white man!" yelled others, brandishing their knives.

"Throw him in the river!"

"Kill him! Drown him! Burn him! Hang him!"

Frightened by that noise and afraid of being stoned to death, the drinkers quickly fled from the tavern, some through the door, making their way through the throng, others through the windows, which fortunately were not too far from the ground. Only the Portuguese remained, laughing to the point of insanity, as if he were taking part in a brilliant farce.

"Bravo! Excellent! Encore!" he yelled, loading his pistol and drawing his kris from his belt.

A Chinese vendor at the front of the group shouted a series of imprecations, hurled a few stones at him, missed, and ended up smashing a large straw covered bottle of *sam sciu*, spilling the liquor onto the ground.

"Ah! Rascal!" yelled the Portuguese, "You'll be the tavern keeper's ruin."

He picked up the stone, flung it at his attacker, and smashed in one of his teeth. Even louder cries emanated throughout the district, drawing still more Chinese, several of which were armed with old harquebuses.

Encouraged by the tavern keeper and his companions, three or four men attempted to enter the tavern, but at the sight of the Portuguese's pistols, they quickly turned about and ran off.

"Stone him!" shouted a voice.

"What about my tavern?" moaned the tavern keeper.

A barrage of stones rained through the tavern door, smashing lanterns, bottles, dishes, terracotta bowls and vases. Realizing that the situation was becoming dangerous, the Portuguese fired his pistols into the air. Seven shots thundered in reply, missing their mark but adding to the noise.

Suddenly several voices shouted, "Make way! Make way!"

"The rajah's guards!"

The Portuguese let out a sigh of relief. The noise, the knives, the assortment of clubs flailing in the air, the shower of stones, the musket fire and the continual influx of people had started to become worrisome.

"Now that I'm out of danger, I can cause even more of an uproar," he said.

He rushed towards a table and knocked it over, shattering the flasks, jars and plates upon it.

"Arrest him! Arrest him!" howled the tavern keeper. "He's destroying everything I own."

"Make way! Make way for the guards!" yelled several men.

A path opened among the crowd and two tall, well-built, dark-skinned men appeared at the door. They wore uniforms of white cloth and had drawn their *draghinasse*.

"Back!" shouted the Portuguese, aiming his pistols at them.

"A European!" exclaimed the two guards in amazement.

"An Englishman," corrected Yanez.

The two guards sheathed their knives.

"We wish you no harm," said one. "We serve your countryman, Rajah Brooke."

"What do you want with me?"

"To escort you to safety."

"And to some jail no doubt!"

"That's up to the rajah."

"You're going to take me to him?"

"Yes, sir."

"Fine then, lead the way. I have nothing to fear from Rajah Brooke."

The two guards placed the prisoner between them then unsheathed their *draghinasse* once again to protect him from the rage of the throng.

"Make way!" they yelled.

Their numbers greatly increased, the Chinese did not move, wanting to lynch the European at all costs.

The two guards, however, did not back down. Dispensing vigorous kicks and administering blows with the flat of their swords, they opened a path and lead the prisoner down a narrow lane, threatening to kill anyone who dared to follow.

After having shouted all kinds of curses and imprecations at Yanez, the guards and even the rajah himself who they accused of sheltering thieves and scoundrels, the crowd dispersed, leaving the tavern keeper and his four melancholy scullery boys to tend to the damage.

Sarawak was not a large city. It took less than five minutes for the two guards to reach the rajah's villa. It was made of wood, just like all the other Western style houses that crowned the surrounding hills. The British flag fluttered from the rooftop, an Indian armed with a rifle and a bayonet guarded the main entrance.

"Are you taking me to see the rajah?"

"Not at this hour," replied one of the guards. "His Excellency is asleep."

"So where am I going to pass the night?"

"We'll assign you a room."

"As long as it's not some wine cellar."

"We'd never do that to one of the rajah's countrymen."

The Portuguese was led up some stairs and into a small room. It contained a hammock made of coconut fibres and a few pieces of European furniture. Mats of nipa leaves covered the windows; a lamp hung from the ceiling, bathing the room in a dim light.

"Good Lord!" he exclaimed, rubbing his hands happily. "I'll sleep like a babirussa."

"Is there anything else we can get you?" asked one of the guards.

"Just let me sleep," replied Yanez.

One of the guards left the room, the other sat down beside the door, took out an areca nut wrapped in a betel leaf and popped it into his mouth.

An opportunity to get some information, thought Yanez.

He rolled up a cigarette, lit it, took a few puffs and approached the guard.

"Young man, are you from India by chance?" he asked.

"Bengal, sir," replied the guard.

"Have you been here long?"

"Two years."

"Have you ever heard speak of a pirate they call the Tiger of Malaysia?"

"Yes."

Yanez barely suppressed a cry of joy.

"Is it true the Tiger is here?" he asked.

"I don't know; I heard some pirates came ashore after a battle on the river, about twenty or thirty miles from here."

"Where?"

"We don't know their exact location, but we'll find out soon enough."

"How?"

"The rajah has excellent spies."

"I heard a British ship ran aground near Cape Tanjong-Datu a few months ago."

"Yes," replied the Indian. "A warship from Calcutta."

"Who went to assist her?"

"Our rajah aboard his ship, the *Royalist.*"

"Did they rescue the crew?"

"Yes, everyone, including an Indian prisoner sentenced to life on some island."

"An Indian prisoner!" exclaimed Yanez, feigning surprise. "Who was he?"

"His name was Tremal-Naik."

"What was his crime?" Yanez asked anxiously.

"They say he killed several Englishmen."

"The wretch! Is he still here?"

"They're holding him in the fort."

"Which one?"

"The one on the hill. There's only one fort in Sarawak."

"Is it garrisoned?"

"There are about sixty men there, including the crew from the shipwrecked vessel."

Yanez grimaced.

Sixty men! he thought. Not to mention cannons.

He began to pace about the room, thinking over what he had just heard. He continued for several minutes, then stretched out on the hammock, asked the guard to dim the lamp, and closed his eyes. Despite the many thoughts running through his head, the Portuguese slept as deeply as if he were aboard the *Pearl of Labuan* or in the Tiger of Malaysia's fortified hut. When he awoke, a ray of sunlight was beaming through the nipa leaves that served as blinds.

Yanez glanced at the door; the guard was no longer there. Once his prisoner had fallen asleep, he had left, certain that such a man would not have escaped through a window.

"Excellent," said the Portuguese. "Let's take advantage of the situation."

He jumped down from the hammock, washed his face, raised the mats covering the window and took a deep breath of the cool morning air.

Sarawak looked lovely with its wooden villas and lush green forests; its large river, shaded by superb trees, teemed with prahus, canoes, and longboats. Chinese, Dyaks, Bugis, and Macassars crowded the streets and lanes as they busily went about their day.

The Portuguese quickly scanned the city, his gaze passing from the exotically shaped houses and brightly coloured roofs of the Chinese district, to the towering nipa huts mounted on posts in the Dyak quarter. At last they came to rest upon the hills, where he spotted a small church and not too far from it, a fort of solid construction.

The Portuguese studied it attentively.

"If that's where they're keeping Tremal-Naik," he murmured, "how are we going to free him?"

At that same moment, a voice from behind him said, "The rajah will see you now."

Yanez turned about and found the Bengali standing before him.

"Ah! It's you, my friend," he said with a smile. "How is Rajah Brooke this morning?"

"He's waiting for you, sir."

"Let's go shake his hand then."

They left the room, went up another set of stairs and entered a type of drawing room whose walls disappeared behind weapons of all shapes and sizes.

"The rajah is in the study," said the Bengali.

What am I going to say? thought the Portuguese. Watch your step, Yanez. You're dealing with a cunning old wolf.

He braced himself, opened the door and entered the study; there in the middle of the room, at a table strewn with maps, sat the Rajah of Sarawak.

Chapter 3
Rajah James Brooke

James Brooke, to whose bravery all of Malaysia and the maritime fleets of the east and west are deeply indebted, deserves a few lines of history. This daring man, who through bloody battles and tremendous efforts earned the title 'Exterminator of Pirates', descended from the family of Sir Robert Vyner, baronet, Lord Mayor of London during the reign of Charles II. When he was still a young man, he enrolled in the Indian army as an ensign standard bearer. Gravely wounded in a battle against the Borneans, he resigned his commission and retired to Calcutta. A quiet life, however, did not suit young Brooke, a cold and practical man with incredible energy and an appetite for danger.

Once his wound had healed, he returned to the seas of Malaysia and explored every corner. That voyage marked the beginning of his reputation; his fame would soon spread throughout the globe.

Malay pirates ruled those waters; their incessant butchery and plundering kept local tribes living in fear. Angered by the pirates' brutality, their wanton destruction, and their flourishing slave trade, he decided to liberate the waters of Malaysia and, in so doing, free its people and make the sea safe for navigation.

James Brooke tenaciously fulfilled his objectives. Having overcome the obstacles and opposition he encountered from his government in the execution of his bold plan, he armed a small schooner, the *Royalist*, and in 1838 set sail for Sarawak, a small city in Borneo that then numbered no more than 1500 inhabitants. His timing could not have been worse.

The population of Sarawak, perhaps incited by Malay pirates, was attempting to overthrow its ruler, the Sultan Muda Hassim, and a civil war raged with extreme anger. Brooke immediately offered the sultan his help, took command of the troops, and after numerous battles quelled the rebellion in less than twenty months.

When the campaign was over, he took to the sea in an expedition against pirates and slave traders. With his crew, battle hardened from two years of campaigning, he put his plans for complete eradication into action, fighting, destroying and torching his enemies. It is impossible to calculate the numbers of pirates he executed, the number of ships and prahus he sank, the number of enemy strongholds he burned to the ground. He was cruel and merciless, perhaps too much so.

Once he had defeated the pirates, he returned to Sarawak. Sultan Muda Hassim, appreciative of the great services Brooke had rendered, made him rajah of the small city and its surrounding district.

In 1852, the year in which these events are about to unfold, James Brooke was at the height of his power; with but a gesture he could make the Sultan of Varauni tremble, even though the sultan ruled the largest kingdom on the island of Borneo.

Hearing Yanez enter, the rajah quickly stood up. Though close to the fifty year mark, and despite the ravages of a gruelling lifestyle, he was still a strong, vigorous man with indomitable energy. However, several wrinkles lined his brow, and his white hair announced the onset of old age.

"Excellency!" said Yanez with a bow.

"Welcome," said the rajah, returning the greeting.

The reception was encouraging. Though his heart had started to pound upon entering the room, Yanez managed to relax.

"What happened last night?" asked the rajah, after having offered Yanez a chair. "My guards reported that you fired your pistols a few times. You shouldn't irritate the Chinese, my friend, there are a good number of them in Sarawak and many have no great love for Europeans."

"I'd just come off of an incredibly long march, Excellency, and I was dying of hunger. When I found myself standing before that Chinese tavern, I could not resist the urge to eat and drink, so I went in, even though I knew I didn't have so much as a shilling in my pockets."

"What!?!" exclaimed the rajah. "Not so much as a shilling? Tell me then, what brings you here? I know all the foreigners in my state, but I've never seen you before."

"It's my first visit to Sarawak," said Yanez.

"Where are you from?"

"Liverpool."

"What ship brought you here?"

"My yacht, Excellency."

"May I have your name, sir?"

"Lord Giles Welker of Closeburn," Yanez replied smoothly.

The rajah proffered his hand and the Portuguese shook it warmly.

"It gives me great pleasure to receive a Lord from noble Scotland," said the rajah.

"Thank you, Excellency," replied Yanez with a bow.

"Where did you leave your yacht?"

"At the mouth of the Palo."

"How did you get here?"

"I marched over two hundred miles, through forests and swamps, living off of fruit like a savage."

The rajah looked at him in surprise.

"Were you lost?" he asked.

"No, Excellency."

"Was your yacht shipwrecked?"

"No, sunk by volleys of cannon fire, after it was looted of all it contained."

"By who?"

"Pirates, Excellency."

The rajah jumped up, his eyes blazing, his face filled with terrible rage.

"Pirates!" he exclaimed. "Haven't all those wretches been destroyed?"

"It would appear not, Excellency."

"Did you get a look at the leader of those pirates?"

"Yes," said Yanez.

"Could you describe him?"

"Handsome features, black hair, tanned skin, incredible strength."

"Ah, him!" exclaimed the rajah excitedly.

"Who?"

"The Tiger of Malaysia."

"I've heard that name before. Who is he?" asked Yanez.

"A powerful man, Milord, with the courage of a lion and the ferocity of a tiger. He's the leader of a band of fearless pirates. Three days ago, he dropped anchor at the mouth of my river."

"What daring!" exclaimed Yanez, barely containing a shudder. "Did you attack him?"

"Yes, and I defeated him. But victory came at a great cost."

"Ah!"

"I lost sixty of my men in that battle. We had the Tiger surrounded, but before we could take him, he set fire to his powder room and blew up his ship. Took one of mine along with it."

"So he was killed?"

"I doubt it, Milord. I ordered my men to search for his body, but they did not find it."

"Then he's still alive?"

"I suspect he's found refuge in the forests along with his men."

"Do you think he'll attempt to attack the city?"

"He has the capacity, but he won't find me unprepared. I've bolstered my defences with loyal Dyak troops, and I've sent several of my Indian guides to patrol the forest."

"Wise precautions, Excellency."

"The least I could do, Milord," laughed the rajah. "But please, continue your story. When did the Tigers attack you?"

"Two days ago, I set sail from Varauni and pointed my bow towards Cape Sirik. I'd planned to visit the main cities of Borneo, before heading back to Batavia and India."

"Were you on a pleasure cruise?"

"Yes, Excellency. I'd been at sea for eleven months."

"Continue, Milord."

"At around sunset on the third day, my yacht dropped anchor near the mouth of the Palo. I went ashore and headed into the forest, alone, hoping to capture a couple of babirussa or a dozen toucans. I'd been walking for two hours, when I heard a cannon blast then a second, then a third, then a furious, incessant exchange of artillery. Frightened, I ran back towards the coast. But it was too late. The pirates had boarded my yacht, killed the crew, and started looting the vessel. I remained hidden then once they had sunk my ship and sailed off, I rushed to the shore.

"The tip of the mainmast stood a half-foot above the water; it was all that remained of my ship. I scanned the waves for survivors and spotted the bodies of my crew being dashed against the reef.

"In desperation, I wandered about the mouth of the river for the entire night, yelling out the names of my crewmen, but in vain. When morning came, I set out, following the coast, making my way through forests, swamps and rivers, feeding off of fruit and whatever birds my carbine could procure. When I reached Sedang, I sold my watch and my weapon, my last remaining possessions, and I rested for forty-eight hours. Having purchased new clothes from a Dutch colonist, a pair of pistols and a kris, I set off once more and arrived here, starving, exhausted, and penniless."

"What are your plans now?"

"I have a brother in Madras and a few estates in Scotland. I'll write and have him send me a few thousand pounds then I'll take the first ship back to England."

"Lord Welker," said the rajah, "I place my home and my purse at your disposal, and I'll do everything in my power to ensure you are not bored during your stay in my kingdom."

An expression of joy spread across Yanez's face.

"But, Excellency..." he stammered, pretending to be embarrassed.

"Milord, I would do as much for any of my countrymen."

"How can I thank you?"

"Should I visit Scotland one day, you'll return the favour."

"I swear it, Excellency. My estates will always be at the disposal of you and your friends."

"Thank you, Milord," said the rajah with a smile.

He rang a bell. An Indian servant appeared.

"This gentleman is my friend," said the rajah, pointing to the Portuguese. "My house, my purse, my horses, and my weapons are at his disposal."

"As you wish, Rajah," replied the Indian.

"What are your plans for the day, Milord?" asked the prince.

"A walk around the city, and, with your permission, Excellency, I'd like to venture into the forest. I love to hunt."

"Will you join me for lunch later?"

"It would be my pleasure, Excellency."

"Pandij, show our guest to his room."

The Portuguese left the study and followed the Indian to the guest quarters.

"You may go," he said to the servant. "I'll ring if I need you."

Once alone, the Portuguese studied his new surroundings. It was a vast room papered with a beautiful Tonga floral print, furnished with refinement and lit by two windows that looked out onto the hills. There was a good bed, a small table, chairs made of the finest bamboo, Chinese spittoons, a beautiful gilded lamp that must have come from Europe and several weapons of European, Indian, Malay and Bornean design.

Excellent, thought the Portuguese, rubbing his hands happily. His new friend Brooke was treating him like a lord. Soon Yanez would show him just what kind of Lord Welker he was, but he had to be careful, he knew he was dealing with an old wolf.

A sharp whistle from outside interrupted his thoughts. The Portuguese started.

"Kammamuri," he murmured. "You're taking a great risk, my friend."

Chapter 4
In the forest

He closed the door, locking and bolting it as a precaution, then cautiously approached the window. Forty paces from the villa, in the cool shadow of a sago palm, stood the Maratha, leaning against a long bamboo rod capped by a sharp, undoubtedly poisoned, metal tip. Not without surprise, the Portuguese spotted a small horse standing next to him. Two large baskets of nipa leaves were strapped to it, filled to the brim with sago bread and various kinds of fruit.

"The Maratha is more cautious than I thought," murmured Yanez. "He looks like one of those suppliers for the mines."

He rolled up a cigarette and lit it. The small flame immediately drew Kammamuri's attention.

He's spotted me, thought Yanez, but he isn't moving. Good, caution above all.

He quickly signalled the Indian to wait, then drew away from the window, went to the small table and opened the drawer. He found several sheets of paper, an inkwell, pens and a purse that jingled metallically when he shook it.

"My friend has thought of everything," laughed the Portuguese.

He took out a sheet of paper, ripped it in half and wrote in tiny script:

> Be careful and keep your eyes open. Meet me at the
> Chinese tavern.

He rolled up the piece of paper and pulled down a long, hardwood tube from the wall. It was hollow and armed at one end with an iron bayonet held in place with strips of rattan fibre. About a meter and a

91

half in length, the Dyak sumpitan or blowpipe is the most destructive weapon in the native arsenal. Warriors use it, of course, raised to the mouth, and can strike from a hundred yards with extraordinary precision; at sixty yards the force of their "blow" is sufficient to kill a monkey, and at twenty yards to send the arrow half its length into the enemy's flesh. In wartime, arrows are dipped in gum harvested from an upas tree, a poison so strong it can kill a man in minutes.

"I bet I've still got it," said the Portuguese, examining the weapon.

He took down an arrow, wrapped the note around it and slid it into the tube. One strong blow propelled it to the Maratha's side. Kammamuri quickly picked it up and removed the slip of paper.

"Time to go," said Yanez, once Kammamuri had run off.

He slung a double-barrelled shotgun over his shoulder and went out, receiving a respectful salute from a guard as he left the villa. In less than a quarter of an hour he arrived at the tavern and spotted the Maratha's horse standing near the door.

"Better get the money ready," mumbled the Portuguese. "I foresee a tempestuous welcome."

He peered inside the tavern. In a corner, seated before a terracotta bowl full of rice, was Kammamuri, and behind the counter, wearing a pair of smoky quartz glasses, stood the tavern keeper, busily scribbling upon a sheet of paper with a large brush, more than likely going over his books.

"Hey," yelled the Portuguese, upon entering.

The tavern keeper raised his head. Recognizing his client from the previous night, he jumped to his feet and rushed towards him, threateningly brandishing his oversized pen.

"Scoundrel!" he howled.

The Portuguese was ready for him.

"I've come to pay you," he said, throwing a handful of coins upon the table.

"Great Buddha!" exclaimed the tavern keeper, rushing towards the money. "Eight pounds! I beg your pardon, Señor..."

"Enough; bring me a bottle of Spanish wine."

The tavern keeper rushed off, returned with a bottle and placed it before Yanez, then ran to a gong that hung over the door and began to beat it furiously.

"What are you doing?" asked Yanez.

"Saving your life, sir," he replied. "I must inform my friends that you've paid me, otherwise who knows what could happen to you in the next couple of days."

Yanez threw another ten pounds upon the table.

"Tell your friends that Lord Welker would like to offer them a round of drinks," he said.

"So you're a prince then," yelled the tavern keeper.

"Yes, now leave me be."

The tavern keeper picked up the money then went out to meet his friends, who, summoned by those furious notes, came rushing from all corners armed with knives and bamboo sticks. Yanez sat down before Kammamuri and uncorked the bottle.

"What's new, my good Maratha?" he asked.

"Terrible news, Señor Yanez," replied Kammamuri.

"Is Sandokan in danger?"

"Not yet, but they could find his hiding place at any moment. The forests are teeming with guards and Dyaks. Last night, I was stopped and interrogated, and the same thing happened this morning."

"What did you tell them?"

"I managed to pass myself off as a supplier to the Poma mines."

"You're a clever fellow, Kammamuri. Where's Sandokan now?"

"Six miles from here, camped out in an old abandoned village. He's bolstering his defences, preparing for a possible attack."

"We'll go and see him."

"When?"

"As soon as we've finished this bottle."

"You have news?"

"I've learned where they're keeping your master."

The Maratha jumped to his feet, almost beside himself with joy.

"Where is he? Where is he?" he whispered.

"In the fort, guarded by sixty British sailors."

The Maratha slumped back into the chair, discouraged.

"We'll rescue him all the same, Kammamuri," continued Yanez.

"When?"

"As soon as we're able to."

"Thank you, Señor Yanez."

They left the tavern. The Portuguese led the way; Kammamuri followed a few steps behind, leading the horse by its bridal.

"Hurrah for Lord Welker!" yelled a voice.

"Hurrah for his lordship! Long live the generous son of Europe!" yelled several other voices.

The Portuguese turned about and spotted the tavern keeper surrounded by a large band of Chinese men, each raising a jar.

"So long, gentleman!" he yelled.

"Long live his generous lordship!" thundered the Chinese.

Having left the Chinese quarter and its exotic shops filled with silk, tea, fans, glasses, clogs, hats, clothes, lanterns, weapons, amulets, spittoons, bamboo chairs, and rolls of Tung floral paper brought in from the ports of the Celestial Empire, they entered the Malay district and made their way up into the forest.

"Be careful," Kammamuri instructed the Portuguese. "I spotted several pythons this morning and came across some tiger tracks."

"I've spent a lot of time in the forests of Borneo, Kammamuri," replied Yanez. "There's no need to fear for my safety."

"You've been here before?"

"No, but I've crossed the forests of the Kingdom of Varauni several times."

"In battle?"

"Sometimes, yes."

"Did you fight against the Sultan of Varauni?"

"Yes, we're proud enemies. He despises the pirates of Mompracem because we've thrashed his fleet in every encounter."

"Tell me, Señor Yanez, was the Tiger of Malaysia always a pirate?"

"No, my friend. Once long ago, he was a powerful rajah in Northern

Borneo, but an ambitious Englishman bribed his troops to lead the population in revolt. They killed his mother, father, brothers and sisters and took his throne."

"And that Englishman still lives?"

"Yes."

"You haven't taken your revenge?"

"He's too powerful. However, the Tiger of Malaysia will not let him go unpunished."

"And you, Señor Yanez, why did you join Sandokan?"

"I didn't join him, Kammamuri; I was taken prisoner while sailing towards Labuan."

"Didn't Sandokan kill his prisoners?"

"No, Kammamuri. Though Sandokan is ferocious with his enemies, he is always generous towards others, especially towards women."

"And he always treated you well, Señor Yanez?"

"He loves me like a brother!"

"Will you return to Mompracem once you've freed my master?"

"It's likely, Kammamuri. The Tiger of Malaysia needs great distractions to stifle his pain."

"What pain?"

"The pain he feels over the loss of Marianna Guillonk."

"He loved her that much?"

"Immensely."

"It's almost unbelievable that such a ferocious, terrifying man could have fallen in love."

"And with an Englishwoman at that," added Yanez.

"Whatever became of Marianna Guillonk's uncle?"

"We've lost word of him."

"So he could be anywhere, even here?"

"Anything's possible."

"Are you afraid of him?"

"Perhaps a little, but..."

"Halt!" yelled a voice.

Yanez and Kammamuri froze.

Chapter 5
Poison and Narcotics

Two men had suddenly appeared from behind a cetting, a climbing bush that produces a poisonous sap strong enough to kill an ox in minutes. The first was a tall, thin, nervous-looking Indian dressed in white cloth and armed with a long, silver-plated carbine. The second was a well-built Dyak; his teeth had been blackened with the juice from a siuka bush and his limbs were adorned with an extraordinary collection of pearls and brass rings. He wore a cotton chawat about his hips, a red handkerchief about his head, and a veritable arsenal of weapons. A rattan noose was wrapped about his waist, a blowpipe was slung about one of his shoulders and a formidable parang, a heavy, wide-bladed sword inlayed with pieces of brass, which the Dyaks use to behead their enemies, hung from his side. Completing the arsenal was a kris with a poisoned serpentine blade.

"Halt!" repeated the Indian, coming forward.

The Portuguese quickly gestured to Kammamuri and then advanced, his right index finger resting on the trigger of his rifle.

"Who are you and what do you want?" he asked the Indian.

"I patrol this forest for the Rajah of Sarawak," he replied. "And you?"

"I am Lord Gilles Welker, a friend of Rajah Brooke's."

The Indian and the Dyak presented their arms.

"Is that man in your employ, Milord?" asked the Indian, pointing to Kammamuri.

"No," replied Yanez. "I met him in the forest, and he asked if he could walk with me. He's afraid of tigers."

"Where are you going?" the Indian asked the Maratha.

"As I told you this morning, I'm a supplier for the placers in Poma," replied Kammamuri. "Why must you interrogate me every time we meet?"

"Because those are the rajah's orders."

"You can tell your rajah that I am one of his loyal subjects."

"You may pass."

Kammamuri caught up to Yanez who had continued on along his way, while the two spies returned to their hiding place behind the poisonous bush.

"What do you make of those men, Señor Yanez?" asked the Maratha, once they were out of earshot.

"The rajah is a clever old fox."

"Perhaps we should make a little detour."

"An excellent idea, Kammamuri. Those two spies may grow suspicious and decide to follow us."

"We'll lose them soon enough."

Kammamuri stepped off the path and turned left, followed by the horse and the Portuguese.

Minutes later, they entered the forest and were soon forced to slow their stride. Thousands upon thousands of trees intertwined with rattans and vines, blocking their advance at every turn. Unmoved by the beauty of the colossal camphor trees, sago palms, rubber trees, mangosteens and pinang palms, the Maratha and the Portuguese drew their krises and began to hack away.

After having gone a half mile, jumping over fallen timber, fighting through bushes, and slicing through roots and creepers to open a path, the two pirates arrived before a canal filled with black, fetid water. Kammamuri cut down a branch and measured its depth.

"Two feet," he said. "Saddle up, Señor Yanez."

"Why?"

"We'll ride up the canal for a good bit to hide our tracks. If the two spies are following us, we'll loose them soon enough."

"Well done, Kammamuri."

The Portuguese mounted the horse and the Maratha climbed on behind him. After a brief hesitation, the horse waded into the foul-smelling water and made its way forward, lurching and slipping as it advanced up the muddy riverbed.

Once they had gone eight hundred paces, they returned to shore. Yanez and the Maratha dismounted, put their ears to the ground and listened.

"I don't hear anything," said Kammamuri.

"Me neither," said the Portuguese. "Is the camp far?"

"I'd say about a mile and a half at least. We should hurry, Señor."

After a few more steps, they spotted a narrow path among the bushes and rattan leading into the depths of the forest. Once the two pirates reached it, they began to pick up speed. A half hour later, two men jumped up from behind a thicket and ordered them to halt. Kammamuri whistled.

"Come forward," replied the two sentries.

They were two pirates of Mompracem, armed to the teeth. At the sight of Yanez, they let out a cry of joy.

"Captain Yanez!" they yelled, running towards him.

"Good morning, men," said the Portuguese.

"We thought you were dead, Captain."

"It takes a lot to pierce the hide of a Tiger of Mompracem; where's Sandokan?"

"Three hundred paces from here."

"Keep your eyes open, my friends. The rajah has many spies in the forest."

"We know."

"Excellent, well done, men."

The Portuguese and the Maratha doubled their pace and soon reached the camp that had been set up near an old, abandoned kampong. All that remained intact in the village, which in its time must have been fairly large, was a single hut made of nipa leaves, erected upon posts more than thirty feet high. Some pirates were building shelters while others were putting up a wall of spikes to defend the camp against a sudden attack by the Rajah of Sarawak.

"Where's Sandokan?" asked Yanez, after having been warmly received by his men.

"Up there," replied a pirate. "Did you encounter the rajah's soldiers, Captain Yanez?"

"I'll tell you what I told the sentries, my Tigers," said the Portuguese. "Keep your eyes open; the forest is teeming with the rajah's spies."

"Let them show themselves if they dare!" yelled a Malay, clutching a heavy parang. "The Tigers of Mompracem do not fear the rajah's dogs."

"Captain Yanez," said another, "If you should meet one of those spies, tell him we've set up camp here. It's been five days since our last battle and our weapons are beginning to rust."

"Wait a bit, my friend, you'll have work soon enough," replied Yanez.

"Long live Captain Yanez!" yelled the tigers.

"Hey! Brother!" yelled a voice from on high.

The Portuguese raised his head and spotted Sandokan standing on the small deck of the hut.

"What are you doing up there?" yelled the Portuguese with a laugh. "You look like a pigeon perched in a tree."

Yanez rushed towards a long pole that had been notched in several places and climbed up to the bamboo platform with amazing agility. Once there, however, he discovered he could move no further. The poor man could not find a stable foothold. There were wide gaps between the planks, one wrong move and he'd plunge to the ground.

"It's a trap!" he exclaimed.

"Dyak design, my brother," laughed Sandokan.

"What kind of feet do those savages have?"

"Even smaller than ours, I think. It takes some balance!"

Cautiously leaping from plank to plank, the Portuguese made his way to the hut. It was a good sized shelter divided into three rooms; like the platform, the floor was also made of bamboo slats, but it had been covered with mats.

"What news do you bring?" asked Sandokan.

"There's a lot to tell, little brother," replied Yanez, sitting down. "But first, tell me, where's Ada, I didn't see her in the camp."

"This place isn't very secure, Yanez. The rajah's guards could attack us at any moment."

"Ah, so you've hidden her somewhere."

"Yes, in a secret location on the coast."

"Who's with her?"

"Two of our most loyal men."

"Is she still mad?"

"Yes, Yanez."

"Poor Ada!"

"She'll get better, I assure you."

"How?"

"The shock of seeing Tremal-Naik alive will restore her reason."

"You think so?"

"I'm sure of it."

"Let's hope you're correct."

"So, tell me, Yanez, what have you been up to in Sarawak these past few days?"

"Many things. I've become the rajah's friend."

"How?"

The Portuguese briefly related the adventures of the past two days, describing all that had befallen him and what he had heard. Sandokan listened attentively, without interruption, a smile appearing on his face from time to time.

"So, you're now the rajah's friend," he said, once Yanez had finished.

"Close friend, little brother."

"He doesn't suspect you in the least?"

"I don't think so; but he knows you're here."

"We must free Tremal-Naik as soon as possible. Ah! What I'd give to squash that infernal Brooke as well!"

"Leave the rajah be for now, Sandokan."

"He's been too merciless with our brethren, Yanez. I'd give half my blood to avenge the thousands of Malays murdered by that horrible wretch." [3]

"True, Sandokan, but, remember, we only brought sixty men."

A sinister light flashed in the Tiger of Malaysia's eyes.

"You know what I'm capable of, Yanez," he said darkly.

"Yes. But you can never be too cautious, Sandokan."

"Well, so be it, I'll be cautious. We'll set sail once we've freed Tremal-Naik."

"It may turn out to be more difficult than we originally thought, Sandokan."

"And why is that?"

"The small fort is armed with several cannons and at least sixty European soldiers."

"Sixty men aren't much..."

"The fort is close to the city. At the sound of the first cannon blast, the rajah would send his troops to reinforce the garrison; you'd be trapped between two fronts."

Sandokan bit his lip and sneered.

"And yet, we have to rescue him," he said.

"So what are we going to do?"

"We'll have to be clever."

"You have a plan?"

"Like all Borneans, I've always loved to work with poison. It's amazing what you can do with a single drop. Kill a man, put him to sleep, pass him for dead, even make him go mad. It's a powerful weapon."

"You spent a lot of time working with poison during our sojourn in Java. I remember when a powerful narcotic saved you from the gallows."

"My studies are about to bear fruit, Yanez," said Sandokan.

He reached into his jacket and drew out a small leather box, opened it and showed the Portuguese twelve tiny vials, each one containing a white, green or black liquid.

"Good Lord!" exclaimed Yanez.

---

[3] James Brooke was merciless towards Malay pirates; even his countrymen disapproved of his cruelty.

"There's more," said Sandokan, opening a second small box that contained several pungent little pills. "These are another kind of poison."

"What do you plan to do with those pills and liquids?"

"Listen to me carefully, Yanez. You said that Tremal-Naik is a prisoner in the fort?"

"Yes."

"Do you think the rajah will give you permission to visit it?"

"I hope so. It would be silly to deny a friend such a small favour."

"Then you'll enter and ask to see Tremal-Naik."

"And what'll I do once I seen him?"

Sandokan drew several black pills from the second box and placed them in his friend's hand.

"These pills contain a type of poison that does not kill; they merely suspend life for 36 hours."

"I understand. I'll have Tremal-Naik swallow one."

"Or dissolve one in a pitcher of water."

"When his jailers find him, they'll think him dead, take him to the cemetery and bury him."

"And we'll go dig him up in the middle of the night," added Sandokan.

"A magnificent plan, Sandokan," said the Portuguese.

"It shouldn't be that much of a risk."

"It's just a matter of getting access to the fort."

"If the rajah refuses, try bribing one of his men. Do you have any money?"

The Portuguese undid his jacket and vest, then raised his shirt to reveal a bulging money belt wrapped about his waist.

"I'm carrying sixteen diamonds with a combined value of a million pounds."

"If you need more, just ask. My pouch contains twice as much, and we have enough gold in Batavia to purchase the entire Portuguese fleet."

"Yes, we certainly aren't short of money, Sandokan. The sixteen diamonds should do for now."

"Take these pills and these two vials as well," said Sandokan. "The green one contains a narcotic that'll put a person to sleep for twelve hours; the red one contains a poison that kills instantly and leaves no trace. Who knows, they may prove useful."

The Portuguese hid the pills and vials, slung his rifle around his shoulder and got up.

"Are you leaving already?"

"It's a good stretch to Sarawak, little brother."

"When are you going to put our plan into action?"

"Tomorrow."

"You'll have Kammamuri inform me of the outcome?"

"Of course. Good-bye, little brother."

He climbed down the dangerous ladder, saluted the Tigers, then headed back into the forest and attempted to get his bearings. He had gone six or seven hundred meters, when the Maratha drew up beside him.

"More news?" asked the Portuguese, coming to a stop.

"Just one thing, but it may be serious, Señor Yanez," said the Maratha. "A pirate just returned to camp and informed the Tiger that he had spotted a band of Dyaks led by an old white man about three miles from here."

"If I come across them, I'll wish them good hunting."

"Wait, Señor Yanez," said the Maratha. "The pirate said he was almost positive it was the same old man that had sworn to hang you and the Tiger."

"Lord James Guillonk!" exclaimed Yanez, turning pale.

"Yes, Señor Yanez, Sandokan's uncle... the uncle of his late wife."

"Impossible! Impossible! Which pirate spotted him?"

"The Malay Sambigliong."

"Sambigliong!" stammered Yanez. "That Malay was with us when we kidnapped Lord James' niece, he stopped his lordship from smashing in my skull. Good Lord! I'm in great danger."

"What do you mean?" asked the Maratha.

"If Lord Guillonk reaches Sarawak, all is lost. He'll recognize me in an instant. Then he'll have me arrested and hung. Tell Sandokan I'll keep my guard up and that he should try to capture the old man. Goodbye, Kammamuri. I'll meet you tomorrow morning at the Chinese tavern."

Feeling uneasy, the Portuguese resumed his march towards the city, straining his ears, and carefully scanning his surroundings, afraid of finding the old man before him at any moment. Fortunately, the only sounds to break the silence were the sharp cries of giant arguses and black cockatoos as they flitted among the trees.

It took five hours for Yanez to make his way through the sea of bushes and thickets. He reached Sarawak just as the sun was setting, famished and worn out by his exertions. Realizing it was too late to dine with the rajah, he headed instead for the Chinese tavern.

After a magnificent meal washed down by several bottles, he returned to the villa. Before entering, he asked the guard if an old European man had arrived, but, receiving a negative reply, he went up to his room. The rajah had retired several hours earlier.

"So much the better," murmured Yanez. "A hunter that returns without so much as a parrot could raise suspicions in that distrustful old fox."

He placed his pistol and kris beneath his pillow, stretched out on the bed and closed his eyes.

Chapter 6
Tremal-Naik

Despite his exhaustion, the good Portuguese could not sleep. The image of the old man Sambigliong had spotted near the village remained fixed in his mind. Could it really have been Marianna's uncle leading a band of Dyaks?

Though he tried to convince himself that the Malay must have been mistaken, that Lord Guillonk must have been far off, perhaps in Java or India, or better yet in England, he simply could not relax. His restless mind began to play tricks on him; he thought he heard the old man's voice in the corridor, then footsteps advancing towards his room, then gunfire echoing throughout the palace.

He jumped out of bed repeatedly, cautiously peering through the door and windows, to check if sentries had been posted to prevent his escape. He fell asleep towards dawn, a fitful sleep, of short duration, troubled by nightmares. He awoke to the peals of a gong sounding in the street.

He got up, got dressed, hid two small pistols in his pockets and headed towards the door. Just as his hand touched the doorknob, some-one knocked.

"Who is it?" he asked anxiously.

"The rajah awaits you in his study," said a voice.

Yanez felt a shiver run down his spine. He opened the door and found an Indian servant standing there before him.

"Is the rajah alone?" he asked, attempting to appear calm.

"Yes, Milord," replied the Indian. "He requests you join him for tea."

"I'll go at once," said Yanez, heading towards the study.

The rajah sat before a small table, a silver tea service lay out before him. When Yanez entered, he rose with a smile and proffered his hand.

"Good Morning, Milord!" he exclaimed. "You got back late last night."

"Forgive me, Excellency, for missing our lunch appointment, it was not on purpose, I assure you," said Yanez, drawing comfort from the rajah's smile.

"What happened?"

"I got lost in the forest."

"Even though you had a guide?"

"A guide!"

"I've been informed that you travelled with an Indian, a man claiming to be a merchant supplying the placers in Poma."

"Who informed you of that, Excellency?" asked Yanez, struggling to keep his composure.

"My spies, Milord."

"They appear to be highly trained, Excellency."

"True," smiled the rajah. "I take it you met the Indian by chance, then?"

"Yes, Excellency."

"How far did you travel together?"

"Just to a small Dyak village."

"Would you like to guess who that man was?"

"What do you mean?" asked Yanez, forcing himself to utter those words.

"A pirate," said the rajah.

"A pirate! Impossible, Excellency."

"Quite true in fact."

"But he did not attempt to rob me, or slay me for that matter!"

"The pirates of Mompracem can be generous at times, Milord, just like their leader."

"The Tiger of Malaysia is a generous man?"

"So they say. I've been told he's even given diamonds to those he's defeated in battle."

"Not your typical pirate! Excellency, are you certain that Indian was from Mompracem?"

"Positively! My spies spotted him talking with some of the Tiger's men. But he won't be doing that for much longer. My guards have probably captured him by now."

At that instant, sharp cries emanated from the street, quickly followed by the loud peal of a gong.

Yanez, pale and nervous, rushed towards the window to get a glimpse of what was happening and to conceal his growing uneasiness.

"Good Lord!" he gasped, turning pale. "Kammamuri!"

"What's happening?" asked the rajah.

"They're bringing my Indian friend here, Excellency," he replied, having instantly regained his composure.

"Just as I predicted."

He leaned over the windowsill and looked down.

Four guards, armed to the teeth, were leading Kammamuri towards the villa, his arms tightly bound with solid rattan rope. The prisoner was not offering the least bit of resistance, nor did he appear frightened. He advanced calmly, looking about indifferently as they made their way through the crowd of cackling Dyaks, Chinese and Malays.

"Poor man!" exclaimed Yanez.

"You feel for him, Milord?" asked the rajah.

"A bit, I must confess."

"That Indian is a pirate."

"I know, but he was very kind to me. What are you going to do with him, Excellency?"

"I'll make him talk. Once I've learned the Tiger of Malaysia's whereabouts, I'll assemble my guards and attack."

"And if the prisoner refuses to talk?"

"I'll hang him," replied the rajah coldly.

"Poor devil!"

"All pirates receive the same sentence, Milord."

"Undoubtedly. When are you going to question him?"

"I don't have time today, I have to receive a Dutch ambassador, but I'll be free tomorrow and I'll make him talk."

A light flashed in the Portuguese's eyes.

"Excellency," he said after a brief hesitation. "Would it be possible for me to assist you?"

"If you so desire."

"Thank you, Excellency."

The rajah picked up a small silver bell from the table and gave it a ring. Dressed in yellow silk, a Chinese servant with a *bianzi* a meter long entered, carrying a porcelain Ming teapot full of hot tea.

"I hope you like tea," said the rajah.

"I wouldn't be British," smiled Yanez.

After draining several cups of that delicious beverage, the two men stood up.

"What are your plans for today, Milord?" asked the rajah.

"I thought I'd explore the city," replied Yanez, "maybe even visit the fort, with your permission of course."

"You'll find some of our countrymen there, Milord."

"Really!" exclaimed Yanez, feigning ignorance.

"I rescued them several weeks ago; they were on the verge of drowning."

"Castaways?"

"Precisely. I've put them up in the fort while they're waiting for another ship to arrive. In the meantime, they're keeping an eye on an Indian Thug I have imprisoned there."

"What? A Thug! An Indian Thug!" exclaimed Yanez. "Oh! I'd love to see one of those deadly stranglers."

"Really?"

"Oh, yes."

The rajah reached for a sheet of paper, jotted down several lines, folded it and handed it to the Portuguese who took it excitedly.

"Give this to Lieutenant Churchill," said the rajah. "He'll show you the Thug, and even give you a tour of the fort; there's not much to see, but you may find it interesting."

"Thank you, Excellency."

"Will you dine with me this evening?"

"I would be delighted, sir."

"Excellent. Until this evening, then. Good day, Milord."

Relieved at finally being able to leave the study, Yanez quickly went back to his room.

"Reason this out, Yanez," he murmured, once he was alone. "You've got to play your hand cleverly, you must not get caught."

He went to the window and began to think. He remained rooted there, motionless, eyes fixed on the fort, for ten or twelve minutes, frowning from time to time.

"I've got it!" he exclaimed at one point. "My dear Brooke, Yanez has a few cards up his sleeve, and if they're played well, the escape will be a work of art. Good Lord! Sandokan himself couldn't have done better."

He went to the table, picked up a pen and jotted the following words on a small piece of paper:

Tremal-Naik,

Kammamuri has sent me to rescue you. If you wish to regain your freedom and be reunited with your beloved Ada, swallow these pills at midnight.

Yanez,
A friend of Kammamuri's

He took out two small pills, wrapped them tightly in the note, and hid the tiny package in his jacket pocket.

"The British will assume he's dead, take him out of the fort and bury him," he murmured, rubbing his hands happily, "I'll send Kammamuri to inform Sandokan! My dear James Brooke, I fear you've underestimated the Tigers of Mompracem."

He put on a straw hat, tucked his kris in his belt, then left the room and slowly made his way down the stairs. As he advanced along a corridor, he spotted an Indian armed with a bayonet, standing guard before a door.

"Is this where they're keeping the pirate," asked the Portuguese.

"Yes, sir," replied the sentry.

"Take care he doesn't escape, my friend. He's a dangerous man."

"I'll keep my eyes open, Milord."

"Well done, young man."

He saluted the soldier then went down some more stairs and into the street, an ironic smile slowly spreading across his lips. Walking towards the hill, he spotted the fort, its imposing mass rearing out of the dark green forest.

"Take heart, Yanez," he murmured. "There's a lot to do."

He calmly traversed the city, making his way through the thick crowds of Dyaks, Malays and Chinese, chatting in various tongues as they sold fruit, weapons, clothes and toys from Canton. After a short walk, he came to a path shaded by tall durian and areca trees leading into the forest and up to the fort.

Half way up, he encountered two British sailors on their way to the city, perhaps off to receive one of the rajah's orders, or to check on the arrival of any new ships.

"Good morning, gentlemen," smiled Yanez. "Is Lieutenant Churchill up there?"

"Last we saw of him, he was smoking by the main gate," replied one of the two.

"Thank you, my friends."

He resumed his march and after a long detour reached the top of the hill, the fort stood at the centre of a large clearing. Leaning on his rifle, a sailor guarded the gate, chewing tobacco. A few paces away, a tall naval officer with a large red moustache lay among the grass, smoking a pipe. Yanez halted.

"A sahib!" exclaimed the lieutenant, surprised by that sudden appearance.

"You must be the man I'm looking for," said the Portuguese.

"What can I do for you, sir?"

"I have a letter for Lieutenant Churchill."

"I'm Lieutenant Churchill, sir," said the officer, getting up and moving towards him.

Yanez pulled out the rajah's letter and handed it to the British officer.

"At your service, Milord," he said, after carefully reading its contents.

"Would it be possible to see the Thug?"

"Absolutely, sir."

"Take me to him, then. I've always wanted to meet one of those terrible stranglers."

The lieutenant stuffed his pipe into his pocket and led Yanez into the fort. They crossed the small courtyard, past four old rusting cannons, and entered a building constructed of teak wood, strong enough to withstand a blast from a six or eight pound cannon ball.

"Here we are, Milord," said Churchill, coming to a halt before a sturdy door that had been double bolted. "The Thug's in there."

"Is he fierce?"

"Tame as a kitten," smiled the Englishman.

"Then we won't need our weapons."

"He's never harmed any of us; still, I wouldn't enter without my pistol."

The lieutenant drew back the two bars, opened the door a crack, and peered inside.

"He's asleep," he said. "We may enter, Milord."

Yanez shuddered. A sudden thought had crossed his mind. There was a slight chance the prisoner could accidentally give him away. The Indian could refuse to accept the note and the pills, and, in so doing, expose the plan to Lieutenant Churchill.

Steady, Yanez, he thought. This is not the time to panic.

He stepped through the doorway and entered. He found himself in a small cell; the walls were of teak wood, the only light came through a small barred window. In a corner, stretched out on a bed of dried leaves, wrapped in a small blanket, rested 'the Thug' Tremal-Naik, Kammamuri's master, Ada's fiancé.

He was a handsome man, about five and a half feet tall, with skin the color of bronze. He had a strong chest, muscular limbs, and a proud face. Yanez had fought alongside Chinese, Malays, Javans, Africans, Indians, Bugis, Macassars and Tagalis, but never, aside from Sandokan, had he met a man of such strength and noble bearing.

Though asleep, the prisoner appeared tormented. His chest rose breathlessly, his lips trembled, his hands clutched at the air.

"Quite a specimen," exclaimed Yanez.

"Shh, listen," murmured the lieutenant.

A soft cry escaped the Indian's lips.

"Ada!" he exclaimed

Then his brow darkened and the vein in his temple swelled to twice its size.

"Suyodhana," murmured the Indian, his voice laced with hatred.

"Tremal-Naik!" yelled the lieutenant.

At the sound of his name, the Indian awoke, sat up and fixed his eyes upon the lieutenant.

"What do you want?" he asked.

"You have a visitor."

The Indian's gaze shifted to Yanez, who was standing a few paces behind Churchill. A disdainful smile spread across his lips, bearing teeth as white as ivory.

"Am I a beast?" he asked. "What is..."

He started and fell silent. Unseen by the lieutenant, Yanez had quickly signalled that he was a friend.

"Why are you in here?" asked the Portuguese.

"Why do you think?" said Tremal-Naik sadly.

"Is it true you're a Thug?"

"No."

"They say you've strangled several people."

"That's true, but I'm not a Thug."

"You're lying."

Tremal-Naik jumped to his feet in anger, but another gesture from the Portuguese quickly restored his calm.

"If you allow me to raise my cloak, I'll show you my tattoo; the mark of the Thugs."

"Stay back, Milord!" exclaimed the lieutenant.

"What are you afraid of? I'm not even armed," said the Indian.

Yanez approached the bed of leaves and crouched down by Tremal-Naik.

"Kammamuri," he whispered.

The Indian's eyes flashed with understanding. With one sweep of his arm, he raised his mantle and picked up the small packet containing the pills the Portuguese had let fall to the ground.

"Did you see the tattoo?" asked the lieutenant who as a precaution had drawn his pistol.

"He doesn't have one," replied Yanez, standing up. "Would that mean he's not a Thug?"

"Who knows? It could be anywhere, on his arm, on his back...."

"I don't have one," said Tremal-Naik.

"How long has he been here, Lieutenant?" asked Yanez.

"Two months, Milord."

"Where are they taking him?"

"To some penitentiary in Australia."

"Poor devil! Let's go, Lieutenant."

The officer opened the door and left. Pretending to take a final look, Yanez quickly turned around and signalled Tremal-Naik a last instruction: obey.

"Would you like a tour of the fort?" asked the lieutenant, once he had closed and barred the door.

"I think I've just seen the best part," replied Yanez. "It was a fascinating experience. Thank you, lieutenant. I'll be going now."

"My pleasure, Milord. Have a good day."

113

Chapter 7
Kammamuri Escapes

While Yanez was making preparations to rescue Tremal-Naik, poor Kammamuri, gripped by a thousand fears and anxieties, was plotting his escape. He did not fear being hung or shot like a common pirate; he feared being subjected to some kind of terrifying torture and forced to confess all he knew, and, in so doing, put the lives of his master, the unhappy Ada, the Tiger of Malaysia, Yanez and all the intrepid men of Mompracem at risk.

Upon being locked in the room, he had tried to escape through the window, only to be thwarted by solid iron bars, impossible to cut through without a file or an axe; he then attempted to smash through the floor, hoping to land in a vacant room below, but after almost breaking his fingers, he was forced to renounce that plan as well. As a last resort, he had attempted to strangle the Indian that brought him his food, but just as he was on the verge of success, other guards rushed in to stop him.

Convinced of the futility of his efforts, he crouched down in a corner, determined to die of hunger rather than taste food that could have been laced with some mysterious drug. He would be skinned of his flesh layer by layer before he would be tricked into uttering a single word.

Ten hours had passed and he had not moved so much as a single muscle. The sun had set and darkness had invaded the room, when suddenly he heard a hiss followed by a soft thud. Without making a sound, he got up, looked about and listened. He heard nothing but the hoarse cries of the Dyaks and Malays passing through the square.

He silently approached the window and peered through the metal bars. There, near a giant areca tree that cast its shadow over much of the square stood a man wearing a large hat, clutching what appeared to be a stick. Kammamuri recognized him immediately.

"Señor Yanez," he murmured.

He thrust an arm through the bars and made several gestures. The Portuguese raised a hand and signalled a quick reply.

"Understood," whispered Kammamuri. "Well done, Señor!"

He left the window and made his way to the opposite wall. He looked about carefully, then knelt down and picked up a tiny arrow with a ball of paper wrapped about its tip.

"I never would have guessed Señor Yanez could use a blowpipe," he mumbled.

He unrolled the paper and found two tiny, black, sharp-smelling pills. Poison or narcotics, he wondered, as his eyes fell upon the scribbled instructions. He returned to the window and carefully read the following lines:

> All is going well. Unless something unexpected happens, we'll rescue Tremal-Naik tomorrow night. I've enclosed some sleeping pills. Find a way to feed them to your guard, then escape. I'll meet you near the fort tomorrow at noon.
>
> Yanez

"Well done, Señor Yanez," murmured the Maratha, deeply moved. "You think of everything."

He leaned against the metal bars and began to meditate. A light knock on the door tore him from his thoughts.

"Here we go!" he mumbled.

Without a sound, he quickly approached the table upon which lay a tureen of rice, several kinds of fruit and two large glasses of tuwak. He slipped the pills into the liquid and watched as they instantly dissolved.

"Who's there?" he asked.

"Your dinner," replied a voice.

The door opened and an Indian guard armed with a large scimitar and a long-barrelled pistol inlaid with mother-of-pearl cautiously entered. He carried a talc lantern in one hand and a basket full of provisions in the other.

"Aren't you hungry?" asked the guard, his eyes resting upon the full glasses and the untouched food.

The Maratha glared at him.

"There's no need to worry, my friend," continued the guard. "The rajah is a generous man. He's not going to hang you."

"But he would poison my food," said Kammamuri, feigning terror.

"Is that why you haven't eaten anything?"

"Of course."

"You fasted in vain, my friend. No one has poisoned your food."

"You say that, but would you drink a glass to prove it?"

"If you insist!"

Kammamuri picked up the doctored glass and handed it to the guard.

"Drink this," he said.

Having no reason to be suspicious, the Indian placed the glass to his lips and gulped down a good part of its contents.

"Hey..." he said hesitatingly. "What did they put in this tuwak?"

"Nothing," said the Maratha, his eyes riveted on the guard.

"My legs feel strange."

"Ah!"

"My head is spinning... I can't see... I..."

The words died on his lips. His eyes popped open and he lurched forward as if shot in the chest, then fell to the ground unconscious.

Kammamuri quickly relieved the guard of his pistol and scimitar. Fearing the noise had attracted the others, he approached the door, weapons drawn, and listened attentively, but not a single footstep echoed down the hallway.

"So far so good!" he sighed. "If my luck holds, I'll be out of the city in ten minutes."

He disrobed the Indian, quickly donned his shorts, jacket and sash then wrapped on his turban in a way that concealed most of his forehead and eyes. Once clothed, he sheathed his scimitar and tucked the pistol into his belt.

Moving quietly, he opened the door, checked to see if anyone was around, then walked the length of the dark, deserted corridor, went down the stairs, past the sentry and out onto the square.

"Is that you, Labuk?" asked a voice.

"Yes," replied Kammamuri, without turning about, fearing he would be recognized.

"May Shiva protect you."

"Thank you, my friend."

The Maratha walked off quickly, carefully scanning his surroundings, ears straining to pick up the slightest sound. He kept close to the houses, hiding whenever he thought he spotted one of the rajah's guards at the end of a street or lane. Ten minutes later, he reached the foot of the hill; the moon shone brightly, bathing the fort in light. He stopped and listened.

Music from the Chinese quarter reached his ears, the notes mingling with the songs of the Dyak and Malay boatmen along the river. But not a single sound emanated from the rajah's palace or the main square.

"I'm safe!" he murmured after several anxious minutes. "They haven't noticed my escape."

He rushed into the forest of tall mangosteens, beautiful mango trees and chaotic cettings that covered the hill. Fighting his way through bushes, fording ponds of black, muddy water and jumping from tree to tree to avoid leaving tracks, in less than an hour he arrived, unseen, to within a rifle blast of the fort. He climbed a tall tree and settled among its branches. It was the perfect hiding place; he could watch, undetected, all that transpired upon the hill as he waited for the Portuguese to arrive.

The night passed uneventfully. At four in the morning, the sun suddenly appeared on the horizon, slowly lighting the river as it wound through the city's fertile farmlands, thick forests and surrounding plantations. A few hours later, the Maratha, still atop his observation post, spotted two men leaving the fort at a run.

"I wonder what's happening?" murmured Kammamuri. "It looks serious. Could they have learned of my escape?"

To avoid being spotted by the men running down the path, he climbed up higher among the leaves and anxiously waited for events to unfold. An hour later, the two Englishmen reappeared, walking back up towards the fort, followed by an officer and a European dressed in white, a small black box hanging from his belt.

"A doctor?" wondered Kammamuri, turning pale. "Something's happened to my master! What's keeping Señor Yanez!"

He slid to the ground and crawled towards the path, determined to interrogate the first person he saw, but the clock struck twelve, then one, two, and three, without so much as a sailor or guard passing his way.

Towards five o'clock, a man in a large straw hat with a pair of pistols tucked in his belt appeared at the turn in the path. Kammamuri recognized him immediately.

"Señor Yanez!" he exclaimed.

The Portuguese was advancing slowly, carefully scanning his surroundings as if looking for someone; at the sound of that voice he came to a halt. Spying Kammamuri, he picked up his pace. Upon reaching him, he pushed the Indian into a thicket and said, "If you'd been spotted by a guard, you'd have been arrested immediately and even I wouldn't have been able to help you a second time; you have to be more careful, my friend."

"Something terrible has happened in the fort, Señor Yanez," said the Maratha. "I had a terrible premonition and I left my hiding place."

"A premonition! What kind of premonition?"

"A feeling that my master is dying. I saw a man that looked like a doctor rush in there."

"Yes, your master has created quite a stir among the guards."

"My master!"

"Yes, my friend."

"Is he sick?"

"He's dead."

"Dead!" exclaimed the Maratha, swaying slightly.

"There's no need to worry, my friend. They think he's dead, but he's very much alive, I assure you."

"Ah! Señor Yanez, what a shock you just gave me! Did you give him some kind of drug?"

"I gave him some pills that suspend life for thirty-six hours."

"And they'll think he's dead?"

"Without question."

"How are we going to rescue him?"

"They're probably going to bury him tonight."

"And we'll dig him up and take him to safety!" said the Maratha excitedly. "Where are they going to take him?"

"We'll know soon enough. We'll follow the burial party as soon as they leave the fort."

"When do we rescue my master?"

"Tonight."

"The two of us?"

"You and Sandokan."

"I'll inform him immediately. Will you be coming with us?"

"I can't."

"Why not?"

"The rajah is giving a ball tonight in honour of the Dutch ambassador; I'll arouse suspicions if I don't attend."

"Look!" exclaimed the Maratha, his eyes anxiously fixed upon the fort.

"What is it?"

"Some men are leaving the fort."

"Good Lord!"

He pushed aside the branches of the thick bush and cast his gaze upon the top of the hill.

Two sailors had left the fort with a stretcher, transporting a body wrapped in a shroud. Two more sailors, carrying spades and hoes, and a guard followed close behind.

"Time to go," said Yanez.

"Where are they going?" Kammamuri asked anxiously.

"Down the opposite side of the hill."

"They're going to bury him in the cemetery!"

"It looks like it. We'll go around the forest, try not to make any noise."

They left the thicket and headed in among the trees. They slowly made their way to the far end of the fort, jumping over fallen timber, fighting through bushes and slicing through thick roots. Once they reached the other side of the hill, Yanez came to a halt.

"Where are they?" he wondered.

"There they are, down there," said the Maratha.

The small squad was within sight, moving down a narrow path towards a tiny patch of grass surrounded by superb trees. In the centre, protected by a modest fence, was a space bristling with wooden crosses and white gravestones.

"That must be the cemetery," said Yanez.

"Are they heading there?" asked Kammamuri.

"Yes."

"What a relief, Señor Yanez. I was afraid they'd throw my poor master into the river."

"The same thought crossed my mind."

The sailors entered the cemetery, halted in the middle, and placed Tremal-Naik upon the ground. Yanez watched them move about the gravestones for a few minutes, as if searching for something then they picked up their shovels and began to dig.

"The loose earth will mark the spot," the Portuguese told the Maratha.

"Could my master die of asphyxiation?" asked Kammamuri.

"No, my friend. Now run immediately to Sandokan, tell him to gather his men and to come rescue your master."

"What about you?"

"I'll meet up with you tomorrow at the camp and we'll set sail for Mompracem. Now go, my friend."

The Maratha did not wait to be told twice. He drew his pistol and disappeared into the jungle.

Chapter 8
Yanez in a trap

Towards ten in the evening, when Yanez arrived in Sarawak, he was surprised to find the city bustling with excitement. Dressed in their best clothes, crowds of Chinese, Dyaks, Malays, Macassars, Bugis, Javanese, and Tagalis crisscrossed the streets and lanes, shouting and laughing as they made their way towards the main square in front of the rajah's palace. They had undoubtedly received news of the party their prince was giving and were flocking in great numbers, certain of a good time and hoping, perhaps, for some free food and drink.

"Excellent," murmured the Portuguese, rubbing his hands happily. "With all this commotion, Sandokan will get into the city unnoticed. An excellent distraction, my dear Brooke! I am grateful."

Using his elbows, and, at times, his fists to advance, he reached the square in five minutes. Numerous torches cast their light upon the houses, the nearby trees and the rajah's palace, defended, for the occasion, by a double row of well-armed guards. A large throng of people had crowded into that space, their drunken cries filling the air as they enjoyed the celebration. The good citizens of Sarawak danced enthusiastically to the sounds of the music emanating form the villa, crowding against the houses and trees, even knocking against the row of guards from time to time.

"Guess I'm a little late," laughed Yanez. "Let's hope my prolonged absence hasn't caused his Excellency any worry."

He identified himself to the guards, went up the stairs and entered his room to prepare for the evening.

"Is everyone having a good time?" he asked the Indian servant the rajah had placed at his disposal.

"Very much so, Milord."

"Who's on the guest list?"

"A few Europeans, Malays, Dyaks and Chinese."

"Quite a mix. I guess there's no need for formal dress, just as well, I didn't bring my eveningwear."

He brushed his clothes and put away his weapons, concealing a small pistol in one of his pockets as a precaution. He headed towards the ballroom, but stopped at the entrance, his face displaying great surprise.

Though the room was not vast, it had been decorated with impeccable taste. Large Venetian mirrors adorned the walls, brightly painted Dyak mats covered the floor; numerous bronze lamps from Europe hung from the ceiling, bathing the room in their warm light. Beautiful vases of Chinese porcelain, brimming with bright red peonies and large magnolias, adorned the tables, sweetening the air with their heavy fragrance.

There were no more than fifty guests but so many costumes and so many different kinds of people! There were four Europeans dressed in white, about fifteen Chinese dressed in bright silk, ten or twelve Malays in long Indian robes; five or six Dyak leaders with their women, wearing next to nothing but adorned with hundreds of bracelets and necklaces strung with tiger teeth. Macassars, Bugis, Tagalis and Javanese hopped about like madmen, ready to complain violently every time the Chinese orchestra comprised of twenty flautists and four performers of *piene-kia* (an instrument comprised of sixteen black rocks), played a tune they could not dance to.

He entered the room and headed towards the rajah, the only man attired in black evening dress; he was chatting with a portly Chinese man, most likely one of Sarawak's principal merchants.

"Looks like everyone's having fun," he said.

"Ah!" exclaimed the rajah, turning towards him. "You've arrived, Milord! I've been expecting you for a couple of hours."

"I made it all the way up to the fort then got lost on the way back."

"Did you attend the prisoner's funeral?"

"No, Excellency. A little too gloomy for my taste."

"What do you think of the party?"

"The festivities seem a bit chaotic."

"My dear friend, we're in Sarawak. Chinese, Malays and Dyaks do not know any better. Find yourself a lovely young Dyak and join the dance."

"I find it impossible to dance to this kind of music, Excellency."

"A definite advantage," laughed the rajah.

A cry suddenly erupted behind them, loud enough to be heard above the noise.

Yanez and the rajah immediately turned about and caught a glimpse of a man with a long white beard quickly retreating through the doorway.

"What's happening?" asked the rajah.

Several people headed towards the door but were quickly turned away.

"Wait here, Milord," said the rajah.

Yanez did not move. That cry, which seemed so familiar, had shaken him to the depths of his soul. He turned pale as signs of worry spread across his face. Where had he heard that cry before? He thrust a hand into his pocket and silently loaded his pistol, determined to use it if necessary.

The rajah re-entered and Yanez immediately noticed a frown upon his brow. The pirate grew even more nervous.

"Is everything alright, Excellency?" he asked, making an extraordinary effort to appear calm.

"Yes, Milord," replied the rajah.

"But that cry?" insisted Yanez.

"A friend of mine."

"What happened?"

"He suddenly felt sick. Nothing to worry about."

"Yet..."

"Yes?"

"That did not sound like a cry of pain."

"You are mistaken, Milord. Now, why don't you find yourself a nice Dyak woman and dance a polka."

The rajah moved away and began to talk with one of his guests. Yanez, however, stood motionless, his eyes riveted on his host's every move.

"Something's up," he murmured. "Eyes open, Yanez."

Pretending to head off, he went and sat behind a group of Malays. He kept his eyes fixed on the rajah, noting that his host would often scan the room, as if searching for someone. Yanez started.

"He's looking for me," the pirate mumbled. "Well, my dear Brooke, I'll play a trick on you before you can play one on me."

Affecting a great deal of calm, he stood up, circled the room two or three times then stopped two paces from the door. One of the rajah's servants was standing there. He gestured for him to approach.

"Who screamed a few moments ago?" he asked.

"One of the rajah's friends," replied the Indian.

"What was his name?"

"I do not know, Milord."

"Where is he now?"

"In the rajah's study."

"Is he sick?"

"I do not know."

"Can I see him?"

"No, Milord. Two guards have been posted in front of the door, and they've been ordered not to let anyone enter."

"Do you know who he is?"

"I don't know his name, sir."

"Is he British?"

"Yes."

"How long has he been in Sarawak?"

"I believe he arrived shortly after the battle at the mouth of the river," he said.

"The battle against the Tiger of Malaysia?"

"Yes."

"Is he one of the Tiger's enemies?"

"Yes, he's been searching for him in the forest."

"Thank you, my friend," said Yanez, pressing a rupee into the servant's hand.

Troubled by that new bit of information, he left the hall and headed towards his room. Once inside, he closed the door and drew the bolt as a precaution. He pulled a pair of pistols and a poisoned tipped kris from the wall, then opened the window and peered over the windowsill.

A double row of Indians, armed with rifles, surrounded the house. Just beyond them, a crowd of two or three hundred people danced frenetically, filling the air with savage cries.

Escaping through the square was impossible, yet he had to leave the palace immediately. The danger was palpable. He froze, struck by a sudden thought.

"That cry..." he murmured, turning pale once again. "It must have been... yes! Lord Guillonk! Sambigliong said he'd seen him leading a band of Dyaks in the very forest Sandokan was using as a hiding place... Yes, it must have been him!"

He rushed towards the table and picked up the pistols. Though Yanez was determined not to kill Marianna Guillonk's uncle, he would defend his own life.

He went to the door and drew back the bolt. It refused to open. He pushed against it with his shoulder, but to no effect. A cry escaped his lips.

"They've locked me in," he said. "I'm trapped."

He looked for another way out, but there were no other options aside from the two windows that gave out onto the square. The rajah's guards had not moved, the crowd continued to dance.

"Damn party!" he exclaimed angrily.

At that moment there was a knock at the door. He raised his pistols and yelled, "Who is it?"

"James Brooke," replied the rajah.

"Are you alone?"

"Yes, Milord."

"Enter, Excellency," said Yanez ironically.

He stuck his pistol in his belt, crossed his arms and with head held high, calmly waited for his formidable enemy to appear.

Chapter 9
Lord James Guillonk

The rajah entered.

He was alone, unarmed, and still dressed in black; however, he was no longer the smiling, jovial host of earlier on. His face had turned pale, not in fear, but in rage; his eyes had hardened, a frown now lined his brow and an ironic smile was slowly spreading across his lips. The Exterminator had awakened.

He stood in the doorway for a moment, glaring daggers at Yanez, then entered the room. The door immediately shut behind him.

"Sir," he said firmly.

"Excellency," said Yanez in an equal tone.

"I gather you know why I'm here."

"Yes, Excellency. Please make yourself comfortable."

The rajah sat down upon a chair; Yanez leaned against the desk, resting his arm within reach of his kris.

"Sir," continued the rajah calmly. "Do you know what they call me in Sarawak?"

"James Brooke."

"No, they call me the Exterminator."

Yanez bowed and smiled.

"A terrible nickname, Excellency," he said.

"I bear it proudly. Now, let's cast off our masks and talk."

"Very well, Excellency."

"If I were to land on Mompracem..."

"What story is this?" exclaimed Yanez.

"Allow me to finish, sir. If I were to land on Mompracem and ask the Tiger of Malaysia or his lieutenant for hospitality and later they learned I was one of their most hated enemies, what would become of me?"

"Good Lord! If you announced you were James Brooke, I imagine the Tiger of Malaysia or his lieutenant would order you hung."

"Well, Señor Yanez de Gomera..."

"Señor Yanez de Gomera!" interrupted the Portuguese. "Who says I'm Yanez de Gomera?"

"A man that has dealt with you before!"

"So I've been betrayed?"

"No, I'd say you've been discovered."

"I want this man's name, James Brooke!" yelled Yanez, taking a step towards the rajah.

"And if a refuse?"

"I'd force it out of you."

The rajah laughed.

"You dare threaten me," he said. "There are ten men behind that door, armed to the teeth, awaiting my order to enter and arrest you. You wish to know your accuser's name? Very well, let's have no secrets."

He clapped his hands three times. The door opened and a tall, elderly man with a long white beard and a well-tanned face slowly entered the room.

Despite himself, Yanez cried out in surprise.

He had recognized the man immediately. It was Lord James Guillonk, Marianna's uncle, a sworn enemy who had vowed to hang the two captains from Mompracem. Sambigliong had not been mistaken.

"Do you recognize me, Yanez de Gomera?" his lordship asked dully.

"Yes, Milord," replied the Portuguese, instantly recovering from his initial shock.

"I knew it was only a matter of time before I caught up with my niece's kidnappers."

"Kidnappers? Lady Marianna left of her own accord. Make no mistake, Milord, she loved the Tiger of Malaysia."

"It matters little whether she loved or hated the pirate. She was taken from me, Lord James Guillonk, her uncle, reason enough for me to hunt you down. Yanez de Gomera, I've been searching for you for the last two years. Do you know why?"

"I can't even guess, Milord."

"Vengeance."

"I told you, Lady Marianna was not kidnapped. What vengeance do you claim?"

"Vengeance for the pain of depriving me of my only family, vengeance for the humiliation I had to bear and vengeance for the atrocities you committed against my country. Where's my niece? Is it true she's dead?"

"Your niece, the Tiger of Malaysia's wife, is resting in peace in the cemetery of Batavia, Milord," Yanez said sadly.

"Undoubtedly murdered by her infamous abductor."

"No, Milord. Sandokan, that bloodthirsty, heartless pirate you've been hunting for so long, will mourn Lady Marianna Guillonk for many years to come."

"Sandokan!" exclaimed his lordship with unimaginable hatred. "Where is he?"

"Your nephew, Milord, is somewhere in the forests of Sarawak."

"What brings him here?"

"He's come to rescue an unjustly condemned man who just happens to be in love with another member of your family, Ada Corishant."

"You're lying," howled his lordship.

"Who is this condemned man?" asked the rajah, jumping to his feet.

"I cannot say," replied Yanez.

"Lord Guillonk," said the rajah. "Are you related to any Corishants?"

"My niece's mother had a brother named Harry Corishant. He was stationed in India, but I've been told he was killed."

"Did he have a daughter named Ada?"

"Yes, she was kidnapped by Indian Thugs a few years back."

"Do you think she's still alive?"

"I doubt it."

"Well then..."

"This pirate is lying."

"Milord," said the Portuguese, raising his head and looking the old man squarely in the eyes. "If I were to swear on my honour that I have told you the truth, would you believe me?"

"Pirates have no honour," said Lord Guillonk disdainfully.

Yanez turned pale as his hand ran instinctively to the butt of his pistol.

"Milord," he said gravely. "If you were not Lady Marianna's uncle, there'd be a bullet lodged in your head. This is the fourth time I've spared your life, do not forget it."

"Well then, tell us your tale. Perhaps I will believe you."

"As I said, the Tiger of Malaysia is here to rescue an unjustly condemned man, a man in love with Ada Corishant."

"Where's my niece?"

"With the Tiger of Malaysia."

"Where?"

"I cannot say."

"Why not?"

"You would attack Sandokan and either kill him or take him prisoner. Promise me that you'll allow him to set sail for his island, and I'll tell you where he is and what he's up to."

"I'll never make such a promise," said the rajah, intervening. "It's time for the Tiger of Malaysia to answer for his crimes; he's bloodied these waters far too long."

"Nor shall I," added Lord Guillonk. "I've been planning my revenge for over two years."

"Well then, gentleman, have me flogged, choose whatever torture you desire, I will not utter another word."

Unbeknownst to Yanez, while he had been speaking, two Indians had entered through the window and had silently approached the desk, waiting for a signal to attack.

"So that's all you have to say?" said the rajah, making a quick, imperceptible gesture to his men.

"Yes, Excellency," Yanez replied firmly.

"Well then, sir, I, James Brooke, Rajah of Sarawak, place you under arrest!"

At the sound of those words, the two Indians attacked the Portuguese, knocked him to the floor and tore away his pistols.

"Wretches!" yelled the prisoner.

With Herculean effort, he pushed them away, but other soldiers rushed into the room and quickly gagged and bound him.

"Should we kill him?" asked one, unsheathing his kris.

"No," replied the rajah. "He still has a lot to tell us."

"Do you think he'll talk?" asked Lord Guillonk.

"Without question, Milord," replied Brooke.

At a sign from him, a soldier left the room and returned a short while later carrying a silver tray upon which rested a glass full of green liquid.

"What is that?" asked his lordship.

"A special lemonade," said the rajah, "that'll loosen our friend's tongue."

"It's drugged?"

"Just a bit of opium and a few drops of yuma."

"An Indian beverage?"

"Yes, Milord."

At a sign from him, two soldiers removed Yanez' gag, pried open his mouth and forced the lemonade down his throat.

"Watch, Milord," said the rajah. "He'll soon tell us all we want to know."

Despite his resistance, the prisoner was gagged once again so that his cries would not disturb the party guests in the nearby hall.

Five minutes later, his face, pale with rage, began to change shade and his eyes began to sparkle like an angry serpent's. Though he continued to struggle against his bonds, his movements grew slower and slower, until finally, they stopped altogether.

"Remove the gag," said the rajah.

An Indian quickly obeyed. Yanez, enraged just moments ago, began to laugh frantically and with such force that one would have thought he had suddenly gone insane. He talked without pause, jumping from topic to topic, telling tales of Mompracem, the Tigers, and Sandokan, as if sitting among old friends.

"He's gone mad," said Lord Guillonk, not hiding his surprise.

"No, Milord," said the rajah. "The lemonade induces laughter. It lowers one's defences. We'll have no problem getting the truth out of him now. Yet another of the truly remarkable discoveries I made in India."

"He'll tell us where we can find the Tiger of Malaysia?"

"We have but to ask."

"Yanez, my friend," said his lordship, turning to address the Portuguese, "Tell me about the Tiger of Malaysia."

The chords that bound his wrists and ankles having been removed, at the sound of his lordship's voice, the Portuguese jumped to his feet.

"The Tiger?" he asked. "The Tiger... Ha! Ha!... The Tiger of Malaysia... Who hasn't heard of the Tiger? Is it you, old man?... Never heard of the Tiger?... The invincible Tiger? Ha!... Ha!... Ha!..."

"Is the Tiger nearby?" asked the rajah.

"Yes, right here, under the rajah's very nose. And that idiot Brooke doesn't even know it... Ha!... Ha!"

"This man's insulting you, Excellency," said Guillonk.

"It matters not," shrugged the rajah. "He'll soon deliver the Tiger of Malaysia into our hands."

"Continue then, Excellency."

"Tell me, Yanez, where is Sandokan?"

"You don't know? Ha!... Ha! You don't know where Sandokan is! He's here, right here," said Yanez, continuing to laugh.

"Where exactly?"

"Where? He's..." he fell silent. Perhaps a flash of sanity had sharpened his wits at the moment he was about to betray his friend.

"What's the matter?" asked the rajah. "Don't you know where he is?"

Yanez laughed convulsively for several minutes.

"Of course I do," he replied. "He's in Sarawak."

"You're not telling the truth, Yanez."

"Yes, I am. I know! Ha! Me! Not know where Sandokan is... Ha!... Ha!... You're crazy."

"Well then, tell me, where is he?"

"In the city, yes, he must have arrived by now, probably on his way to exhume Tremal-Naik... and then we'll laugh; yes, we'll laugh over how we faked his death and outsmarted that idiot James Brooke... Ha! Ha!"

The rajah and Lord Guillonk looked at each other in amazement.

"Faked his death!" they exclaimed in unison.

"Yes, Tremal-Naik! The Indian Thug! He's alive!"

"Ah! The wretch!" exclaimed the rajah. "Continue, Yanez, my friend. When are they going to exhume Tremal-Naik?"

"Tonight... and tomorrow we'll laugh. Oh, how we'll laugh!... Ha!... What a great trick!... Ha!... Ha!"

"And Sandokan will be there?"

"Yes, Sandokan, this very night... Ha! Ha! We will enjoy ourselves tomorrow... and Tremal-Naik will be happy... Oh! So happy, so happy!..."

"That's enough," said the rajah. "We know what we must do, Milord."

They left the room and went into the study were the captain of the guards had been waiting. He was a tall handsome Indian of proven courage and cunning, one of the rajah's old companions at arms.

"Kallooth," said the prince. "How many loyal men do you have at your disposal?"

"Sixty. All Indians," replied the captain.

"Have them ready to leave in ten minutes."

"It shall be done. Anything else?"

"Station four guards in Yanez's room. They are to kill him if he tries to escape. Now go!"

The Indian saluted and quickly left the room.

"Will you be joining us, Milord?" asked the rajah.

"There's no need to ask, Excellency," replied Lord Guillonk. "I hate the Tiger of Malaysia."

"Yet, he is your nephew, Milord," smiled the rajah.

"I do not recognize him as such."

"Well, if fortune smiles upon us, tomorrow, Malay piracy will forever lose two of its greatest leaders."

Chapter 10
In the cemetery

While events were unfolding in the rajah's villa, Sandokan was rapidly making his way towards the city. Within two hours of Tremal-Naik's burial, the good Maratha had reached the pirates' camp and relayed Yanez' message. Sandokan had immediately set off with his men, armed to the teeth and ready for battle.

It was a beautiful night; stars twinkled like diamonds as the moon cast its soft blue light over the immense forest. An almost perfect silence reigned over all, broken only by the soft rustling of leaves whenever a light breeze blew in from the sea.

A carbine beneath his arm, his eyes open, his ears straining to pick up the slightest noise, Sandokan led his men forward, the Maratha following a few steps behind.

The pirates marched in single file, fingers resting on the triggers of their rifles, cautiously advancing over the dried leaves and dead branches, carefully scanning their surroundings to avoid an ambush. At ten o'clock, just as the festivities were commencing in the capital, the pirates reached the outskirts of the immense forest. To the east the river sparkled like a long silver ribbon, partly illuminating the houses and cottages along its shores. Sandokan's sharp eyes immediately spotted the rajah's villa, its brightly lit windows standing out prominently against the night.

"Looks like there's dancing in Sarawak tonight."

"An excellent distraction, Captain," replied the Maratha.

"Take us to the cemetery. Try to keep us as far from the city as possible."

They left the forest and made their way across a vast field marked by beautiful groves of fruit trees. Though at times the wind carried a mix of cries and laughter from the city, the countryside remained deserted. Nevertheless, Kammamuri remained ever vigilant. He knew the out-skirts of the city teemed with spies, ready to run to the rajah at the first sign of a pirate attack. The Maratha doubled his pace and led the pirates into the woods at the base of hill beneath the fort. Twenty minutes later, he signalled for the men to halt.

"What's the matter," asked Sandokan, drawing up beside him.

"We're close to the cemetery," said the Maratha.

"Where is it?"

"Over there, Captain, in that field."

Kammamuri pointed to a fence a short distance away, beyond it, sev-eral gravestones gleamed white in the moonlight.

"Do you hear anything?" asked Sandokan.

"Just the wind," replied the Maratha.

Sandokan whistled. The pirates rushed forward and circled around them.

"Tigers of Mompracem," he said. "We must be cautious. James Brooke is a sharp, suspicious man who'd gladly relinquish his throne to smash the Tiger of Malaysia and his men."

There was a murmur of agreement.

"We'll take a few precautions to ensure we're not interrupted. Sambig-liong, take eight men and set up a perimeter a thousand paces from the cemetery. If you see or hear anything suspicious, send someone to warn me."

"Understood, Captain," replied the pirate.

"Tanauduriam, take six men and set up a perimeter five hundred paces from this spot. If you see or hear anything suspicious, follow the same procedure."

"It shall be done, Captain."

"Aier-Duk, take four men and take position halfway up that hill. There's a small fort up there, someone may come down to patrol the area."

"As you wish, Tiger."

"Go then, when I blow my whistle, make your way back towards the cemetery."

As the three squadrons went off, the remainder of the men, led by the Tiger of Malaysia and Kammamuri, headed down towards the fence.

"Do you know where he's buried?" Sandokan asked Kammamuri.

"In the middle of the cemetery," replied the Maratha.

"In a shallow grave?"

"I can't say exactly. Captain Yanez and I watched the proceedings from the foot of the hill. Are you sure my master's still alive?"

"Oh, yes, but he won't awaken until tomorrow afternoon. In the meantime, we'll return to camp, then, once Yanez has joined us, we'll go find Ada."

"And then?"

"Then we'll set sail immediately. If James Brooke discovers what we've done, we won't have a moment's peace."

They had arrived at the gate, Sandokan first, followed by the Maratha and the pirates. They headed towards the center of the cemetery and halted before an unmarked grave. The loose soil indicated it had been freshly made.

"This must be it," said the Maratha excitedly. "Poor master!"

Sandokan drew his scimitar and carefully began to dig away at the ground. Kammamuri and the pirates drew their krises and did the same.

"Did they bury him in a shroud or a coffin?" asked Sandokan.

"In a shroud," replied Kammamuri.

"Be careful men, we don't want to injure him accidentally."

Digging cautiously, removing the soil with their hands, they had reached a depth of two feet, when the tip of a kris hit against something solid.

"I struck something," said a pirate, quickly drawing back his arm.

"The body?" asked Sandokan.

"Yes," replied the pirate.

"Start scooping out the soil."

The men reached into the opening and started tossing dirt about in all directions. It wasn't long before they caught a glimpse of Tremal-Naik's burial shroud.

"Try and pull him out," said Sandokan.

The pirates grabbed the shroud, gathered their strength, and began to pull. Bit by bit, the dirt gave way as the body came to light.

"My master!" cried the Maratha, his voice trembling with joy.

"Put him down here," said Sandokan.

Tremal-Naik was set down near the grave. The shroud was damp and showed no signs of life.

"Let's see," said Sandokan.

Kris in hand, he carefully sliced down the length of the material and drew Tremal-Naik's body from the shroud.

The Indian appeared dead. His muscles were rigid, his bronze skin had turned drab and grey, his eyes had rolled back so only their whites were visible, and his lips were parted and stained with blood. Anyone setting eyes upon him would have immediately concluded that he had been killed by a powerful poison.

"My master!" repeated Kammamuri, kneeling down beside him. "Are you sure he isn't dead, Captain?"

"I guarantee it," replied Sandokan.

The Maratha rested a hand on Tremal-Naik's chest.

"His heart isn't beating," he said, terrified.

"But he isn't dead, I swear."

"Can't you revive him now?"

"I'm afraid that's impossible."

"And tomorrow at..."

The Maratha did not finish his question. A sharp whistle from the field had cut him off; someone was sounding the alarm.

Sandokan, who had knelt down near Tremal-Naik, quickly jumped to his feet and scanned the meadow.

"Someone's coming," he said.

A pirate was rushing towards the fence, waving his scimitar, the blade sparkling in the moonlight.

Moments later, after having jumped the fence, he was at Sandokan's side.

"Is that you, Sambigliong?" asked the Tiger of Malaysia with a frown.

"Yes, Captain," said the pirate, panting slightly after such a long run. "We're about to be attacked."

"Attacked!" repeated Sandokan, his hand running to the hilt of his scimitar.

"Yes, Captain. A band of armed men has just left the city and is marching towards us at full speed," said Sambigliong.

"How many?"

"At least sixty."

"And you're certain they're heading here?"

"Yes, Captain."

"How can this be? Yanez must have been discovered... Heaven help James Brooke if he's harmed him!"

"What are we going to do?" asked Sambigliong.

"First, we'll gather our men."

He placed a small whistle to his lips and blew three short breaths.

"There are fifty-six of us," he said, "all brave warriors; we could battle a hundred men."

"Two hundred," said Sambigliong, waving his scimitar. "At the Tiger of Malaysia's command, we'll attack Sarawak and set it ablaze."

"There's no need for that," said Sandokan. "Now listen, I have a plan. Sambigliong, take eight men into that grove of trees on the right. Tanauduriam, take another eight and hide in that grove on the left."

"Yes, sir," said the two captains.

"And you, Aier-Duk, select three men and take position in the middle of the cemetery."

"Yes, captain."

"You'll pretend to be digging a grave."

"Why?"

"So the guards will approach without fear. The rest of us will hide behind that wall. When the time comes, I'll give the signal to attack."

"What will the signal be?" asked Sambigliong.

"A rifle blast. Once you hear it, fire your carbines then draw your scimitars and attack."

"An excellent plan!" exclaimed Tanauduriam. "They'll be caught in a crossfire."

"Take your positions!" commanded the Tiger.

Sambigliong and Tanauduriam led their men into their respective groves. The Tiger of Malaysia knelt down behind the wall, surrounded by the remainder of his men, while Aier-Duk and his companions took position near Tremal-Naik and began to dig.

Moments later, two columns of Indians led by a man in white appeared in the meadow. They advanced silently, rifles in hand, ready to attack.

"Kammamuri," said Sandokan, his eyes fixed on the enemy, "Can you make out who that man in white is?"

The Maratha frowned, eyes narrowing, as he studied the on comer.

"Captain," he said excitedly, "I'm almost certain it's Rajah Brooke."

"The Rajah..." exclaimed the Tiger, his voice marked with hatred. "Coming to challenge me in person! It will be his final battle!"

"You're going to kill him!"

"With the first blast of my rifle."

"No, Captain."

The Tiger of Malaysia turned to face Kammamuri, a menacing look upon his face.

"Captain Yanez could be his prisoner."

Sandokan fell silent.

"That's true."

"Wouldn't it be better to capture the rajah? We could make an exchange."

"An excellent idea, Kammamuri. You can't imagine how I hate that man. He's slaughtered many of our brethren."

"Yanez is worth more than the rajah."

"You're right, my friend. Yanez is his prisoner, I can feel it."

The Indians had arrived to within four hundred meters of the cemetery. Not wanting to be spotted by Aier-Duk and his men, they had dropped to the ground, crawling forward towards their prey.

"Ten more paces," murmured Sandokan, fingering the trigger of his carbine.

Unexpectedly, the advance stopped. At a sign from the rajah, the Indians fanned out and surrounded the meadow.

Brooke undoubtedly suspected a trap.

Once they had formed a semicircle, the soldiers cautiously resumed their advance. Sandokan, who had been crouching behind the wall, stood up. He levelled his carbine, aimed, and fired. The shot tore through the silence that reigned over the cemetery. An Indian leading a band of men fell to the ground, a bullet lodged in the middle of his forehead.

Chapter 11
The Battle

The sound of the shot had not yet faded, when frightening cries arose from the meadow.

Ten, fifteen, twenty rifle shots tore from the bushes with lightning speed. Fifteen Indian soldiers, half wounded, half dead, fell to the ground before they could think to use their weapons.

"Forward, my Tigers!" howled the Tiger of Malaysia as he leaped over the wall followed by Kammamuri, Aier-Duk and the others. "Attack those dogs."

Sambigliong and Tanauduriam rushed out of the bushes, scimitars in hand, leading their men into battle.

"Long live the Tiger of Malaysia!" they howled.

Finding themselves under attack, the soldiers reacted quickly, randomly firing their rifles. Three or four pirates fell, covered in blood.

"Forward, Tigers!" repeated the Tiger.

Emboldened by their captain, the pirates rushed at the enemy line, mercilessly attacking all that stood before them. Frightened by such brutality, the Indians drew back, colliding in the scramble. Scimitar flailing, the Tiger of Malaysia quickly split the wall of soldiers in two. Ten pirates rushed in through the breach and attacked the Indians from the rear. Realizing they had no hope of victory, the soldiers scattered in all directions, fleeing for their lives.

However, a small group, led by James Brooke, refused to surrender.

Spotting his enemy, Sandokan attacked with even greater fury.

Kammamuri, Aier-Duk and Tanauduriam immediately followed with their men, while Sambigliong led his band after the escapees to prevent them from regrouping and forming a second offensive.

"Surrender, James Brooke," yelled Sandokan.

The rajah replied by firing his pistol and killing a pirate.

"Attack, Tigers!" howled Sandokan, as he toppled a soldier about to fire upon him.

Though the enemy resisted tenaciously, it did not take long for the Tigers of Mompracem to open a path with their scimitars and poisoned krises. Kammamuri and Tanauduriam rushed towards the rajah and knocked him to the ground as Aier-Duk and his companions ran after the men fleeing across the meadow.

"Surrender!" yelled Kammamuri, as he relieved the rajah of his sword and pistols.

"I surrender," replied James Brooke, quickly realizing the futility of any further resistance.

Sandokan advanced, still clutching his scimitar.

"James Brooke," he said mockingly, "You are my prisoner."

Having been felled by Tanauduriam's steel fist, the rajah stood up and looked the captain of the pirates in the eye.

"Who are you?" he asked, his voice choked with rage.

"Sandokan, the Tiger of Malaysia."

"Well, what may the Rajah of Sarawak do for the illustrious pirate?"

"You'll answer a few questions."

An ironic smile spread across the rajah's lips.

"What makes you think I'll answer?" he asked.

"Oh, you will! If I have to, I'll use fire to make you speak. I hate you, James Brooke; I hate you the way the Tiger knows how to hate. You've shown no mercy to the pirates of Malaysia, and I'd like nothing more than to avenge those you murdered so ruthlessly."

"They inflicted misery and devastation on everyone they encountered. Was it not my right to exterminate them?"

"Men of your race murdered my family and destroyed everything I held dear. Was it not my right to seek vengeance? But enough talk of rights, answer my questions."

"Ask away."

"What have you done with Yanez?"

"Yanez!" exclaimed the rajah. "A good friend of yours?"

"A very good friend, James Brooke."

"Yes, I can imagine."

"Is he your prisoner?"

"Yes."

"I suspected as much. When did you discover his true identity?"

"This evening."

"How did you capture him?"

"You ask a lot of questions for a pirate."

"Are you refusing to answer?"

"No, perish the thought."

"Speak then."

"Do you know Lord Guillonk?"

Sandokan started. A frown formed upon his brow.

"Yes," he replied hoarsely.

"Your uncle, I believe."

Sandokan did not reply.

"Your uncle recognized Yanez and had him arrested."

"Him!" exclaimed Sandokan. "Him again! And where is Yanez now?"

"In my villa, under lock and key."

"What are you going to do with him?"

"I haven't decided yet, I'll have to think it over."

"You'll think it over?" exclaimed the Tiger of Malaysia with a smile that would have made any other prisoner tremble. "Do you not realize, James Brooke, that you are in my hands? Do you not realize, James Brooke, that I hate you? Do you not realize that, come the morning, you may no longer be Rajah of Sarawak?"

Despite his extraordinary courage, the rajah turned pale.

"You're going to kill me?" he asked, a trace of nervousness in his voice.

"If you do not accept my proposal," Sandokan said coldly.

"Proposal? What kind of proposal?"

"An exchange. You for Yanez."

"He's that important to you?"

"Very."

"Why?"

"He is my brother. Do you accept?"

"I accept," said the rajah, after a minute's reflection.

"Now allow my men to bind and gag you. Your soldiers could return with reinforcements and attempt to attack us."

"We're leaving the cemetery?"

"Yes, we're going to a safer place."

"Fine, I won't put up any resistance."

Sandokan motioned to Kammamuri. Four pirates stepped forward, carrying stretchers made of woven branches. The first was empty; the second was occupied by Tremal-Naik and the others by two gravely injured Dyaks from Sambigliong's squadron.

"Bind and gag the rajah," Sandokan ordered the Maratha.

"Yes, Captain."

They bound the rajah with solid cords, gagged him with a silken handkerchief then placed him upon the empty stretcher.

"Where are we going, Captain?" Kammamuri asked.

"Back to camp," replied Sandokan.

He placed a silver whistle to his lips and blew three sharp notes. The pirates that had gone off in pursuit of the soldiers rushed back, along with Sambigliong and Aier-Duk. Sandokan counted his men. Eleven were missing.

"They're dead," said Tanauduriam.

The squadron quickly marched into the forest, circling the hill dominated by the fort. Sambigliong and Tanauduriam, at the head of a band of ten pirates, led the march, carbines in hand, ready to fire at the first sign of the enemy. The stretchers followed, carrying the rajah, Tremal-Naik and the wounded. Aier-Duk, and the remainder of the men, brought up the rear.

They advanced quickly and reached the abandoned village at five that morning, without having encountered a single soul. The pirates had reinforced it with solid walls and trenches. Sandokan ordered several men into the forest to watch out for enemy troops then untied the rajah, who had not attempted to utter a word throughout the entire trip.

"If it isn't too much of an imposition, I'd like you to write a short note, James Brooke," said Sandokan, offering him a pencil and a piece of paper.

"What would you like me to write?" asked the rajah, managing to maintain an air of tranquility.

"That you've been taken prisoner. The Tiger of Malaysia offers to release you in exchange for the man they know as Lord Welker."

The rajah took the piece of paper, placed it upon his knees and began to write.

"Just a moment," said Sandokan.

"Is there something else?" asked the Englishman, arching his eyebrows.

"Add that if Yanez is not here within four hours, I'll hang you from the tallest tree in the forest."

"Very well."

"Oh, one more thing," said Sandokan.

"Yes?"

"Tell them not to attempt to free you. I'll hang you at the first sign of an armed squadron."

"You seem obsessed with hanging me," the rajah said ironically.

"I do not deny it, James Brooke," Sandokan replied menacingly, "Finish your letter."

The rajah wrote as instructed then handed the letter to Sandokan.

"Excellent," he said, after having read it. "Sambigliong!"

The pirate rushed to his side.

"Take this letter to Sarawak," said the Tiger, "and deliver it to Lord James Guillonk."

"Should I go armed?"

"No, and leave your kris behind. Once you've delivered the letter, return to camp."

"I'll run like a horse, Captain."

The pirate hid the letter in his sash, tossed his scimitar, axe and kris to the ground, and ran off.

"Aier-Duk," said Sandokan, turning to the pirate standing nearby. "Keep a close eye on our prisoner."

"You can count on me, Captain," replied the Tiger.

Sandokan armed his carbine, summoned Kammamuri who had gone to sit by his sleeping master's side, and left the village, heading towards a hill from which could be seen the city of Sarawak.

"Do you think they'll release Captain Yanez?" asked the Maratha.

"Yes," replied Sandokan. "He'll be here within two hours."

"Are you sure?"

"Positive. The rajah is worth as much as Yanez."

"Keep your guard up, Captain," said the Maratha. "Indians can cross a forest without making a sound."

"There's no need to fear, Kammamuri. My pirates are just as clever. Not a single enemy will approach our camp undetected."

"Do you think the rajah will pursue us once we've released him?"

"Undoubtedly, Kammamuri. As soon as he's back in Sarawak, he'll assemble his guards and Dyaks and set off on our trail."

"So we'll be forced to fight a second battle."

"No, we'll set sail immediately."

They soon reached the summit of the hill, which towered several meters above the forest. Sandokan arched his hands above his eyes to shade them from the sun and carefully scanned the surrounding countryside. The river sparkled like a bright silver ribbon as it flowed past the city and in among the luxuriant vegetation of the forests and plantations.

"Look over there," said Sandokan, pointing to a man running towards the city.

"Sambigliong!" exclaimed Kammamuri. "If he maintains that pace, he'll be back within two hours."

"Let's hope."

The two men sat down at the base of a tree, their eyes still fixed upon the city.

An hour passed uneventfully, then a second, dragging on for what felt like a century. Finally, towards ten, a squadron of people appeared near a grove of chestnut trees.

Sandokan jumped to his feet, signs of worry marking his habitually impassive face. Though a bloodthirsty pirate, he had great affection for his loyal friend Yanez.

"Where is he? Where is he?" Kammamuri heard him murmur.

"The man in white in the middle of the squadron. Look!" said Kammamuri.

"Yes, yes, I see him!" exclaimed Sandokan with indescribable joy. "It's him! Yanez!"

He remained there, completely motionless, leaning forward, his eyes fixed on that man in white, then once the squadron disappeared beneath the trees, he rushed down the hill at full speed and ran towards the camp.

Two pirates that had been standing watch in the forest arrived at the same moment.

"Captain," they yelled, "They're brining Señor Yanez."

"How large is the escort?" asked Sandokan, barely able to control himself.

"Twelve men, counting Sambigliong."

"Armed?"

"No, sir."

Sandokan placed his whistle to his lips and blew three sharp notes. Within minutes, the pirates had assembled around him.

"Prepare your weapons," said the Tiger.

"Sir!" yelled James Brooke, sitting at the base of the tree, carefully guarded by Aier-Duk. "Are you going to ambush my men?"

The Tiger turned to face the Englishman.

"James Brooke," he replied gravely, "The Tiger of Malaysia keeps his word. In five minutes, you'll be free."

"Who goes there?" yelled a sentry stationed two hundred meters from the trenches.

"My friends," replied Sambigliong's familiar voice, "Lower your rifles."

Chapter 12
Tremal-Naik's Resurrection

The squad emerged from the forest; Sambigliong, one of the rajah's officers, ten unarmed Indian soldiers and Yanez, his arms and legs unbound.

At the sight of his friend, Sandokan could no longer contain himself. He ran to meet him, pushed away the Indian guards, and clutched the Portuguese to his chest. It was hard to believe that such a display of affection could come from a man known as the Tiger of Malaysia, a pirate that had bloodied the waters of the South China Sea for so many years.

"Yanez!... My brother!" he exclaimed, his voice choked with joy.

"Sandokan, my friend!" yelled the Portuguese, no less moved by the reunion. "I feared I'd never see you again!"

"I'd never let that happen, Yanez. From now on, we'll always fight side by side."

"Yes, little brother! Taking the rajah prisoner was a brilliant move. I've always said you were a great man. What happened to Tremal-Naik?"

"He's not far from here."

"Alive?"

"Alive, but still unconscious."

"And Ada?"

"Still mad, but she'll regain her reason soon enough."

"Sir," said a voice at that moment.

Sandokan and Yanez turned about. James Brooke was standing there before them with his arms crossed. Though he appeared calm, he had turned slightly pale.

"You're free to go, James Brooke," said Sandokan. "The Tiger of Malaysia keeps his word."

The rajah bowed slightly and walked off. But after going a few paces, he suddenly turned about and walked back.

"Tiger of Malaysia," he said, "When shall we meet again?"

"Already planning your revenge?" asked Sandokan, his voice laced with irony.

"James Brooke does not forgive."

Sandokan studied him silently for several instants, almost surprised that that man still dared challenge him, then raised his right arm and pointed it towards the sea

"Mompracem lies in that direction. The waters about it are red with blood and filled with the ships of conquered foes. Approach those shores, and you'll hear the roar of the Tiger and his men moving against you. Do not forget, James Brooke, the Tiger and his men thirst for blood."

"Expect a visit."

"When?"

"In the coming year."

A smile crossed the pirate's lips.

"It'll be too late," he said.

"Why?" the rajah asked, surprised.

"By then, you'll no longer be the Rajah of Sarawak. There's talk of an insurrection in this state of yours; Pangeran Macota will soon be sitting in your place."

The rajah turned pale and took a step back.

"Muda Hassim's nephew? Why invent such things?" he asked uneasily.

"I haven't invented anything, Milord," replied Sandokan.

"What do you know? You must know something."

"It's probable."

"Probable?"

"That's all I'm going to say," said Sandokan.

"Well then, thank you for the warning."

He bowed once again, joined his guards and quickly set off towards Sarawak.

Sandokan, arms crossed and stone faced, followed the rajah with his eyes. Once Brooke had disappeared, a sigh escaped his lips.

"That man is going to cause us a lot more trouble," he murmured. "I can feel it."

"What's the matter, Sandokan?" asked Yanez, drawing near. "You seem nervous."

"I have a bad feeling, brother," said the pirate.

"What?"

"The rajah still has a score to settle with us."

"Do you think he'll attack?"

"I can feel it in my heart."

"Don't put too much stock in premonitions, little brother. We'll leave these shores in two or three days, the rajah won't dare follow us to Mompracem. What's the plan now?"

"We'll head for the bay. I don't feel safe here."

"Let's go then. But what about Tremal-Naik?"

"He won't wake up before noon."

Sandokan gave the signal to depart and the squadron set off once again, following a small trail into the forest. Carbines in hand, Sandokan, Yanez and ten of their most courageous men led the way. The stretcher-bearers followed close behind, then the rest of the pirates, in pairs, eyes scanning both sides of the path, ears straining to detect the slightest sound.

They had gone about half a mile, when Aier-Duk who had gone ahead to scout the path, suddenly halted and cocked his rifle. Yanez and Sandokan rushed to his side.

"Don't move," said the Dyak.

"See something?" asked Sandokan.

"A shadow darted across that thicket."

"Man or animal?"

"I think it was a man."

"It could have been a Dyak," said Yanez.

"Or one of the rajah's spies," said Sandokan.

"Think so?"

"I'm almost certain. Aier-Duk, take four men and scout the surroundings. We'll keep moving forward."

The Dyak summoned four pirates and headed into the forest, crawling among the bushes, branches and roots.

They resumed their march, advancing through rows of sontar trees[4]. A short while later, Aier-Duk and his men returned to the squadron. They had scoured the forest and though they had not spotted anyone, the pirates had come across some fresh footprints.

"Were there many?" Sandokan asked uneasily.

"Four sets," replied the Dyak.

"Boots or bare feet?"

"Bare feet."

"They could have been Dyaks. We'll pick up the pace, it isn't safe here."

For the third time, the squadron set off, carefully scanning the trees and bushes. Three-quarters of an hour later, they reached the shore of a large river that emptied into a vast, semicircular bay.

Sandokan pointed to a small island about three hundred fifty meters away, shaded by beautiful groves of sago palms, mangosteens, durian and arenghe trees. It was defended by an ancient but sturdy Dyak fort, constructed of thick teakwood beams strong enough to withstand cannonballs of medium calibre.

"Is that where they're keeping the Guardian of the Temple?" asked Yanez.

"Yes," replied Sandokan.

"You couldn't have found her a better place. The bay is beautiful and the island is well defended. If James Brooke decides to attack us, he'll have quite a fight on his hands."

"The sea is only five hundred paces from the island, Yanez," said Sandokan, "They could easily attack by ship."

---

[4] A type of palm renowned for its sugary sap; the tribes of Malaysia use its leaves as writing paper.

"We'll defend ourselves."

"We don't have any cannons."

"Our men are brave."

"True, but there aren't many of them and..."

"What's the matter?"

"Quiet! Did you hear that?"

"What, Sandokan?"

"I thought I heard a branch snap."

"Where?"

"In the middle of that thicket."

"Could there really be spies about? I'm starting to feel nervous, Sandokan."

"Me too. Let's go. Best we reach the island as soon as possible. Aier-Duk!"

The Dyak approached the Tiger.

"Take eight men and set up camp here," said Sandokan. "If you spot anyone buzzing about, come and warn me."

Sandokan, Yanez and the others set off towards the bay. Making their way through the thick forest lining the shore, they soon reached a small inlet, where a launch had been hidden beneath a mass of reeds and laurel branches.

The Tiger cast a rapid glance about; though he did not spot anyone, he appeared uneasy.

"One of my men should have been guarding this launch," he said.

"He's probably returned to the fort," said Yanez.

"Without the launch!?!... Yanez... my heart is racing... Something bad has happened, I can feel it."

"Bad? What do you mean?"

"I think Ada's been kidnapped."

"Impossible!"

"Quiet!"

"Another sound?"

"Yes, Captain Yanez," confirmed a pirate, as the men drew their weapons.

There was a slight movement among the thickets a hundred paces from the shore.

"Who goes there?" yelled Sandokan.

"Mompracem," replied a voice.

Minutes later, a pirate emerged from the bushes clutching his rifle. He was panting and sweating, as if he had just come from a long run.

"Long live the Tiger!" he exclaimed, spotting the captain.

"Where were you?" asked Sandokan.

"Scouting the forest, Captain."

"Where's the Guardian?"

"In the fort."

"Are you certain?"

"I placed her under Koty's guard two hours ago."

Sandokan let out a sigh of relief.

"I was beginning to get worried," he said. "How is she?"

"Fine."

"What was she doing when you left?"

"She was sleeping the last time I saw her."

"Did you see anyone?"

"No, but Koty spotted a man marching along the shore this morning. He was eyeing the fort quite suspiciously. Once he realized he was being watched, he immediately disappeared."

"Did you find him?"

"I searched for him but without success."

"One of the rajah's spies?" asked Yanez.

"It's probable," replied Sandokan, suddenly preoccupied.

"Scouting for a possible attack?"

"Who knows?"

"What are we going to do?"

"Get out of here as quickly as possible."

The two captains and their men jumped into the launch, crossed the two hundred meters that separated them from the island and landed at the base of the fortress. Koty stood at the gate, waiting for them.

"Is the Guardian still asleep?" asked Sandokan.

"Yes, Captain."

"Anything suspicious to report?"

"No."

"Let's go see her then," said Yanez.

Sandokan pointed to Tremal-Naik who had been set down upon a patch of grass and leaves.

"It's just a few minutes before noon," he said. "Let's wait until he revives."

He ordered his men to enter the fort then sat down beside the Indian and closely examined his face. Yanez stretched out beside him.

"How long before he awakens?" he asked, after drawing several puffs of his cigarette.

"Soon, Yanez. See, his skin is slowly reverting to its natural shade; his blood is starting to circulate."

"Are you going to take him to Ada?"

"Not immediately, but he'll see her before nightfall."

"What if she doesn't recognize him? What if she doesn't regain her reason?"

"She will."

"I have my doubts, little brother."

"Well then, we'll try I little test."

"What kind of test?"

"You'll see soon enough."

"Why so much mys..."

"Shhh!"

Tremal-Naik's lips trembled; his chest rose almost imperceptibly.

"He's waking," murmured Yanez.

Sandokan bent over the Indian and placed a hand on his forehead.

"Yes, it shouldn't be long now," he said.

A second breath, stronger than the first, caused Tremal-Naik's chest to rise once more. His lips moved slightly, his hands closed slowly then his eyes opened, looked about and came to rest upon Sandokan.

He remained that way for several moments, too stunned to move, then, suddenly, he sat up and exclaimed, "Alive! I'm... still alive!"

"And free," said Yanez.

The Indian looked at the Portuguese and recognized him immediately.

"You!... you!..." he exclaimed. "What happened? How did I get here?"

"Good Lord!" exclaimed Yanez, laughing. "Have you forgotten the pill I gave you back at the fort?"

"Ah!... Yes!... I remember... you came to see me... Sir, thank you for having freed me!"

Tremal-Naik had rushed to Yanez's feet. The Portuguese immediately picked him up and clutched him affectionately to his chest.

"How kind you are, sir!" exclaimed the Indian, beside himself with joy. "Free! I'm free! Thank you, sir, thank you!"

"That's the man you should be thanking, Tremal-Naik," said Yanez, pointing to Sandokan, who, deeply moved, had not once taken his eyes off the Indian. "You owe your freedom to the Tiger of Malaysia."

Tremal-Naik rushed towards Sandokan, embraced him and said, "You are my friend!"

At that moment, a cry of joy erupted from behind them. Kammamuri, who had just left the fort, was running towards them yelling, "Master! Master!"

Tremal-Naik rushed towards the loyal Maratha and clutched him to his chest. The two men embraced at length, unable to utter a word.

"Kammamuri, Kammamuri!" the Indian finally exclaimed. "I never thought I'd see you again. How did you get here? I thought the Thugs had killed you!"

"No, master, no. I escaped to find you."

"To find me! You learned where I was?"

"Yes, master, I found out all I could. Ah! Master! The tears I shed after that fateful night. I can hardly believe you're standing here before me. I'll never leave your side again, master! I promise!"

"As do I, Kammamuri."

"We'll live on Mompracem with Señor Yanez and the Tiger of Malaysia. What noble men, master! If you knew how much they've done for you, if you knew how many battles..."

"There's no need to go into detail, Kammamuri," said Yanez. "Other men would have done as much."

"That's not true, master. No men would ever have done what Señor Yanez and the Tiger of Malaysia did for you."

"But why go to such great pains to help me?" asked Tremal-Naik. "I've never met either of you gentlemen before."

"Because you're Ada Corishant's fiancé," said Sandokan, "And my wife was Ada Corishant's cousin."

Hearing that name, the Indian took a step back, rocking slightly as if he had just been stabbed in the chest. He buried his face in his hands and murmured, "Ada!... My beloved Ada!..."

A sob emanated from his chest and two tears, perhaps the first he had ever shed, rolled down his bronze cheeks. Sandokan approached, lowered the poor Indian's hands, and said kindly, "Why the tears, Tremal-Naik? This is a joyous day."

"Ah, sir!" murmured the Indian. "If you knew how much I love that woman! Ada! Ah, my Ada!"

A second sob tore through the Indian's chest as new tears welled in his eyes.

"There's no reason to be so sad, Tremal-Naik," said Sandokan. "You'll see your beloved Ada again."

The Indian raised his head. A flash of hope shone in his dark eyes.

"Is she safe?"

"Safe!" said Sandokan. "She's here, on this island."

A savage cry erupted from Tremal-Naik's lips.

"She's here!... Here!" he yelled, looking about desperately. "Where is she? I want to see her! I want to see her! Ada! Ah!... My beloved Ada!..."

He attempted to rush towards the fort, but Sandokan quickly grabbed his arm and held him back.

"Wait, there's something you should know," he said. "She's mad."

"Mad!... Ada, mad!" yelled the Indian. "What! How?! I have to see her, sir! I have to see her! If only for a moment..."

"You'll see her, I promise."

"When?"

"In a few minutes."

"Thank you, sir! Thank you!"

"Sambigliong!" yelled Yanez.

The Dyak, who was carefully examining the walls of the fort to ensure they could sustain an attack, rushed forward at the sound of his name.

"Is the Guardian still asleep?" asked Sandokan.

"No, Captain," replied the pirate. "She left several minutes ago with her guards."

"Where did they go?"

"Towards the shore."

"Come, Tremal-Naik," said Sandokan. "And no matter what happens, you must remain calm."

Chapter 13
The Two Tests

It was two o'clock in the afternoon. A magnificent sun blazed over the sparkling azure waters of the bay, as a cool, light breeze blew in from the sea, whispering mysteriously through the leaves of the surrounding trees.

Quiet reigned over the small island, broken only by the monotonous roar of the waves lapping against the shore. At times black cockatoos and large pheasants would flutter by, filling the air with their chatter.

Tremal-Naik, barely able to contain his excitement, Sandokan, Yanez and Kammamuri marched quickly towards the northern tip of the small island, making their way through a dense tangle of rubber trees and climbing vines. When they arrived to within forty paces of the shore, one of the madwoman's guards shot up from behind a bush.

"Where's my Ada?" asked Tremal-Naik, rushing towards him.

"On the beach," replied the pirate.

"What's she doing?" asked Sandokan.

"Staring at the sea."

"Where's the other guard?"

"A few paces from here."

"The two of you may go back to the fort."

Tremal-Naik, Sandokan, Yanez and the Maratha rapidly made their way through the remainder of the trees and came to a stop on the outskirts of the forest. A soft cry escaped the Indian's lips.

"Ada!" he exclaimed.

He was about to rush towards the beach, but Sandokan, expecting that reaction, quickly grabbed his wrist.

"She's mad," he said. "You must remain calm."

157

"I'll control myself."

"Go then. We'll wait for you here."

Sandokan, Yanez and Kammamuri sat down upon the fallen trunk of a tree while Tremal-Naik, barely managing to contain his excitement, headed towards the shore.

There, a few paces from the sea, in the shade of a beautiful carnation tree, sat the Guardian of the Temple of the East, her arms crossed upon her magnificent golden breastplate. Her hair fell to her shoulders in a shower of midnight curls; her eyes gazed into the waters as the waves gently caressed her feet.

Tremal-Naik, barely breathing, eyes aflame, his face no longer hiding his emotion, rapidly approached his fiancée, taking care not to make any sudden, startling noises. When he arrived to within two paces of her, he came to a stop. She appeared not to have noticed him.

"Ada!... Ada!..." exclaimed the Indian, his voice choked with emotion.

The madwoman did not move.

As he gently reached to take her arms in his, the Guardian shot to her feet. She stared at the Indian fixedly, then took two steps back and murmured, "The Thugs!..."

"Ada!... My darling Ada!" cried the Indian desperately. "It's me Tremal-Naik!"

"The Thugs!" she repeated, looking blankly at the man before her.

Tremal-Naik let out a cry of pain and anger.

"Don't you recognize me, Ada? Tremal-Naik, the tiger hunter of the Black Jungle? Ada! Come back to me, Ada! Remember how we met in the jungle? Remember the night I saw you in the Sacred Pagoda? You must remember the terrible night the Thugs took us prisoner! Ada!... Come back to me! Ada... Your Tremal-Naik, Ada, try to remember!"

The madwoman had listened to those words without batting an eyelash, without making a single gesture. She could not remember a thing. Madness had extinguished all feeling in the unfortunate young woman's heart.

"Ada," continued Tremal-Naik, no longer able to restrain his tears, "Look at me closely, my sweet, Ada. How can you not remember your

Tremal-Naik? Why are you so quiet? Why don't you look at me? Why don't you rush into my arms?"

The poor Indian burst into sobs and buried his face in his hands.

Suddenly the madwoman, who had impassively watched the growing desperation of the man she had once loved, took a step forward and knelt beside him. Her face had turned pale and her dark eyes flashed brightly.

"Why are you crying?" she murmured.

Tremal-Naik raised his head.

"Ada!..." he shouted, reaching out to her. "Do you recognize me?"

The madwoman studied him silently for several minutes, frowning repeatedly, as if trying perhaps to remember where she had seen the Indian's face.

"Why are you crying?" she repeated.

"Because you no longer recognize me, Ada," said Tremal-Naik. "Look at me, look at me."

She bent down towards him, then took a step back and began to laugh.

"The Thugs! The Thugs!" she exclaimed.

She turned around and went off, heading towards the fort.

Tremal-Naik let out a cry of despair.

"Great Shiva!" he exclaimed, as fresh tears rolled down his cheeks. "All is lost! She doesn't recognize me anymore!"

He sank to his knees in desperation, then immediately jumped back to his feet and set off after the madwoman who was about to disappear into a grove of trees.

He had not gone more than five paces when two strong arms brought him to a halt.

"Get a hold of yourself, Tremal-Naik," said a voice.

It was Sandokan; Yanez and Kammamuri stood at his side.

"But, sir," babbled the Indian.

"Get a hold of yourself," repeated Sandokan. "All is not yet lost."

"She no longer recognizes me. How I longed to hold her in my arms again, after such torture, after so much anguish! It's over, it's over!"

159

murmured the poor Indian.

"There's still hope, Tremal-Naik."

"Why lie to myself, sir? She's mad, she'll never recover."

"She'll recover, this very night, you have my word."

Tremal-Naik fixed tear-filled eyes upon the Tiger of Malaysia.

"Is it truly possible?" he asked. "You've already been so generous, you've done so much for me, but if you can accomplish this last miracle, my life is yours."

"I will perform this last miracle, Tremal-Naik," said Sandokan gravely. "You have my word."

"When?"

"Tonight."

"How?"

"You'll know soon enough. Kammamuri!"

The Maratha came forward. The young man's eyes, just like his master's, were welled with tears.

"Yes, Captain," he said.

"Were you in the temple the night your master entered Suyodhana's cavern?"

"Yes, Captain."

"Do you remember the conversation between your master and the leader of the Thugs?"

"Word for word."

"Come with me to the fort."

"What about us, what should we do?" asked Yanez.

"I don't require your help for the moment," said Sandokan. "Go for a walk. Don't come back to the fort before nightfall. I'm going to prepare a surprise for you."

Sandokan and the Maratha went off towards the fort. Yanez took Tremal-Naik by the arm and the two set off, following the shore.

"What do you think he's up to?" Tremal-Naik asked the Portuguese.

"I have no idea, Tremal-Naik, but knowing him, it's sure to be extraordinary."

"Do you think he'll be able to restore her sanity?"

"I believe so. The Tiger of Malaysia has many skills."

"If only he were to succeed!"

"He'll succeed, Tremal-Naik. Is this Suyodhana still alive?"

"I believe so."

"Is he powerful?"

"Very, Señor Yanez. He commands an army of stranglers. Thousands of men."

"Sounds like it would be difficult to get to him."

"I'd say almost impossible."

"For others, perhaps, but not for the Tiger of Malaysia. Who knows, one day the Tiger of Malaysia and the Tiger of India may meet face to face."

"You think so?"

"I'd bet on it. Are the Thugs still headquartered on the island of Rajmangal?"

"I don't think so. During my trial, I gave the British the exact location of their lair. Several ships were dispatched to Rajmangal, but they returned without having found so much as a single strangler."

"They escaped?"

"Every one of them."

"Are the Thugs rich?"

"Extremely rich, Señor Yanez. They do not content themselves with just strangling. They attack caravans; they've even sacked entire villages."

"Worthy opponents! The Tiger of Malaysia would enjoy himself. Who knows, perhaps one day, when we tire of Mompracem, we may head for India and measure ourselves against Suyodhana and his followers."

"Do you intend to return to Mompracem?"

"Yes, Tremal-Naik," said Yanez. "Tomorrow, we'll send several of our men to Sarawak to buy prahus and then we'll set sail for our island."

"Will you be taking me with you?"

"We'll assign an escort of brave pirates to take you to Batavia. We have a small villa there; a new home for you and Ada."

"That's too generous, Señor Yanez," said Tremal-Naik, deeply moved. "You've already done so much for us."

"Add to that a pile of diamonds worth a few million, my dear Tremal-Naik."

"I can't accept that."

"You should never refuse the Tiger of Malaysia, Tremal-Naik. It would only irritate him."

"But..."

"There's no need to object, Tremal-Naik. A million is a mere trifle to us."

"You are very wealthy?"

"Extremely."

The sun had set while they were talking, and it was quickly growing dark. Yanez studied his watch by the pale light of the stars.

"It's nine o'clock," he said, "We can go back to the fort."

He scanned the vast stretch of water one last time, but not sighting anything, he turned about, left the beach and headed into the forest. Tremal-Naik, sad and thoughtful, eyes to the ground, followed close behind. Several minutes later, the two men arrived at the fort. Sandokan was sitting in front of the entrance, calmly smoking his pipe.

"I've been waiting for you," he said, moving towards them. "All preparations have been made."

"What preparations?" asked Tremal-Naik.

"All that is necessary for Ada to regain her reason."

He took his two friends by the arm and led them into a vast hut that occupied most of the fort's enclosure. In other times, it must have housed a garrison and a large quantity of provisions and munitions.

Tremal-Naik and Yanez let out a cry of surprise.

In only a few hours, Sandokan, Kammamuri and the pirates had completely transformed that hut into a dark cavern that reminded Tremal-Naik of the Temple of the Indian Thugs, where the grim Suyodhana had taken his frightening revenge.

Torches bathed the room in a ghostly blue light. Large tree trunks had been erected about the room like columns, adorned with clay figures of the gods of India. A frightening statue, also of clay, stood in the center of the room. It had four arms, a long tongue, and its feet rested upon the body of a slain man. A tiny fish swam in a small basin set before it.

"Where are we?" asked Yanez, looking about in amazement.

"In the pagoda of the Indian Thugs," said Sandokan.

"Who made all these ugly monsters?"

"We did, brother."

"In only a few hours?"

"You'd be amazed what you can accomplish when you set your mind to it."

"Who's that ugly monstrosity with the four arms?"

"Kali, the goddess of the Thugs," replied Tremal-Naik, having recognized her immediately.

"What do you think, Tremal-Naik, does our hastily constructed pagoda resemble the one in the Thugs' lair?"

"Yes, Tiger of Malaysia. What do you plan to do?"

"Only a strong shock can restore Ada's sanity."

"I agree, Sandokan," said Yanez, "I think I understand. You're going to re-enact the events in the pagoda the night Tremal-Naik confronted Suyodhana."

"Yes, yes, that's it exactly. I'll play the leader and recite the words he spoke that terrible night. Our men will play the Thugs. Kammamuri has told them what to do."

"Let's begin then."

Sandokan placed a silver whistle to his lips and blew a sharp note. Immediately, thirty Dyaks, naked to the waist, entered the great hut and took position on either side of the goddess. Each man wore a rattan noose about his waist and had a Nagi painted upon his chest.

"Why are their chests marked like that?" asked Yanez.

"All Thugs bear that tattoo," replied Tremal-Naik.

"Kammamuri hasn't forgotten a single detail."

"Are you ready?" asked Sandokan.

"Ready," replied the Dyaks.

"Yanez," said Sandokan, "you're going to play an important part."

163

"What must I do?"

"You'll play Ada's father and lead the remainder of our men. They're going to pretend to be Indian Sepoys. Kammamuri will tell you what to do."

"Understood."

"When I attack you outside the fort, you'll fall before Ada and pretend to die."

"You can count on me, little brother. Places everyone."

Tremal-Naik, Yanez and Kammamuri left the room, as Sandokan took his place before the statue of the Goddess Kali. The Dyaks, dressed as Thugs, lined up alongside him. At a sign from the Tiger, a pirate moved towards a type of gong that had been found in a corner of the fort and struck it twelve times. As the last peal faded, the door to the hut opened and two Dyaks entered, leading the Guardian.

"Advance, Guardian of the Temple of the East," said Sandokan gravely, "Suyodhana commands you."

At the sound of that name, the madwoman came to a halt and freed herself from the pirates' grasp. Her eyes widened, took in Sandokan, fell upon the rows of Dyaks then came to rest upon the Goddess Kali.

Her body trembled visibly and a frown formed upon her brow.

"Kali," she murmured, a trace of terror lining her voice. "The Thugs..."

She took a few more steps forward, alternately casting glances upon Sandokan, the pirates, and the frightening statue in the centre of the room. As she advanced, she ran her hand three times along her brow, as if trying to remember some horrible scene.

Suddenly Tremal-Naik burst into the pagoda and ran towards her yelling, "Ada!"

The young woman came to an immediate halt; an expression of anxiety spreading across her extremely pale face. As she turned to look at Tremal-Naik, the madness appeared to be fading from her eyes.

"Ada!" he repeated, his voice almost a shriek. "Come back to me!"

At that instant, they heard a voice cry, "Fire!"

Several shots sounded outside the entrance to the pagoda, and a group of men led by Yanez burst into the room; the Dyaks, like the Thugs upon that fatal night, fled in all directions.

Ada did not move. At one point, she started then leaned forward as if awaiting a final command.

Sandokan had stopped at one end of the pagoda, his eyes fixed upon her. Did he know what the mad woman was waiting for? Perhaps, for just as the ferocious Suyodhana had done that fateful night he thundered, "We'll meet again in the jungle!"

He had just uttered those words when a sharp cry erupted from the madwoman's lips. Arms raised, her face twisted with emotion, she took a step forward, rocked slightly, and fell into Yanez' arms.

"Dead! She's dead!" Tremal-Naik howled desperately.

Sandokan placed a hand upon the guardian's chest and felt a faint heartbeat.

"She's fainted," he said.

"Then she should be fine," said Yanez.

"If only that were true!" exclaimed Tremal-Naik, through tears of relief.

Kammamuri had returned with some water. Sandokan splashed a few drops in the young woman's face and waited for her to awaken. Several minutes passed then a deep sigh left her lips.

"She's about to awaken," said Sandokan.

"Should I remain here?" asked Tremal-Naik.

"No," replied Sandokan. "We'll send for you once we've told her all that's happened."

The Indian cast a long, tender glance upon his beloved and left the room, stifling a sob.

"Do you think it worked, Sandokan?" asked Yanez.

"I'm almost certain," replied the pirate. "These two unfortunate souls will soon be reunited."

"And we..."

"Shh, Yanez, she's opening her eyes."

The young woman was starting to regain consciousness. She let out a second sigh, longer than the first, then opened her eyes and fixed them upon Sandokan and Yanez. Her gaze was no longer clouded, a sure sign she had recovered her sanity.

"Where am I?" she asked weakly, attempting to get up.

"Among friends," said Sandokan.

"What happened?" she murmured. "Was I dreaming? Where am I?... Who are you?"

"You're among friends," repeated Sandokan. "You've been through a lot; you've just regained your sanity."

"My sanity?... My sanity?" the young woman exclaimed in surprise. "It wasn't a dream?... I remember... it was horrible... it was horrible..."

She burst into tears, unable to speak.

"Try to remain calm," said Sandokan. "You're not in any danger. Suyodhana no longer exists, and there aren't any Thugs about. This isn't India, you're in Borneo now."

Ada gathered her strength and slowly rose to her feet. She grabbed Sandokan's hands tightly and said through tears, "In the name of God, tell me all that has happened. I must know."

They were the words Sandokan had been waiting for. With a grave voice, he briefly narrated all that had occurred in India, on Mompracem and finally in Borneo.

"Now then," concluded Sandokan, "If all you've been through hasn't quelled your love for Tremal-Naik, at a sign from you, he'll be at your knees."

"Do I still love him!" exclaimed Ada. "Where is he? Let me see him..."

"Tremal-Naik!" yelled Yanez.

The Indian rushed into the pagoda and fell before Ada's feet.

"Mine!... Still mine!... Tell me again, Ada that you'll be my wife!" he exclaimed.

The young woman placed her hands upon his head.

"Yes, I will be your wife," she said. "My father promised me to you, and I love you."

At that same moment a rifle blast sounded from across the bay. Immediately a voice yelled out, "To arms! Pirates of Mompracem! The enemy approaches!"

Chapter 14
Rajah Brooke's Revenge

At the sound of that cry, the Tiger of Malaysia ran to the door of the hut, filling the air with a roar.

"The enemy here!" he exclaimed through clenched teeth. "How is that possible!?!"

He drew his scimitar, a terrible weapon in the hands of that formidable man, and rushed out of the fort yelling, "To me, Tigers of Mompracem!"

Yanez, the pirates, Kammamuri and the two lovers raced after him, weapons drawn. Even the Guardian of the Temple had drawn a scimitar, ready to fight at the side of her benefactors.

Aier-Duk and his eight men were running down the path to the bay. Sandokan sighted a large squadron of armed men, several Dyaks, Indians and Europeans, among the trees a short distance behind them.

"To arms, pirates of Mompracem! The enemy!" yelled Aier-Duk, racing towards the boat anchored upon the shore.

Six or seven rifle blasts thundered from the forest and several bullets grazed the water.

"Rajah Brooke's troops!" exclaimed Sandokan. "Just when things were at an end! Very well then, James Brooke, I accept your challenge!"

"What shall we do, Sandokan?" asked Yanez.

"We'll fight, brother," replied the pirate.

"They'll block our escape routes."

"What does it matter?"

"We're on an island, little brother."

"Yes, but we're in a fort."

Aier-Duk and his men quickly traversed the small tract of water and reached the island. Sandokan and Yanez rushed towards the brave Dyak and noted that one of his arms was bleeding.

"Were you taken by surprise?" asked Sandokan.

"Yes, Captain, but I didn't lose a man."

"How many men are we dealing with?"

"At least three hundred."

"Who's in command?"

"A white man, Captain."

"The rajah?"

"No, not the rajah; a naval officer, a lieutenant."

"A tall man with a long red moustache?" asked Yanez.

"Yes," replied the Dyak. "He has about forty European sailors at his command."

"That's Lieutenant Churchill."

"Lieutenant Churchill?" asked Sandokan.

"The commander of the fort."

"You didn't see the rajah?" asked the Tiger.

"No, Captain."

Sandokan scowled.

"What's the matter?" asked Yanez.

"The wretch is going to attack by sea," said the pirate.

"Good Lord!" exclaimed Yanez, frowning. "We'll be caught in a crossfire!"

"But we'll fight, and once we're out of powder and cannonballs, we'll attack with our scimitars and krises."

The enemy troops had originally come to a halt six hundred meters from the shore, but now, they were slowly advancing behind the trees and thickets. The musket fire, having ceased for a short time, began to thunder once again.

"Good Lord!" exclaimed Yanez, "It's starting to hail!"

"Back into the fort!" yelled Sandokan. "It's strong enough to withstand these bullets."

168

The pirates, Tremal-Naik, Ada and Kammamuri re-entered the enclosure, after having sunk the boat to prevent the enemy from using it to cross the small strip of water.

They barricaded the entrance with large boulders then opened the numerous loopholes along the walls. Once the final preparations had been made, the Guardian of the Temple was led into the great hut and the pirates took to their battle stations.

"Fire, Tigers of Mompracem!" thundered Sandokan, who had led Yanez and eight of his toughest men up onto the roof of the great hut.

The pirates responded with a war cry, as several rifle blasts filled the air.

"Long live the Tiger of Malaysia! Long live Mompracem!"

In the meantime, the enemy had almost reached the opposite shore, all the while continuing to fire. Several men had begun to cut down trees, perhaps intending to build a raft and sail to the island. However, they soon realized it was not that easy to approach a fort defended by the indomitable pirates of Mompracem. Lethal discharges roared from the enclosure with speed and precision; minutes later, sixteen men lay lifelessly upon the ground.

"Fire, Tigers of Mompracem!" yelled the Tiger of Malaysia, his voice thundering repeatedly as he issued command after command.

"Long live the Tiger! Long live Mompracem!" replied the pirates as they fired their weapons, aiming the bullets into the thick of the enemy attackers.

The rajah's soldiers were soon forced to retreat back into the forest. They had just reached the safety of the trees, when they sighted a dark mass advancing along the opposite shore; a large troop of men had come to bolster their ranks. A terrible shower of bullets immediately rained down upon the fort, towards the rooftop, where Sandokan stood, rifle in hand.

"Good Lord!" exclaimed Yanez as several bullets whistled past his ears. "There're more of them!"

"And ships!" yelled Sambigliong, sitting nearby.

"Where?"

"Look over there, at the end of the bay. There are two... four... seven... a true fleet!"

"Good Lord!" exclaimed the Portuguese. "Little brother!"

"What is it?" asked Sandokan, loading his carbine.

"We're about to be surrounded."

"Don't you have a rifle?"

"Yes."

"And a scimitar, and a kris?"

"Certainly."

"Well then, brother, we'll fight."

Without giving a second thought to the bullets whistling about him, he climbed to the top of the roof and thundered, "Tigers of Mompracem, revenge! The Exterminator is approaching! To the wall; fire upon those dogs!"

The pirates quickly abandoned the loopholes and raced atop the enclosure wall, climbing like cats. Tremal-Naik, Sambigliong, Tanauduriam and Aier-Duk led the charge, inspiring the men through their fearlessness. Rifles soon began to fire with incredible fury. Lights flashed from beneath every tree lining the shore, shots cracking in the night. Hundreds upon hundreds of bullets crisscrossed through the air, whistling sadly as they sped to find their marks.

From time to time, the thundering voice of the Tiger of Malaysia, the curses of the Tigers, the commands of the rajah's officers, and the savage cries of the Indians and Dyaks punctuated the ever-increasing noise. At times, however, triumphant cheers gave way to the shrieks and howls of the wounded and dying. Suddenly a blast emanated through the air, drowning out the sound of the musketry. A cannon had announced its presence.

"Ah!" exclaimed Sandokan. "The rajah's fleet!"

He looked towards the sea. A large silhouette had entered the bay and was heading towards the island; two lanterns, one green, one red, shone from its sides.

"Sandokan!" yelled a voice.

"Keep fighting, Yanez!" replied the Tiger of Malaysia.

"Good Lord! We have a ship at our backs."

"If we have to, we'll board her..."

He did not finish. A light flashed from the bow of the ship and a cannonball took down part of the enclosure.

"The *Royalist*!" exclaimed Sandokan.

The ship rushing to aid the enemy was in fact Rajah Brooke's schooner, the same ship that had attacked and sunk the *Helgoland* at the mouth of the Sarawak.

"Wretch," roared Sandokan, his eyes enflamed with hatred. "Ah! Why couldn't I have a prahu as well? I'd show you what the Tigers of Mompracem can do!"

Another blast thundered from the bridge of the enemy deck and a second cannonball tore down another part of the wall.

The Tiger of Malaysia howled with rage.

"We're done for!" he exclaimed, a note of agony lining his voice.

He rushed down from the roof of the hut, followed by his men, just as a cloud of grapeshot swept across the fort's summit. He climbed up the barricade that still blocked the entrance and yelled, "Fire, Tigers of Mompracem, fire! Show the rajah who we are!"

The battle took on frightening proportions. The rajah's troops, who until then had remained hidden among the trees, made their way towards the beach and unleashed an infernal barrage of fire; the fleet, which until then had maintained a respectable distance, noting that it was now backed by a powerful cannon, began to move forward, determined, or so it seemed, to land upon the island.

The pirates' situation was becoming desperate. They fought with extreme rage, firing upon the ship, then upon the fleet, then upon the troops gathered along the shores of the bay, roused throughout by the voice of the Tiger of Malaysia. However, their numbers were too small to take on such a large enemy!

Bullets rained down upon them, felling the pirates two or three at a time. Grenades spewed from the *Royalist*'s cannons, exploding with terrible violence and knocking down large tracts of the enclosure wall. At three that morning, more reinforcements arrived to assist the attackers: a fast yacht armed with a large cannon. She opened fired immediately and smashed in the remnants of the fort's enclosure.

"We're done for!" murmured Sandokan from atop the barricade as he fired at the advancing fleet, "It won't be long before we're forced to surrender."

By four o'clock only seven people remained in the fort: Sandokan, Yanez, Tremal-Naik, Ada, Sambigliong, Kammamuri, and Tanauduriam. The enclosure no longer provided any kind of shelter, and they had retreated into the great hut, part of which had already been destroyed by the combined cannon fire from the *Royalist* and the yacht.

"Sandokan," said Yanez at one point, "We can't resist much longer."

"As long as we have gunpowder and bullets, we won't surrender," replied the Tiger of Malaysia, his eyes fixed on the enemy fleet, which, though repelled six times, was about to attack again and attempt to land its troops.

"We're not alone, Sandokan. There's a woman with us."

"We can still win, Yanez. We'll let the enemy disembark and fight them man-to-man."

"What if a bullet were to strike Ada? Look, Sandokan, look!"

A grenade launched from aboard the *Royalist* had exploded just then, taking down a large tract of the wall. Several metal fragments made their way into the large room, whistling over the group of pirates.

"They're going to kill my fiancée!" exclaimed Tremal-Naik who had readily leapt in front of the Guardian of the Temple.

"We have to surrender or prepare to die," said Kammamuri.

"We have to surrender, Sandokan," yelled Yanez. "We promised to protect Marianna's cousin."

Sandokan did not reply. Standing by the window, rifle in hand, eyes flaming, lips parted, his face twisted with violent rage, he watched as the enemy rapidly advanced toward the island.

"We have to surrender, Sandokan," repeated Yanez.

The Tiger of Malaysia sighed. A second grenade flew through an opening and struck the opposite wall where it exploded in a shower of burning fragments.

"Sandokan!" yelled Yanez for the third time.

"Brother," murmured the Tiger.

"We have to surrender!"

"Surrender!" yelled Sandokan, his voice no longer human. "The Tiger of Malaysia surrender to James Brooke! Why don't I have a cannon to use against the rajah? Why did I leave so many men behind on Mompracem? Surrender! The Tiger of Malaysia surrender!"

"There's a woman here, Sandokan!"

"I know..."

"She's your wife's cousin."

"I know..."

"We have to surrender, Sandokan."

A third grenade exploded in the room as two heavy calibre cannonballs struck the top of the hut, caving in a good part of the roof. The Tiger of Malaysia turned around and looked at his companions. They were all clutching their weapons, ready to continue the fight, the Guardian of the Temple standing among them. She appeared calm, but a slight uneasiness was evident in her eyes.

"We no longer have any hope," the pirate murmured darkly. "In ten minutes, none of these brave souls will be standing. We have to surrender."

He pressed his hands against his brow.

"Sandokan!" said Yanez.

A loud hurrah drowned out his voice. The rajah's soldiers had finally crossed the expanse of water and were heading towards the fort.

Sandokan shook himself awake. He drew his terrible scimitar and for a moment it appeared as if he were about to rush out of the hut to engage his enemies, but reason soon triumphed and brought him to a halt.

"The final hour has sounded for the Tigers of Mompracem!" he exclaimed painfully. "Sambigliong, raise the white flag."

With a gesture, Tremal-Naik stopped the pirate from fastening some white rags to the barrel of a rifle then advanced towards Sandokan, leading his fiancée by the hand.

"Sir," he said, "if we surrender, no harm will come to Ada, Kammamuri, and myself, but the rajah will not spare you and your men; you'll be hung as pirates. You've saved us; we place our lives in your hands. If there's any chance of victory, give the order to attack and we'll rush at the enemy to the cry of "Long live the Tiger of Malaysia! Long live Mompracem!"

"Thank you, my noble friend," said Sandokan, his voice deeply moved as he pressed the hands of the Indian and the young woman. "Unfortunately, the enemy has already landed and there are only seven of us. We have no choice but to surrender."

"What about you?" asked Ada.

"James Brooke will not hang me," replied the pirate.

"You may proceed, Sambigliong," said Yanez.

The pirate climbed up onto the roof of the hut and waved the white flag. They immediately heard a bugle sound from the deck of the *Royalist*, followed by a loud hurrah. Still clutching his scimitar, Sandokan left the hut, made his way through the courtyard strewn with bodies, weapons and cannonballs, and came to a halt near the remnants of the barricade.

Two hundred of the rajah's soldiers had disembarked and now stood in formation along the shore, weapons levelled, ready to fire. A launch carrying Rajah Brooke, Lord Guillonk and twelve sailors had been lowered from the *Royalist*'s side and was rapidly making its way toward the island.

"That's my uncle," Sandokan murmured sadly.

He sheathed his scimitar, crossed his arms, and waited for the arrival of his two bitterest enemies.

Advancing with great speed, the launch landed near the fort minutes later. James Brooke and Lord Guillonk disembarked and made their way toward Sandokan, a large escort of soldiers following closely behind.

"Are you asking for a cease-fire or are you surrendering?" asked the rajah, saluting with his sabre.

"I'm surrendering, sir," said the pirate, returning the salute.

"I knew it was just a matter of time before I defeated the indomitable Tiger of Malaysia," he said. "Sir, I place you under arrest."

Sandokan proudly raised his head and cast a menacing look upon the rajah.

"Rajah Brooke," he hissed. "I still have five Tigers of Mompracem at my command, a small number, but enough to wage battle against your men. At a sign from me, they'd attack and kill you and your escort. You'll arrest me after I've ordered them to put down their arms."

"You're not surrendering then?"

"I'm surrendering but only upon certain conditions."

"Sir, allow me to bring a few facts to your attention. You may not have noticed, but my troops have already landed; there are only six of you and two hundred and fifty of us; what's more, I need but wave and every one of their rifles would fire into your chest. I find it strange that even in defeat, the Tiger of Malaysia wishes to dictate conditions."

"The Tiger of Malaysia is not beaten yet, Rajah Brooke," Sandokan said proudly. "I still have my scimitar and my krises."

"Should I order my men to attack?"

"You may do as you wish, after you've heard what I have to say."

"Very well then, proceed."

"Rajah Brooke, Captain Yanez de Gomera, the Dyaks, Tanauduriam, Sambigliong and myself are from Mompracem, and we surrender upon the condition we be tried by the Supreme Court of Calcutta. Furthermore, liberty will be granted to Tremal-Naik, his servant Kammamuri and Miss Ada Corishant. They shall be allowed to go wherever they wish."

"Ada Corishant! Ada Corishant!" exclaimed Lord Guillonk, rushing towards Sandokan.

"Yes, Ada Corishant," replied Sandokan.

"That's impossible!"

"Why's that, Milord?"

"She was kidnapped by Indian Thugs and was never heard from again."

"She's in the fort, Milord."

"Lord James," said the rajah. "Have you ever met Miss Ada Corishant?"

"Yes, Excellency," replied his lordship. "I met her once, a few months before she was kidnapped."

"Would you recognize her if you saw her again?"

"Yes, and I'm sure she'd recognize me as well, even though it's been several years."

"Well then, sir, follow me," said Sandokan.

He led them through an opening and into the great hut. The Guardian of the Temple, Yanez, Tremal-Naik, Kammamuri, Tanauduriam and Sambigliong stood at the centre of the room, rifles in hand, krises clutched between their teeth

Sandokan took Ada by the hand, presented her to his lordship and said, "Do you recognize her?"

Two cries filled the air.

"Ada!"

"Lord James!"

Uncle and niece embraced warmly.

"Sir," said the rajah, turning toward Sandokan, "How did Miss Ada Corishant arrive in your hands?"

"Allow her to tell you herself," replied Sandokan.

"Yes, yes, I want to know!" exclaimed Lord James, embracing the young woman through tears of joy. "I want to know everything."

"Well then, tell him everything, Miss Ada," said Sandokan.

The young woman did not wait to be told twice and briefly narrated her story to his lordship and the rajah.

"Lord James," she said, once she had finished, "I owe my rescue to Tremal-Naik and Kammamuri; and my happiness to the Tiger of Malaysia. Congratulate these men, Milord."

Lord James approached Sandokan who with his arms crossed, had been watching the scene before him.

"Sandokan," said the old man, his voice deeply moved. "You kidnapped my niece, but you have rescued another woman I love just as much. I forgive you and offer you my friendship!"

Though terrible enemies for so many years, the Tiger of Malaysia fell into the old man's arms. When they parted, his lordship's eyes were welled with tears.

"Is it true your wife passed away?" he sobbed.

At that question, the Tiger's face changed frighteningly. He closed his eyes and buried his face in his hands.

"Yes, she's dead," said the Tiger, moaning in agony.

"Poor Marianna! My poor niece!"

"Quiet, quiet," murmured Sandokan.

A sob stifled his voice. The Tiger of Malaysia had begun to cry! Yanez approached his friend, placed an arm on his shoulder and said, "Be strong, little brother. You're still standing before the Exterminator; the Tiger of Malaysia must not show signs of weakness."

Almost in anger, Sandokan wiped away the tears and proudly raised his head.

"Rajah Brooke, I'm at your disposal. My men and I surrender."

"Name your men," said the rajah, his brow darkening visibly.

"Yanez, Tanauduriam and Sambigliong."

"And Tremal-Naik?"

"What! You dare..."

"I dare nothing," said James Brooke. "I'm obeying orders, nothing more."

"What do you mean?"

"Tremal-Naik will be taken prisoner along with your men."

"Excellency!" exclaimed Lord Guillonk. "Excellency!"

"I'm sorry, Milord, but I do not have the power to grant Tremal-Naik his freedom. He was consigned to me, and I have to return him to the British authorities."

"But you've heard Tremal-Naik's story! He's innocent and soon to be my nephew!"

"True, but I cannot ignore orders issued by the Anglo-Indian authorities. A few days from now, a ship transporting convicts will arrive in Sarawak and I'll be forced to deliver him to its commander."

"Sir!" Tremal-Naik exclaimed sadly, "How can you allow them to take me from Ada and send me to Norfolk?"

"Rajah Brooke," said Sandokan, "This is pure treachery."

"Just following orders," replied the rajah. "Lord Guillonk is free to go to Calcutta, deliver this new evidence, and obtain a pardon for Tremal-Naik. I promise, on my part, to support him completely."

Ada, who until then had remained silent, held back by an almost lethal anguish, came forward.

"Rajah," she said sadly, "Do you wish to see my insanity return?"

"You'll have your fiancée back soon enough. Once the Anglo-Indian authorities have reviewed the trial, they will not hesitate to grant Tremal-Naik a full pardon."

"Then allow me to embark with him."

"You!... Nonsense! Are you joking, Miss?"

"I want to be with him."

"On a convict ship! Among that infernal bedlam!"

"I want to be with him," she said exultantly.

James Brooke looked at her with a certain amount of surprise. He appeared taken aback by the young woman's energy and determination.

"Answer me," said Ada, noting that he remained silent.

"Impossible, Miss," he said. "The commander of the ship would not take you aboard. It would be better for all concerned if you accompanied your uncle to India to obtain your fiancé's pardon. Your testimony should be enough to restore his freedom."

"That's true, Ada," said Lord Guillonk. "My testimony would not be enough to pardon him."

"But you're asking me to abandon him once again!" exclaimed Ada, bursting into tears.

"Ada!" said Tremal-Naik.

"Excellency," said Sandokan, advancing towards the rajah. "Grant me five minutes freedom!"

"What for?" asked James Brooke.

"I wish to persuade Miss Ada to go with Lord James."

"Granted."

"Your presence is not necessary; I wish to be alone with them."

He left the hut and led his friends into the enclosure.

"Listen," he said. "I still possess the means to defeat the rajah. Miss Ada, Lord James..."

"Call me uncle, Sandokan," said the Englishman. "You're my nephew after all."

"Thank you, uncle," said the Tiger, moved by those words. "Miss Ada, you must renounce the idea of accompanying your fiancé to Norfolk. Let's try to convince the rajah to keep Tremal-Naik in Sarawak until the authorities in Calcutta have reviewed his trial and decided his fate."

"But it'll be a long separation," said Ada.

"No, Miss, it'll be short, I assure you. I'm just playing for time."

"What do you mean?" asked Tremal-Naik and Lord Guillonk.

A smile crossed Sandokan's lips.

"Tried in India!" he said. "Do you think I'm unaware of the fate awaiting me in Calcutta? The British hate me; I've waged a ferocious war against them. They'd show no mercy and I'm not ready to die just yet."

"Do you have a plan?" asked Lord Guillonk.

"Our fate rests with Pangeran Macota."

"The old Sultan's nephew?" asked Lord James.

"Yes, uncle. He's plotting to reacquire the throne and he's slowly undermining Brooke's power."

"How can we help?" asked Ada.

"Find him and tell him that the Tigers of Mompracem will help him retake his throne. My pirates will land here, take command of his insurrection, attack our prison and set us free."

"But I'm British, nephew," said his lordship.

"I'm not asking you to play any part in this, Uncle James. You cannot conspire against one of your own countrymen."

"Who will do this then?"

"Miss Ada and Kammamuri."

"Oh yes, sir," said the young woman. "You restored my reason and reunited me with Tremal-Naik. My life is yours to command. What must I do?"

Sandokan unfastened his jacket and drew a swollen purse from the folds of his sash.

"Go to Pangeran Macota and tell him that Sandokan, the Tiger of Malaysia, offers these diamonds, worth two million, as a gift to expedite his revolt."

"And what must I do?" asked Kammamuri.

Sandokan removed a ring adorned with a large emerald and gave it to him saying, "You'll sail to Mompracem and show my pirates this ring, tell them that I've been taken prisoner and that they must embark for Sarawak immediately to assist in the insurrection against James Brooke. Let's go back now; the rajah must be growing suspicious."

They entered what remained of the hut. Brooke was waiting for them, surrounded by a group of officers that had just come ashore.

"Well then?" he asked.

"Ada renounces the idea of going with her fiancé, on the condition that you, Excellency, keep the prisoner Tremal-Naik in Sarawak until the Court of Calcutta has reviewed his trial," said his lordship.

"Very well," said Brooke after a few minutes of reflection.

Sandokan advanced, threw his scimitar and kris upon the ground and said, "I am your prisoner."

Yanez, Tanauduriam and Sambigliong also tossed down their weapons.

His eyes damp, Lord James stood between the rajah and Sandokan.

"Excellency," he said, "What are you going to do with my nephew?"

"I'll meet his terms."

"Specifically?"

"I'll send him to India. He'll be tried by the Supreme Court of Calcutta."

"When will he set sail?"

"In forty days, on the postal ship from Labuan."

"Excellency... he's my nephew and I helped to capture him."

"I know, Milord."

"He saved Ada Corishant, Excellency."

"I know, but the matter is out of my hands."

"What if my nephew promised to leave these waters forever? If he promised never to set foot upon Mompracem again?"

"There's no need for that, Uncle James," said Sandokan. "Neither I nor my men fear human justice. When our last hour has sounded, the Tigers of Mompracem will face death with honour."

He approached the old Lord, who was crying silently, and embraced him, then turned towards Ada and Tremal-Naik.

"Goodbye, Miss," he said, pressing the sobbing young woman's hand. "Don't give up hope."

He turned to face the rajah who was waiting for him by the door and said, "At your service, Excellency."

The four pirates and Tremal-Naik left the fort and took their positions in the launches. Once the vessels had pulled away from the shore and were heading towards the *Royalist*, the prisoners cast their eyes upon the island. Ada, Kammamuri and his lordship stood before the fort's entrance, tears bathing their cheeks.

"Poor Ada, poor Uncle James," sighed Sandokan. "But we won't be separated for very long, and James Brooke will lose his throne!"

Chapter 15
Aboard the *Royalist*

Ten minutes later, James Brooke's small schooner triumphantly left the bay and headed out to sea. The rajah's crew had hoisted sails on the fore and mainmasts, and the ship, driven by a fresh breeze, flew over the azure waters of Borneo, a bright wake stretching behind her.

Guarded by four soldiers armed with bayonets, Sandokan and Yanez stood at the stern, their eyes fixed upon Lord Guillonk's yacht, attempting perhaps to catch a last glimpse of their friends. Once the ship had disappeared from view, the Tiger turned towards the Portuguese.

"So this is how it ends!" he exclaimed. "We'll have to answer for a great deal, Yanez."

The Portuguese merely shrugged.

"You're not afraid."

"No," replied Yanez.

"But we're in the Exterminator's hands."

"You're still the Tiger of Malaysia."

"If you were free and I still had my scimitar, I'd wager the Tiger could still defeat the Exterminator, but now..."

"I have faith in you, Sandokan."

A pale smile spread across the lips of the leader of the pirates of Mompracem.

"The Tigers we led into battle have been slain," he sighed.

"There are others on Mompracem ready to take their place."

"Mompracem is far off and we're still prisoners."

"We've escaped from worse situations," said Yanez.

"James Brooke approaches."

After having conferred with his officers, the rajah had come back on deck and was making his way towards the two prisoners. He signalled to the four soldiers to stand down then turned towards the pirates.

"Follow me," he said.

"What do you want of us?" Sandokan asked arrogantly.

"You'll find out at sundown," replied the rajah. "My officers have just held a tribunal and pronounced sentence upon you."

"I do not recognize that as one of their rights."

"I recognize that right and I am the Rajah of Sarawak."

"James Brooke! I wouldn't count the Tiger of Malaysia as dead just yet!" Sandokan yelled menacingly.

"What do you mean?"

"One day, I'll return to Sarawak, leading the Tigers of Mompracem!"

"Ah! You'll soon be quite far from Mompracem," said the rajah, smiling darkly. "Within a month, there'll be an ocean between your island and your new home."

"What new home?"

"The Isle of Norfolk."

Sandokan started. Shock gave way to rage, but he quickly regained his composure and began to speak in a calm voice laced with irony.

"Ah! So you're sending us to live with the British convicts on Norfolk? Not a bad idea, James Brooke! Is the *Royalist* going to undertake the long journey?"

"My ship is of better use to me here."

"Then I imagine we're to be transported by the vessel that was to collect Tremal-Naik."

"Correct."

"Has she already reached Sarawak?" Sandokan asked mockingly.

"She's been anchored off Matany since last night."

"Well then, we'll visit Norfolk, provided of course, that something unexpected doesn't happen."

"What do you mean?" asked the rajah, looking at him suspiciously.

"As you know, James Brooke, when you're at sea, you can never be certain of reaching your destination."

"That's not what you meant. You hope to escape before the ship reaches Norfolk. I'd forget such ideas; it's impossible, I assure you. You're unfamiliar with life aboard a convict ship."

"I'll find out soon enough, sir, the *Royalist* should be within sight of Matany by nightfall."

James Brooke looked at him fixedly for several instants as if attempting to read his soul.

"Follow me," he said.

"Do you wish to clap us in irons so soon?" Sandokan asked sardonically.

"You'll be my guests for the remainder of the journey," James Brooke replied gallantly. "Come."

He led Sandokan and Yanez below deck and halted before a lavishly set table.

"The two of you must be hungry after such a long battle," he said. "It would give me great pleasure if you would join me."

"With pleasure," replied Sandokan, as Yanez bowed silently.

The rajah and the two captains of Malay piracy began to eat with excellent appetite, chatting as if they were the best of friends instead of the bitterest of enemies. They competed in courtesies; they spoke of the sea, of navigation, of ships, of arms and boardings, without once referring to their rivalry, the Isle of Norfolk or Mompracem. An observer would never have guessed that only three hours earlier those formidable men had been engaged in merciless battle, determined to annihilate one another; that one was the 'Exterminator', and the other two led the most feared pirates in all of Borneo.

They got up from the table shortly before nightfall. James Brooke offered them coffee and Manila cigars, then led them onto the bridge, continuing to chat familiarly, to the great amazement of the *Royalist*'s crew. Driven by a favourable breeze, the ship headed swiftly towards Matany, its majestic peak, towering 2900 meters above the sea, soared before them to the west, coloured by the last rays of the sun. As the sun disappeared beneath the horizon, the sea slowly turned from red to black, and the last golden glimmers faded from the waves. Partridges, gannets, sea swifts and petrels wheeled aloft, filling the air with their cries.

The rajah and the two captains of piracy had been walking about the deck for a half hour when the Englishman came to an abrupt halt and cast his eyes towards the bow; he had sighted two bright points shining not too far from Matany. He frowned suddenly and his face, which until then had born a good-natured smile, grew cold and fierce. He turned towards a sailor and said, "Light a flare."

Sandokan and Yanez did not utter a single word. Their eyes were anxiously fixed upon those two bright dots, one red, one green, that heralded the presence of another ship.

Minutes later, a flare was launched from the *Royalist's* stern and exploded in a shower of golden light. Standing on the bow of his small vessel, the rajah stared in expectation at the two bright dots. Suddenly a bluish flare tore through the darkness.

"That's the ship," said James Brooke.

He turned toward Sandokan and Yanez.

"You're no longer my guests," he said brusquely.

"So that's the ship that's taking us to Norfolk?" Sandokan asked flatly.

"Yes," the rajah replied dryly.

"We're ready."

A launch was lowered from the *Royalist's* side, manned by an officer and eight crewmen armed with rifles and axes.

Before descending the ladder, Sandokan approached the rajah, fixed his eyes upon him, and said in a slow, measured voice, "James Brooke, we shall meet again."

An ironic smile spread across the Exterminator's lips.

"You don't believe me?" asked Sandokan.

"Hardly."

"It's unwise to underestimate your enemies, James Brooke. When next we meet, you shall fear the combined might of the pirates of Mompracem and the rebel Dyaks."

"What do you mean?" the rajah asked uneasily. "Pangeran Macota is in my custody and his Dyaks have been disbanded."

"Perhaps things will change. Good-bye, James Brooke! The battle between us is not over yet; sparing my life may prove to be your greatest mistake."

Having said that, Sandokan quickly descended the ladder and took his place among the soldiers followed by Yanez, Sambigliong and Tanauduriam who had also been brought up on deck.

At a quick command from the officer, the launch rowed off towards the two bright dots shining in the darkness. However, before it got very far, Sandokan raised his head and sighted the rajah leaning over the bulwark, looking at him. The pirate waved contemptuously then turned to Yanez and said, "Let's get a look at this convict ship."

"Should be as happy as a funeral," smiled the Portuguese.

"Perhaps, but we'll enliven the festivities," murmured the formidable pirate leader in Bornese.

"What are you up to, Sandokan?"

"I have the beginnings of a plan, my good Yanez. Convicts are a rough lot and desperation makes them fearless. They'll try anything to regain their freedom. Enough talk for now, let's see how events unfold."

Driven by three pairs of oars, the launch quickly flew over the dark waters. Rifles resting on their knees, the soldiers sat in a square about the four prisoners to prevent them from escaping; an impossibility since the launch was more than ten miles from the coast.

An hour later, the vessel became visible, for the moon had risen behind the tall peaks of Matany. It was a large three-masted frigate, an old ship that had seen service with the British squadron of 1830, good vessels in their time, but long since decommissioned. Sandokan and Yanez calmly studied her, admired her tall masting and large hull, then looked at each other and smiled.

"Looks like we'll have a good deal of company," said the former.

Hoarse, savage cries echoed from the interior of that enormous ship, erupting with great commotion, then, suddenly, all fell silent as a voice from the bridge yelled out, "Who goes there?"

"A launch from the rajah's ship," replied the officer.

"Approach!"

With a few strokes the launch arrived beneath the frigate's side. A ladder was quickly lowered.

"Follow me," the officer instructed Sandokan and Yanez.

The two pirate leaders obeyed without objection and climbed up the ladder escorted by four soldiers. When they reached the deck, an officer stepped forward and shined a lantern upon them.

"Your new prisoners, sir," said the rajah's officer. "James Brooke entrusts them to your care."

"So these are the two famous pirates?" asked the lieutenant, casting a scrutinizing glance upon Sandokan and Yanez.

"Yes, sir."

"Two dangerous men."

"Guard them carefully."

"Leave it to us, sir. Convey my best wishes and those of the captain to his Excellency."

"Are you setting sail?"

"Immediately. The wind is favourable."

Once the rajah's envoy and his men had returned to the launch, the frigate tacked and pointed her bow northward. The lieutenant summoned four sailors and indicating Sandokan and Yanez said, "Clap them in irons and take them below deck, we're dealing with very dangerous men."

At those words, Sandokan moved to rebel; Yanez, ever alert, immediately rushed to his side and said quickly, "Calm down, little brother, or your plan will go up in smoke."

"You're right," Sandokan replied through clenched teeth.

The quartermaster stepped forward bearing two sets of leg irons, fastened them around the prisoners' ankles, then pushed them roughly towards the bow saying, "Come, you wretches."

He had not yet finished uttering those words when Sandokan's right arm smashed down upon his shoulder, almost knocking him over the side.

"Wretch?" he hissed. "I am of royal blood, and up until this morning, I was the leader of the pirates of Mompracem. I've killed far better men than you!"

Having witnessed that exchange, the lieutenant quickly stepped between them. However, instead of addressing Sandokan, he violently pushed away the quartermaster and admonished him severely.

"These two men are under the protection of the Rajah of Sarawak and are not common criminals. I'll clap in irons whoever dares insult them."

"I renounce James Brooke's protection," Sandokan said proudly. "I ask no more than to be treated as the others, but I will not tolerate insults!"

After having saluted the officer, they followed the quartermaster, who, from time to time, would look over his shoulder as if afraid of receiving yet another blow from that powerful fist.

When they had reached the bow, they went down a short set of steps and entered the ship's waist. Sandokan and Yanez came to an immediate halt and shuddered in horror.

"What kind of infernal pit is this!?!" asked the Portuguese. "Good Lord, I never thought I'd end up in a place like this. This is the hell of the damned."

"Yes, a hell we'll soon transform," said Sandokan. Then turning towards the quartermaster, he asked, "Where's our place?"

"Down there, towards the stern," replied the sailor."

"Lead the way!"

Chapter 16
The convict ship

A horrible, repugnant spectacle unfolded before them in the waist of that old convict vessel. A sea of bodies, revolting, unwashed, stretched from the crew's quarters to the flat of the stern. Three hundred men, the dregs of England and the British colonies of Asia, lay side by side, almost atop one another, chained to the floor like wild beasts.

And what a range of scoundrels! Young men brutalized by vice and crime, giants of immense size, middle-aged men, still strong and vigorous, and old men with white hair. Thieves, arsonists, murderers, even incorrigible drunkards had been gathered and sent off to the Isle of Norfolk, the worst penitentiary in the Pacific Ocean. Some, weakened by tuberculosis or exhausted by the strain of the long, arduous journey, would never get a glimpse of the giant pine trees that covered that cursed island.

A foul stench emanated from those three hundred bodies blanketing the ship's waist. Two lanterns cast their light upon the convicts, smoky flames flickering with each wave of snores. From time to time, a chain creaked mournfully.

Sandokan and Yanez looked on in horror at that foul display of human flesh.

"What kind of infernal pit is this!?!" the Portuguese exclaimed a second time. "I never dreamed I'd witness such a scene! I'd rather look upon a battlefield bathed in blood, covered with the dead and dying, than upon this sea of bandits..."

"Come," the quartermaster said brusquely.

The two pirate captains and their men followed in silence. They slowly advanced through that mass of sleeping souls, taking great care not to step on anyone, and soon reached the stern. The quartermaster had each man sit beside an iron ringbolt fixed into the planks then ordered them to close their eyes and go to sleep.

"Weren't you ordered to clap us in irons?" asked Sandokan.

"There's no need for that," smiled the sailor. "You're... worthy of respect. Sleep well."

He went off without another a word.

Sandokan and Yanez looked at each other.

"This freedom will favour my plans," said the first.

"What about our leg irons?" objected Yanez.

"We'll have them removed at the appropriate time."

"How are we going to get out of here?"

"I'm slowly formulating a plan, Yanez. James Brooke thinks I'm going to let myself be taken to Norfolk. Well, he's mistaken, my friend. There might be a terrible massacre, but we'll be in control of this old scow before she gets within sight of Cape Sirik."

"You're going to lead the convicts in a revolt?"

"Yes, Yanez."

"You think they'll obey you?"

"Do they not also wish to regain their freedom?"

"What about the crew?"

"They won't be able to resist the attack. They'll surrender."

"And then?"

"We'll head back to Sarawak."

"Again?"

"The Tiger of Malaysia will not accept defeat! I'll force the rajah from his throne. I should have allied myself with Pangeran Macota much earlier, but that matters little now, we'll still raise his Dyaks against James Brooke."

"Do you know Pangeran Macota?"

"I met him several years ago. He'd be the ruler of Sarawak if his uncle hadn't handed the throne to Brooke."

"Where's the Pangeran now?" asked Yanez.

"In Sedang, guarded by several of the rajah's most loyal men."

Suddenly an imperious voice thundered, "Quiet, or you'll get a taste of the lash."

"Guard at the bow," whispered Sambigliong and Tanauduriam, lying behind the two captains.

"Let's try to get some sleep," replied Sandokan. "This is not the time to make plans."

Accustomed to sleeping on the barren ground of the jungles of Borneo, the four men stretched out upon the planks without much discomfort. They closed their eyes and soon fell asleep, gently cradled by the waves breaking against the sides of the old vessel.

During the night, however, Sandokan woke up three times and sat up to observe the convicts sleeping nearby. His eyes rested upon a giant of a man with broad shoulders and muscular arms.

He was about forty years old with a Herculean build, thick red hair, a large forehead and regular features that contrasted greatly with the ferocity of his neighbours. Though he wore the cloth outfit of a convict, his bronzed face and his manner of sleeping indicated he was either a woodsman or a man of the sea.

More than once, Sandokan had been tempted to wake him, but the fear of drawing the attention of the guard leaning upon his rifle at the far end of the ship's waist, held him back.

"Here's a man that could be of great help to us," he murmured. "Until tomorrow then."

After this last thought, he fell asleep once again, his fist clenched near his sash, out of habit, resting where his krises would have been.

The deafening rattle of chains mixed with cries of pain abruptly tore him from his slumber. Two sailors were crossing the ship's waist, snapping their whips in the air.

"Up you scoundrels!" they rumbled.

From time to time, the two whips would fall, harshly striking groups of convicts, unleashing a salvo of moans and curses. The lash they wielded so mercilessly, without regard for who they struck, was the dreaded cat-o'-nine-tails, a deadly instrument and popular form of punishment in penitentiaries and aboard British ships.

The cat draws its name from the nine straps attached to a short handle. Each strap is capped with a small lead ball; they're much worse than the *knuts* used by the Russians or the terrible *courbasc* of hippopotamus skin used by the people of Sudan and Abyssinia. With every strike, the lead balls leave a bloody furrow on the victim's back. Fifteen to twenty blows can break even the strongest man. Fifty blows can kill him.

The terror this device inspires is inconceivable; it is more feared than the gallows. Once, when a band of stranglers began to stalk the streets of London, the authorities merely had to threaten to punish the guilty with fifty blows of the lash to bring the crime wave to an end.

Yanez, Tanauduriam and Sambigliong had immediately sat up so as not to receive one of those brutal caresses. Sandokan, however, after having seen the cause of the noise, lay back down and closed his eyes.

The two sailors, continuing their march, soon arrived before the four pirates. Noting that Sandokan had not obeyed the order, one of the two leaned down and yelled, "On your feet!"

The Tiger of Malaysia did not move. Believing the captain had not heard the sailor's cry, Tanauduriam and Sambigliong moved to shake him. A rapid glance from Yanez held them back. The Portuguese knew Sandokan was not asleep; he therefore must have had a reason to keep his eyes closed.

"On your feet, rascal..." repeated the sailor, making the lash whistle in the air.

Seeing that the command had no effect, the sailor snapped the cat-o'-nine-tails and whipped Sandokan squarely in the chest, slicing through his green silk shirt.

The lash had barely touched his skin when the Tiger of Malaysia jumped to his feet. In a flash, he grabbed the sailor by the small of his back and raised him into the air.

The voice of that formidable man thundered throughout the waist like a piece of artillery.

"Wretch! You dare strike the Tiger of Malaysia?... I'll kill you!..."

The sailor, suffocating beneath that powerful, rib-crushing grip, cried out in pained rage.

His colleague had rushed toward Sandokan, whip raised, ready to strike. However, Tanauduriam and Sambigliong had been keeping a close eye on him. With a quick movement, they tripped the sailor and sent him flying against the planks.

That display of strength and daring made a great impression upon those hardened rascals, toughened by crime and accustomed to admiring courageous and determined men. The pirate's expensive clothing and the large diamond adorning his green and white silk turban reinforced their high opinion, for Sandokan looked more like a Bornean prince than a common thief.

Cries of amazement and admiration filled the air.

"What a man!..."

"What strength!..."

"Well done! Kill that oaf!"

A sharp voice suddenly cried out, "Brothers! I propose we proclaim this good prince, king of the convicts."

A round of applause greeted that strange proposal but was immediately extinguish by the rustle of chains.

The guard had sounded the alarm and a dozen men armed with bayonets, rushed into the ship's waist, ready to assist the two sailors. A lieutenant, the same that had met Sandokan the night before, was in command of the squadron.

"Drop that man!" he shouted, clutching his pistols and aiming them resolutely at Sandokan.

At a sign from Yanez, Tanauduriam and Sambigliong released the second sailor, after first relieving him of his whip.

Hearing the lieutenant's order, Sandokan, turned around.

"Oh! It's you!" he said, "Here's your man; consider this a warning, if he ever attempts to raise his whip to me again, I'll kill him!"

He put down the sailor, pushed him forward and said, "Get out of my sight!"

"I promise no one will lay a hand on you for as long as you remain aboard this ship, as per the orders of his Excellency the Rajah," said the lieutenant. "However, I'm afraid I must place you in irons."

"Go ahead," Sandokan replied coldly.

"I can spare you this humiliation if you give me your word that you will not rebel against my men."

"I'll never make such a promise."

"Clap him in irons," said the lieutenant, turning towards his men.

Two sailors approached Sandokan, took hold of the chains connecting his leg irons, and fastened them to two ringbolts imbedded in the ship's waist. The pirate let them proceed, and when they had finished, grabbed the chains with both arms, wrenched them violently, and ripped the ringbolts out of the planks.

"Here are your rings," he said. "You'll need something a little stronger if you wish to tame the Tiger of Malaysia!"

Surprised beyond belief, the convicts held their breath, eyes riveted upon that man who in such short time had given two examples of his incredible strength and who appeared not to fear those brutal guards. His presence alone was enough to make every man in the ship's waist tremble. Even the lieutenant, seeing the ringbolts destroyed, had remained motionless, standing there, looking at the formidable pirate with incredible amazement.

"Why did you do that?" he asked.

"They were getting in my way," replied Sandokan. Then proudly drawing up to his full height and crossing his arms, he said disdainfully, "There's royal blood in my veins; I will never stand for such humiliation, even if I have to fight your entire crew."

"You'd get yourself killed..."

"The Tiger of Malaysia does not fear death; he has challenged it in more than a hundred boarding raids! Leave me be and I will not attack your men. James Brooke did not order you to insult me or to manhandle me."

"Do you promise to cause no further trouble?"

"One can hope," Sandokan replied disdainfully.

"I promise no one will bother you."

"Very well."

Sandokan went back and sat down among his friends, while the lieutenant went off with his men.

The convicts had not moved. They continued to look at the terrible pirate with a mixture of amazement and admiration, almost as if hypnotized by his defiance.

The giant Sandokan had noticed during the night was the most curious of all. He seemed more surprised than the others and did not take his eyes off the leader of the pirates of Mompracem. The arrival of several sailors, carrying enormous pots and numerous bowls, broke the spell.

"Soup's on!" the convicts exclaimed.

A deafening clatter of chains echoed throughout the ship's waist.

The early-morning distribution of breakfast had begun. Bowls filled with steaming black soup were quickly circulated among those poor unfortunates and just as quickly emptied.

When they came to James Brooke's four prisoners, the sailors gave them their four bowls and added, undoubtedly as per the captain's orders, a jug of wine, some biscuits and some ham.

"Great heavens, what luxury," exclaimed Yanez, as always in an unalterable good mood. "Our shipmates will be jealous."

"They'll get better fare in time," replied Sandokan, devouring his soup.

"Still working on your plan?"

"Do you think I made that scene for the pleasure of lifting that sailor into the air and getting a lash across the chest? I had to show these convicts what I was capable of, and I had to let them know I was the Tiger of Malaysia. There isn't much difference between a pirate and a bandit, brother. You'll see. From now on these men will obey my every command, my simplest gestures."

"I'm starting to believe it, Sandokan. These men only bow to strength."

"Yes, and there's one man in particular that could be of great help to us. He may even be stronger than I am."

195

"The giant sitting nearby, eyeing our food? I'd say the poor devil has a burning desire to share our meal, it is, after all, three times the size of his own."

Sandokan turned around. The man with red hair was staring greedily at their meal. Given his solid build, the convicts' thin rations would hardly have sated his appetite. It was the perfect opportunity to start a friendship.

"Would you like one?" he said, offering him a biscuit.

The convict hesitated for a moment, perhaps ashamed that Sandokan had caught him looking on so hungrily, then quickly stretched out his hand, grabbed the bread and drew it eagerly to his lips.

"Thank you, sir," he murmured in a voice choked with gratitude.

Two tears welled in his eyes and trickled down his bronze cheeks.

"They don't feed you very well, do they?" asked Sandokan, offering him a few more biscuits and a piece of ham.

"No, sir, I've been dying of hunger for seven long weeks," replied the giant, stifling his rage.

"You should mention it to the officers or the captain."

"They don't give much thought to the likes of us. I've begged the sailors several times to add something to my ration, but they merely laughed in my face and called me a wretch. Me! Hell!... If Fortune hadn't turned her back to me..."

"Are you an Englishman?"

"Welsh, sir."

"Were you a sailor?"

"Aboard a frigate, the *Scotland.*"

"So how did you end up on a convict ship headed for Norfolk?"

The giant lowered his eyes, then with a voice broken by sobs murmured, "Because... I killed... a man..."

"One of your shipmates?"

"The quartermaster, sir. He was a bad piece of work, a bully, a scoundrel! It's a blur now... one night I drank... I drank too much... and he had the audacity to slap me. Hit me!... John Fulton... the strongest man in Wales! I lost all control... I saw red... I didn't understand the horror of what I was about to do... I raised my fist and swung at his head... a few minutes later, he was dead!... Cursed be the night that turned an honest sailor into a galley slave, a convict dragging the chains of the damned!..."

The biscuits he had been holding fell to the floor as his hands went to cover his face. Tears streamed through his fingers, and he began to sob uncontrollably.

Sandokan and Yanez studied him in silence.

"My poor mother! I've caused her so much pain, she'll never see her only son again," the giant added sadly a short while later. "I'll be the cause of her death!..."

"You've never thought of regaining your freedom?" Sandokan asked suddenly.

The Welshman quickly raised his head and cast a burning look upon the Tiger of Malaysia.

"Freedom!" he exclaimed. "I'd give my heart's blood to cast eyes upon my mother once more, to see my home, my village! A hopeless dream... I'll spend the rest of my miserable life on that wretched island."

"What if I offered you a chance to escape?"

"What!?!" exclaimed the Welshman with amazement. "Aren't you condemned to life on Norfolk as well?"

"What does that matter?"

"You are the Tiger of Malaysia, the dreaded leader of the pirates of Mompracem. I heard tell of your exploits during my trips to Borneo, and I've seen just now what you are capable of, but escape... Forgive me for saying so... but, it's impossible."

"Look around, John Fulton," said Sandokan. "I'd wager these men share your thirst for freedom."

"To a man, sir."

"And wouldn't they try anything to reacquire it?"

"Of course, sir."

"If we can unite this horde of rascals, you'll see them perform miracles, challenge death like my pirates of Mompracem and compete with them in courage and ferocity. Put some determined leaders at their head, and tell me then if it would be impossible to take this ship."

The Welshman studied the pirate in silence, his amazement increasing with each passing minute. His eyes, wet with tears just a short while earlier, were now shining with hope.

"Freedom!" he rattled. "Yes, unite the men, fight the crew, take the ship! If you succeed, my life is yours!"

"Do you have any influence over these convicts?" asked Yanez.

"Yes, sir," replied the Welshman. "Once I fought a sailor who was being a little too free with the lash, I almost killed him with a blow... It's given me a certain authority. They obey me as if I were their leader."

"Then you'll inform them of our plan. I hope no one will give us away."

"There's no need to fear. They all hate the guards."

"Any idea how many men there are aboard?"

"Eighty sailors and four officers."

"Cannons?" asked Sandokan.

"Two on the quarterdeck," the Welshman replied.

"That could be a problem," murmured Sandokan with a frown. "At the first sign of attack, the crew will entrench themselves on the quarterdeck and fire at us without mercy. We'll have to nail them in place."

"Impossible, Sandokan," said Yanez. "There are guards at the wheel."

"I know, but those two pieces could slaughter us."

The Tiger fell silent, deep in thought.

"Ah!" he exclaimed, striking his forehead after a moment's reflection.

"What is it, little brother?"

"By Allah!" exclaimed Sandokan as a sinister smile spread across his lips. "It's an ambitious plan, and it'll put the ship in danger, but by then we should be close enough to Cape Sirik. Time to get to work, John Fulton. The men will have to be ready for battle within three days."

Chapter 17
The Revolt

While the convicts were preparing for their rebellion, the old frigate calmly sailed through the vast Bay of Sarawak, driven by a cool breeze blowing form shore. Once within sight of the Palo, she tacked slightly and headed north, planning to round Cape Sirik and follow the coast of the Sultanate of Borneo.

That course considerably lengthened the journey, but the ship was assigned to collect all the convicts in the British Indo-Malayan colonies and had to stop in Labuan to pick up more prisoners.

If Sandokan and Yanez had been aware of the frigate's course, they would not have unleashed their rebellion so early on, for the ship would have sailed within sight of Mompracem. Fearing that after rounding Cape Sirik, she would set sail for her final destination, they decided to take the ship as soon as possible. Learning they had sailed past the Palo and the tiny village of Redding, they quickly finalized their strategy.

Plans for the revolt had already been secretly organized. The three hundred convicts had not raised a single objection to the bold designs put forth by the two pirate captains. Norfolk had a sombre reputation; no one was unaware of the mental and physical torture that awaited them on that island prison, and all had unanimously declared themselves ready to make any sacrifice to regain their freedom.

John Fulton, who wielded great influence over those three hundred wretches, thanks to his giant stature and prodigious strength, had also vowed to kill with a blow any man who would not fight or dared reveal their plans.

Four days after the pirates of Mompracem had been brought aboard, all had been prepared. The three hundred scoundrels, divided into six squads, had selected their leaders from those renowned for their determination and bloodthirsty nature; tactics had been formulated, and all had been assigned battle stations throughout the waist. Once lured below, the crew would be divided and overwhelmed by shear numbers.

"We'll strike tonight," Sandokan told the Welshman. "Tell everyone to stand ready; I'll issue final instructions after pipe down."

The giant whispered the message to those beside him then a soft murmur filled the room as the instructions were relayed from man to man. When the bosun piped for silence, the Welshman stretched out on his plank, resting his head near Sandokan and Yanez.

The three hundred convicts lay down and pretended to sleep; however, from time to time, a few men would slowly sit up and fix anxious eyes upon their leaders.

"Listen," the Tiger whispered to the giant who was pretending to snore. "I'd wager you're strong enough to sever your chains."

"Child's play, captain."

"Excellent. Start with yours then free the young man sleeping beside you. He's vital to our plan. Does everyone know the signal?"

"Yes, sir, as soon as they hear us cry, 'Fire!' they'll jump to their feet, ready to act."

"You may begin."

Moving quietly so as not to draw the attention of the guard at the far end of the waist, the Welshman crossed his legs, slid both hands beneath his stomach and snapped the ringbolts enclosing his chains.

"Done," he said, without changing position.

"Now your friend."

John Fulton fixed his eyes upon the guard, waited for him to turn his back, then quickly bent over the young man at his side, sundered his chains, and whispered, "Make your way towards the captain."

The young convict did not move. Eyes mere slits, he watched the guard make his way up the walk. Once the sailor had turned towards the bow, the prisoner crawled silently towards Sandokan.

"Can you hear me?" whispered the Tiger.

"Yes, Captain," replied the young man.

"I'm in need of your services."

"At your orders, sir."

"See that vent over there? It leads into the pantry below. Do you think you can squeeze through it?"

The convict raised his head and quickly scanned the narrow opening.

"It'll take a little work, but I'll get through," he said.

"Do you have of lighter?"

"No."

"Fortunately, Yanez has everything we need."

He turned towards the Portuguese, who was also pretending to sleep, drew a lighter from one of his pockets and handed it to the young man.

"What do you want me to do?" he asked, surprised.

"A simple task," replied Sandokan, "set fire to the pantry."

"What?" asked the convict, believing he had misheard the order.

"Set fire to the ship."

"But we'll burn up as well, Captain."

"If you wish to regain your freedom, you must follow my orders without question. We will not succeed unless I have your full obedience."

"I'm not questioning your orders, sir; what about the guard?"

"Wait till he has his back to you then make your move."

"Yes, sir."

The rascal remained completely still, his eyes riveted upon the guard pacing at the far end of the ship's waist. He waited for the guard to turn on his heel, then, slithering like a serpent, made his way to the vent. Slowly twisting his body into the tight opening, he soon disappeared into the pantry.

"Did he make it?" whispered Yanez.

"Yes," replied Sandokan and the Welshman.

Several anxious minutes passed. The guard had returned to the centre of the ship's waist but seemed not to have noticed the young man's absence, for those three hundred bodies almost formed a single mass. Moments after he had passed, the convict appeared at the mouth of the vent. He climbed out with incredible speed and quickly rejoined the four pirates and the Welshman.

"Mission accomplished," he murmured happily. "I set fire to two cases of lard and smashed open a barrel of oil."

He had just finished uttering those words when a cloud of heavy black smoke erupted from the vent and invaded the ship's waist. Ever vigilant, the convicts shifted slightly, their chains rattling gloomily. The guard, sensing that all was not well, abruptly turned about. A large flame shot out of the opening and raced towards the ceiling, illuminating the sea of bodies.

"Fire!" he cried out.

"On your feet!... Fire!... Fire!" thundered the Tiger of Malaysia.

That second cry was greeted with a raucous, savage roar, followed by a deafening rumble of chains. No longer cowed by the threat of the lash, the convicts had jumped to their feet like one man, ready to engage in battle.

Spotting the flames at the stern of the ship, they began to pull at their chains, cursing and calling out as they attempted to sunder them.

Hearing the guard's cry, the watchmen on deck rushed below. There were about twenty of them, several carried axes and a few had drawn their rifles, but most were unarmed.

Seeing the convicts on their feet, they quickly began to retreat, sensing a revolt. But at the sight of the flames erupting from the pantry, they no longer hesitated; they rushed towards the stern, trampling the men that still lay upon the floor.

It was the moment Sandokan had been waiting for.

"Attack!" he yelled, rushing forward.

The Welshman, Yanez, Sambigliong, Tanauduriam and the young man were quick to follow.

The guard, still at the centre of the ship's waist, seeing those five men rushing determinedly towards him, levelled his rifle.

A shot rang out and the young man who at that moment had rushed in front of the Welshman, wielding a heavy block of wood, fell to the floor, a bullet lodged in his skull. Sandokan leapt like a tiger, pounced upon the guard and grabbed his rifle. The Welshman's fist descended like a blacksmith's hammer, one quick blow to the head sent the sailor crashing to the ground unconscious.

In the meantime, the three hundred convicts had seized the men that had responded to the alarm. Outnumbered, the twenty crewmen were quickly knocked down, disarmed, and stripped of their clothing. Though most could not get up, a few had managed to escape from the hundreds of grabbing arms and had rushed towards the stairs at the bow, howling for help at the top of their voices.

A ferocious roar echoed throughout the ship's waist as the men cheered their first victory.

While the flames intensified, fed by the stores of oil and lard in the ship's pantry, the convicts quickly smashed through their chains with the axes they had taken from the guards.

Twenty seconds later, two hundred men rose to their feet, free from the shackles that had held them prisoner for so many months, a few seconds more and the remainder would be ready to join the battle.

They had only a few weapons: the guard's rifle, ten daggers, a few axes and a half-dozen pistols, but their sheer number gave them the advantage. Sandokan, Yanez, the Welshman and the two Malays, the first armed with an axe, the second with the guard's rifle, and the others with daggers, had taken command of the first squad of men to sunder their chains, planning to rush up onto the deck.

"Attack!" Sandokan howled.

The men wielding axes attacked the iron grating covering the central hatch. Just as Sandokan and his squad were about to move towards the stairs, several volleys thundered from the far end of the ship's waist.

Forty men, armed with rifles and axes, led by the captain and one of his officers, had stormed below and immediately opened fire. That sudden appearance was greeted with cries of rage. Several convicts fell, struck by enemy lead, bloodying the planks in the vast room, while others rushed forward in an irresistible torrent, dragged on the attack by the Tiger of Malaysia, his voice thundering without pause, "Forward! Our freedom lies above!"

At one point, cries of terror emanated from behind the attack columns. The sound of gunshots filled the air. Believing they were being attacked from behind, Sandokan, Yanez and the Welshman quickly turned towards the flat of the stern. Those shots had not been fired from the officers' quarters but from the iron grate sealing the main hatch above them. Several sailors on deck were firing upon the poor wretches attempting to smash through the bars.

"Damn!" howled the Tiger, "If we don't eliminate those men, all is lost."

Caught in a crossfire, smoke growing thicker as the flames blazed towards the officers' quarters, the convicts' situation was growing desperate. Fortunately, the last chains had been sundered, and another mass of men rushed to their aid.

"Attack!" thundered the Tiger of Malaysia.

Enraged by the cruel losses they had suffered and by the smoke pouring in from all sides, the convicts attacked with irresistible force. No one could stop those three hundred men thirsting for freedom; at that moment they equalled, perhaps were even more formidable than, the dreaded Tigers of Mompracem.

The two squads quickly descended upon the forty sailors that had regrouped at the far end of the ship's waist. Volleys of gunfire thundered in quick succession, creating large holes among the unarmed attackers. But what did it matter if many lay on the floor in pools of blood? The others continued to fight, engaging in a desperate struggle among the smoke and sparks invading the ship's waist. They fought with their fists, punching and clawing at their opponents, all the while howling threats to instil fear in their enemies.

Never relenting, Sandokan's axe and the Welshman's powerful arms soon breached the crew's defences.

"Forward! One more effort!" howled the Tiger of Malaysia, waving a blood-soaked arm.

The attack was so violent the forty crewmen did not stand a chance. They attempted to regroup at the base of the steps and repel that torrent of men with their bayonets, but their weapons were pulled out of their hands by hundreds of arms and they were forced to retreat back up the stairs, leaving several of their shipmates lying lifelessly on the floor.

The path now clear, Sandokan rushed up the steps. The Welshman had grabbed an axe and was quick to follow, waving it about menacingly, while Yanez, Sambigliong and Tanauduriam, all three armed with rifles, fired round after round in an attempt to scare off the sailors defending the iron grate covering the hatch.

Driven by blood lust and certain of victory, the convicts crowded behind their captains and stormed onto the frigate's deck with a frightening roar.

The lanterns on the bow and the stern had been extinguished and the ship was cloaked in total darkness. A thick mass of clouds blanketed the sky, blotting out the stars. A hot, sizzling wind whistled through the rigging of the old ship and the sea bellowed dully as the waves crashed against her keel.

Momentarily blinded by the change in light, the convicts had come to a halt; unable to see more than a foot in front of them.

Having reunited, Sandokan, Yanez and the Welshman rushed forward but did not meet any resistance. The crew had disappeared.

"Where have they gone?" asked Sandokan uneasily.

"Look! There at the stern!" yelled Yanez.

Several faint silhouettes were visible through the smoke spewing from the hatch. The frigate's crew had gathered behind the two cannons on the quarterdeck to protect the wheel and have a better command of the deck. However, it appeared they had not given much thought to the imminent danger beneath them. As the deck below continued to burn, the supporting beams could give way at any moment, plunging them into the flames.

"Forward!" howled Sandokan, "One last effort."

He was about to attack, when Yanez grabbed him brusquely and pulled him down onto the deck. An instant later, two tongues of fire shot out from both sides of the quarterdeck, lighting up the night as a hail of grapeshot swept the deck from bow to stern.

Terrible cries filled the air in response to those volleys. Several men jumped back, as others fell to the deck badly mutilated.

Sandokan got back up, still clutching his axe.

"Thank you, Yanez," he said. Then his voice thundered, "Attack!"

Aware that even the slightest hesitation would allow the cannons to unleash another lethal round, the convicts rushed forward, determined to take the crews' last refuge. At one point, an unexpected obstacle stopped their attack. A wall of flames erupted through the grate and invaded the deck. The sails of the main and topmasts, unfurled, caught fire, setting off a monstrous blaze. As the cloth fell in tatters, it singed the hair and burned the faces of the first line of convicts.

"Retreat!" shouted Sandokan.

At the same instant, the two pieces on the quarterdeck thundered with a horrible din, making the old frigate tremble, and another whirlwind of grapeshot sliced through that wall of flame, slaughtering the first wave of attackers.

Rifle shots echoed the cannon blasts, bullets whistled in all directions, disseminating death. The convicts cried out ferociously, but there was little they could do, the fire spewing from the hatch blocked their advance and shielded their enemies.

"Fall back!" thundered the Tiger of Malaysia.

The attackers retreated towards the bow, stumbling over their dead and dying comrades. They crowded upon the forecastle, behind the foremast and the capstan. Those that had the good fortune to possess a rifle quickly reloaded and attempted to respond to the relentless hail of bullets fired by the crew.

Though the convicts continued to crowd into the far end of the ship, they were still not out of danger. The number of dead and wounded continued to mount as the torrents of lead relentlessly found their marks. Sandokan, Yanez and the Welshman took shelter behind the capstan for a quick consultation. The cruel losses they had suffered had reduced their number to two hundred, and their situation was about to turn desperate. The crew's stronghold remained impregnable, and the ship was about to go up in flames.

"What are we going to do?" asked the Welshman.

"We must resist at all costs," replied Sandokan.

"The ship's going up in flames," said Yanez.

"Take a hundred men and try to put out the fire. There are two pumps here; you'll probably find some buckets in the crew's quarters."

"The pumps are within range of the crews' rifles, Sandokan."

"Have the men build a barricade with barrels, beams and whatever else they can find."

"What about us?" asked the Welshman.

"Once we've tamed the fire, we'll attempt another attack."

"We only have about twenty or so rifles, sir."

"Our numbers will make up for our lack of weapons. I doubt the crew will be able to resist for very long."

"Why's that, sir?"

"The fire has already invaded the ships' waist; if the sailors remain on the quarterdeck, they'll be swallowed into that blazing furnace beneath their feet. Now, let's build a barricade."

While Yanez and his men grabbed tubs and buckets to fight the fire that threatened to destroy the ship, Sandokan and the Welshman, assisted by the remainder of the convicts, built a barricade between the fore and mainmasts.

It was not an easy task. The two pieces of artillery would spray the deck from time to time, while fragments of flaming rope, sails, and wood rained down from the burning mainmast. The crews' musket fire decimated their numbers; the dead could no longer be counted, and corpses continued to pile up in those places most exposed to artillery fire. But despite the flames and incessant gunfire, the convicts, led by Sandokan and the Welshman, succeeded in raising a barricade of boxes, beams, barrels, hammocks, yardarms, chains and anchors.

About twenty men, those that had managed to secure rifles, immediately took position and fired at the quarterdeck. Those discharges, however, had no great effect, for the wall of fire and the clouds of smoke kept their target well out of sight.

What's more, the ship had begun to rock, further throwing off their aim. During the battle, the sea had grown fierce and large waves now smashed against the frigate's sides, knocking the vessel about. The wind had picked up as well. Violent gusts descended upon the masting, whistling through the rigging and rattling the sails, as they fed the flames. The mainmast was ablaze, filling the air with sparks, making the waters shimmer in the firelight.

Despite the convicts' tenacity and the fire devouring the deck below, the crew had not given up. Though they knew they could no longer quell the revolt, they continued to defend themselves with desperate bravery, attempting to inflict disastrous losses upon their attackers. Certain they could not retake the ship, they were determined to destroy it, even sink it, in hope of drowning that horde of convicts like a pack of wild beasts.

The two pieces on the quarterdeck did not let up for a single minute. When the crew ran out of grapeshot, they fired cannonballs, smashing the bulwarks, caving in the forecastle, damaging the masts, and demolishing the crew's common room.

Furious at being held in check by that small band of men, the Tiger of Malaysia attempted to lead an attack on the quarterdeck, but three times the wall of fire brought him to a halt.

Several men, the most daring, had managed to pass through the blaze unscathed, only to fall before they could reach the quarterdeck, killed by the volleys of the crew.

The battle had been raging for two hours, when suddenly, the enemy fire, which had been gradually diminishing, came to complete stop. Fearing a sudden attack, Sandokan summoned all available men on deck and ordered them to stand ready. However, several minutes passed without a shot; total silence reigned over the stern.

"What are they up to?" Sandokan asked uneasily.

He made his way towards the mainmast, challenging the rain of sparks that fell from the yardarms, but could not make out anything due to the smoke. He was about to rush forward, when the Welshman pulled him back and shouted, "Back, sir! The mast's about to fall!..."

Sandokan jumped back behind the barricade. An instant later, the mainmast, now stripped of shrouds and backstays, its base consumed by the flames, crashed down upon the port bulwarks with a tremendous noise, dragging the topgallant, royal masts and yardarms into the sea.

The bulwarks shattered beneath that sudden blow; for a moment the frigate rolled to one side, but almost immediately regained her balance, with only a slight list to starboard.

Its housing destroyed by the fire burning below, the mizzenmast gave way a minute later. Unfortunately, instead of falling towards one of the remaining bulwarks, it fell along the deck, knocked down a dozen men and severed the foremast rigging with one blow.

Ignoring the cries of the wounded, Sandokan and the Welshman rushed to the quarterdeck. They ran through the clouds of smoke spewing out of the hatch and came to a halt at the base of the steps.

"They're gone!" shouted Sandokan.

It was true. Protected by the wall of fire, the crew had taken advantage of the rebels forced inaction, lowered the launches in the waters off the stern and rowed away. However, before abandoning ship, they had hauled down the flag, spiked the two cannons and nailed them in place.

Sandokan and the Welshman rapidly made their way up to the quarterdeck and leaned over the bulwark. Several bright dots sparkled in the distance to the south of them.

"They'll try to reach the coast," said Sandokan.

"What about us?" asked the Welshman.

"We'll do the same, if possible," replied the Tiger of Malaysia.

"If possible!"

"The ship's starting to sink."

"You don't think we'll be able to contain the fire?"

"Yanez is making headway, but it matters little now. We can only count on the foremast and the strength of our arms; I doubt the prisoners know much about ship repair."

"I don't think there are any seamen among them, but I hope they'll help us," said the Welshman.

"We'll know soon enough," replied Sandokan. Then raising his voice he thundered, "The ship is ours! The crew has escaped!"

There was a loud cheer then a voice shouted, "To the barrels! Let's celebrate our victory."

"To the barrels!" replied a hundred voices. "Let's drink!"

Chapter 18
Shipwrecked

The old frigate had been taken but at what a price! Of the three hundred convicts, one hundred and fifty lay on deck, horribly mutilated by the volleys of grapeshot that had thundered from the two cannons on the quarterdeck. Sixty more lay gravely injured.

What's more, the ship, reduced to a deplorable state, barely remained afloat. Though the fire had been put out, it had caused irreparable damage in those few hours. The pantry had been completely destroyed, the waist devoured by flames, the quarterdeck threatened to crash in at any moment, the stern decks had cracked in places, and the mizzen and mainmasts had been lost. Even the bow had suffered serious damage from the rain of projectiles that had streaked across the deck. The forecastle would not stand much longer, its supports having been severed, the bowsprit had lost its harpoons and the bulwarks had been smashed in various places when the mainmast and the mizzenmast had fallen.

Strewn with bodies, the deck was a horrendous site. Unfazed by their surroundings, the convicts rushed en masse towards the ship's waist, planning to raid the stores for whatever alcohol they could find. Aware of their intentions, Sandokan raced into the centre of the throng, brandishing his axe menacingly.

"Take care of the wounded, you wretches!" he howled.

The Welshman had rushed to his side, wielding an iron rod, a weapon more destructive in those mighty arms than a piece of artillery.

The convicts replied with laughter.

"To hell with the wounded!" yelled some.

"Let them die!" howled others.

"Gin?... Brandy?... Arak?!... Time for a drink, my friends! Hurrah for the galley! Make way! Make way!"

The Tiger of Malaysia howled with rage. "I'll kill all that do not obey!" he thundered, blocking their path as he raised his axe.

"To hell with that nigger!" yelled a convict. "He won't stop me from draining a barrel of arak."

A hard-looking man with a square, pockmarked face and a long scar upon his brow, advanced towards Sandokan, clutching a large bowie knife.

"I'll either open a keg of arak or I'll spill your blood."

"Back or I'll kill you," replied Sandokan, staying the Welshman who was about to strike the convict with the iron rod.

"This savage thinks he can squash me like a bug," sniggered the convict.

"Well said, Paddes!" shouted a crazed voice.

The convict rushed toward Sandokan.

"Make way! I want to drink!" he howled.

The words had barely escaped his lips when he fell to the ground dead.

"Take care of the wounded!" Sandokan repeated menacingly. "I've given you your freedom, you will obey my orders!"

The convicts hesitated for an instant, mulling over what they had just seen. At the sight of Yanez, Sambigliong and Tanauduriam rushing over to assist with rifles drawn, they decided to comply. Upon reflection, many had quickly realized they would never make it to shore without the assistance of those men.

"At your orders, Captain," said several of them. "Listen, mates! Let's lend a hand to those poor devils at death's door."

The convicts scattered about the decks, checking through the mounds of the dead and pulling out the groaning bodies of their injured friends. Those desperate souls were carried down into the ship's waist to the crews' hammocks and tended to as best as possible. There were sixty in total and almost all were in serious condition with no hope of recovery. When the last man had been carried down, those rascals, lacking any feeling of humanity, headed off in all directions, intending to loot the ship as they searched for food and spirits.

Sandokan did not attempt to intervene, for he realized he would have to resort to further violence and risk being attacked by that horde of scoundrels. Besides, he had to take care of the ship; she was beginning to drift across the waves, threatening to tip on her side.

The sea had grown restless during the battle; a hot wind blew from the south and was gradually increasing in intensity. Large, towering waves attacked in endless rows, crashing with deafening bellows, violently lifting the old frigate's hull and shaking her severely. The foremast trembled beneath the weight of its sails, raising fears it could come toppling down at any moment.

Lightning streaked the sky, lighting enormous clouds as thunder echoed gloomily from their depths.

Sandokan, assisted by Yanez, the Welshman, the two pirates and a few volunteers, had pushed the mainmast into the sea so as to raise the frigate's port side. The topgallant and royal sails were lowered to relieve the pressure on the foremast; only the foresail and topmast sail remained unfurled.

To give the ship greater stability, he ordered two jib sales hoisted up the bowsprit and the topsails raised to a yardarm tightly fastened to the mizzen box.

"Do you think we'll make shore?" asked the Welshman.

"It'll be a struggle," replied Sandokan, "but we'll reach the coast of Borneo."

"Any idea where we are?"

"Near Cape Sirik, I think."

"Not easy sailing, or so I've been told."

"There's no shortage of reefs, but it'll matter little if the ship runs aground. Once we reach land, we'll make new plans."

"What about the crew. Any chance they'll return and attack?"

"There's still many of us, they wouldn't stand a chance."

"You're right; they probably headed towards the nearest shore."

"I agree. The sea's getting worse. I wouldn't want to face those waves in a launch! Ah! Those rascals are coming back. Let them get drunk; at least they won't be in our way."

Howls of joy emanated from the waist. The convicts had undoubtedly found the food supply, stumbled upon some barrels of alcohol, and were now preparing to celebrate their reacquired freedom with a drunken feast.

"Leave them be," said Sandokan, noticing that Sambigliong and Tanauduriam had rushed to grab their rifles. "Come, we've got to take care of the ship."

"What are you planning to do with all these rascals?" asked Yanez. "I'm beginning to have enough of their company."

"We'll get rid of them at the first opportune moment," replied Sandokan. "I have no desire to take them to Mompracem."

"What if we lead them against James Brooke?"

"Do you think they'd obey me? They'll abandon us as soon as we reach land."

"We definitely won't hold them back, little brother. May the devil take them all."

At that moment, the convicts erupted onto the deck like a pack of wolves, triumphantly carrying four barrels of gin they had found in the depths of the hold, a barrel of Spanish wine and a notable quantity of biscuits, hams, cheese and lard that had somehow miraculously escaped the fire.

It was all they had been able to find and they were preparing to devour it, without a thought to how they would eat the next day. The galley had been entirely destroyed by the fire along with all the food stores brought aboard for the long voyage, caution would have therefore warranted the rationing of any provisions they had found, but not a soul had paused to think about the future.

In a flash, those rascals set up some tables, lit a large number of torches and lamps, fixed them upon the bulwarks and hung them from the ropes, then began their feast among shouts, laughter, curses, hurrahs and toasts, without giving the slightest thought to the waves that had started to attack the old ship, nor to the hurricane that was menacingly approaching.

They devoured the stores like starving wolves, dipping their glasses without pause into the open kegs and barrels, alternating glasses of gin with glasses of wine, howling at the top of their voices, quarrelling, embracing, at times rolling in the blood clotted along the bulwarks.

From the stern, standing by the wheel, Yanez, Sandokan, the Welshman and the two Tigers of Mompracem gazed impassively upon that monstrous feast.

A flash of lightning had illuminated the shore to the east; however, they did not know if they had sighted an island or the coast of Borneo. Though it had only been visible for an instant, it had been enough for Sandokan and Yanez to measure the distance and determine their options.

"It could be Cape Sirik," said the Portuguese, "or one of the small islands to the north of it."

"I agree," replied Sandokan.

"We could reach it by dawn; the wind is driving us north, but we'll try to set a course for it."

"It won't be easy, Yanez; we can only keep a few sails hoisted, the rudder doesn't work very well and the waves are getting worse."

"So much the worse for those drunkards."

"Gentleman," the Welshman said at that moment, "The wind is picking up and the foremast is starting to rattle, I fear it may come crashing down at any moment. We've already lost the port shrouds."

"If it falls, we'll replace it with some yards," replied Sandokan. "Now go to the bow with Sambigliong and Tanauduriam; Yanez and I will take care of the rudder."

"We're on the verge of sinking and all those wretches can do is drink!"

"Leave them be, John; no need to start trouble."

"A likely state we'd be in if the crew was to return with reinforcements!"

"Don't worry about them; they've probably reached the shore by now. Yanez keep her to the wind!"

While the four pirates of Mompracem and the Welshman attempted to sail the vessel to shore, the convicts continued their feast. Some played music, beating out a rhythm on pots and pans brought up from the galley, as others danced about like madmen, falling to the deck in drunken heaps.

Some started gaming, gambling for the money they had found in the officers' quarters and in the sailors' chests on the lower decks. Emboldened by the alcohol, the convicts began to argue and curse. It wasn't long before tempers flared and fights erupted, the onlookers cheering wildly at every blow.

A good number, having drunk their fill and exhausted by the day's events, snored upon the bulwarks, along the forecastle or beneath the quarterdeck, rolling among the dead as the old frigate pitched over the waves.

As the celebrations raged, the storm worsened. Towering ever higher, the waves attacked in endless rows, smashing against the frigate's sides with a deafening roar. The wind whistled through the foremast's sails and rigging, threatening to knock it down at any moment. Lightning flashed to the south as thunder rumbled dully.

Sandokan had taken the wheel, Yanez at his side, as the Welshman, Tanauduriam and Sambigliong worked the sails.

What a fantastic sight that large, partially dismasted ship must have been, knocked about by the waves, lanterns and torches blazing on her deck, as a swarm of drunken men challenged the fury of sea and sky, their howls mixing with the menacing roar of the waves! At one point, however, the celebration came to a sudden stop. A large wave had erupted over the port bulwark and crashed upon the deck, snuffing out torches and lanterns as it tossed the men in all directions. Only then did those drunken scoundrels become aware of the danger looming before them. Cries of joy immediately gave way to cries of terror.

Those that could still stand got up and looked in fear at the waves crashing upon the bulwarks.

All eyes turned anxiously toward the Tiger of Malaysia. Standing on the quarterdeck that formidable man calmly challenged the hurricane, intrepidly guiding the old ship, his face not betraying the least amount of strain.

Despite the vessel's violent rocking, his eyes did not stray from the compass and his hands did not leave the wheel. Seated nearby on an upturned bucket, Yanez calmly watched the waves as they smashed against the bulwarks.

A cry arose among the convicts as fear began to take hold of the men. "Save us!"

Sandokan did not reply. He had raised his eyes and held them fixed towards the east, where a flash of lightning had revealed a violently surging sea.

A convict had rushed upon the quarterdeck and yelled, "Save us, sir."

Sandokan gave him a disdainful look and replied, "Go back to your party!"

"The ship's about to sink, sir."

"And there are sharks about," said Yanez, laughing derisively. "They're hungry."

"We don't want to die!" yelled the convict, turning pale.

"Well then, take the wheel and sail the ship," replied Sandokan.

"But... Sir!"

"Go to hell!" Sandokan yelled furiously.

"Go sleep off your gin," added Yanez.

Believing it best not to insist, the convict made his way back to his friends and said, "Mates, looks like we're in for a swim."

"If we're going to die, we'll drink 'til we drop!" howled a voice.

"Well said, Burthon!"

"Yes! To the barrels! Drink 'til we drop!" howled everyone.

They were about to resume their feast when a second, third, and fourth wave crashed down upon the ship, sweeping the deck from port to starboard.

"Hold on!" yelled Sandokan.

The frigate was rolling frightfully. Her bowsprit raced as if to touch the clouds then buried itself beneath the sea as the stern rose to the heavens. It too would fall as the waters passed, a sullen boom echoing from the depths of her hold.

Tossed about by the incessant waves pounding the deck, the convicts rolled about in all directions, stumbling confusedly. The bodies of the dead twisted among the torrents, dancing to the pitch of the ship. They rolled and bounced, back and forth, until finally they were dragged over the bulwarks and swept away.

The sea swelled and bellowed, hurling frightening waves in all directions.

Yanez stood up and asked, "What's our position, Sandokan?"

"We're among the reefs," the Tiger of Malaysia replied calmly.

"We're going to crash."

"I'm afraid so, brother, the wheel's no longer responding!"

The Welshman, Tanauduriam and Sambigliong drew up before them.

"Sir," said the sailor, "We're surrounded by reefs."

"I know," replied Sandokan.

"And the foremast is about to come crashing down."

"Let it fall."

"But the shore's still far off, sir."

"It can't be more than twenty miles away, John; I caught a glimpse of it during that last lightning flash."

"But how are we going to reach it if the ship smashes against these reefs? All we have left is a small launch barely large enough for three or four men."

"That should hold us," said Yanez.

"What about these poor devils? No, we cannot abandon them," said Sandokan. "They helped us regain our freedom, we owe them a debt."

"Those drunkards! Let them fend for themselves."

"Without them we'd still be on our way to Norfolk."

"True."

"Let's try not to appear ungrateful. Ah!"

Tossed towards the reefs by the breaking waves, the old ship suddenly shook so violently, the men feared they had run aground. Yanez and the Welshman rushed to the bow, where Sambigliong and Tanauduriam, assisted by several of the more sober convicts, were hoisting the foresail and a counter jib, in an attempt to make the frigate tack about.

They sighted a double row of reefs two hundred paces off the side; enormous rocks loomed in the distance, forming a small archipelago. Mountains of water crashed against them with irresistible force, rebounding with deafening roars as the sea raged with fury.

Despite the efforts of Sandokan and his companions, the frigate was swept into a canal among that chaos of rocks and islands. Driven by the wind, she hurtled towards the reefs; collision was imminent.

With death so close at hand, the convicts lost their defiance.

Those that could still stand had rushed to assist Yanez and the Welshman. The others were howling, as if the eleventh hour had already struck, begging for help. No one gave a thought to emptying the barrels rolling wildly about the deck. At one point, Sandokan's voice thundered in warning:

"Look out! We're about to crash!"

Propelled by those mountains of water, the ship flew through the reefs, rolling and pitching as she shot forward. The waves howled about her sides, climbed over the remains of the bulwarks, then crashed on deck, felling all that stood in their way. They heard a formidable crack and the frigate shook from her keel to the tip of her foremast. The mast, already unstable, crashed to the deck with a horrible thud.

Then a second blow, more terrible than the first, echoed gloomily in the hold, and the poor ship, ripped apart by the sharp rocks that had penetrated the keel, rolled onto her starboard side and careened against a rock, just as a large wave swept the deck and smashed twenty or thirty men against the bulwarks.

The Tiger's voice thundered above their cries of fear.

"The ship's been cut in two!"

Chapter 19
Safe

The ship would not hold together for much longer.

Torn apart by the sharp rocks, she was little more than wreckage destined to be demolished by the waves or to slowly sink beneath the waters. Split in half, her keel had broken off and water had erupted into the hold, knocking out the support beams and tearing apart the framework.

Heavy with water and careened against the reef, the frigate ran no danger, at least for the present. The shaking had stopped, but waves continued to pound her deck, threatening to sweep away the convicts at any moment.

Despite the frightening circumstances, Sandokan, Yanez and the Welshman had not lost their cool. They quickly took shelter upon the quarterdeck, the only part of the frigate out of reach of the waves.

Realizing salvation lay above, the convicts slowly made their way towards them, without a second thought to their drunken companions rolling among the corpses strewn about the deck. Those poor unfortunates, unable to walk, were soon dashed against the bulwarks and swept away by the waves.

Only a hundred and thirty remained; the wounded had died in the storm, drowned by the waters that had invaded the ship's waist.

Throughout the night, those wretches fought against death, ringing the four pirates of Mompracem and the Welshman in a tight circle, tenaciously resisting the continual assault of the waves. Luckily, towards two in the morning, the wind began to die down and it appeared as if the waters would soon settle.

After a great deal of effort, Yanez and Sandokan had managed to climb up onto the reef, an enormous rock that rose more than a hundred meters out of the water.

They had hoped to spot the coast of Borneo from its summit; however, even larger reefs lay to the east of them, blocking their view.

"No matter," said Sandokan. "We can't be too far from the coast; we'll make our way there."

"How exactly?" asked Yanez. "All we have is that small launch."

"We'll build a raft."

"You plan to take these wretches with us?"

"We can't abandon them on this reef without food and shelter."

"You think you'll find enough food for all hundred and thirty of them once we reach the shore?"

"There's a tribe of Dyaks near Cape Sirik, they may be able to help us."

"Yes, if they don't eat us first," said Yanez. "They're cannibals."

"If they treat us as enemies, we'll sack their village."

"I hope you don't plan on dragging these bandits with us wherever we go."

"Not in the least," replied Sandokan. "At the first opportune moment, we'll leave them behind and make our way towards Mompracem."

"What about James Brooke?"

"We'll settle our score with him, Yanez. We'll arm a new expedition, return to Sarawak, unite with Pangeran Macota and declare war upon him."

"I hope nothing bad has happened to Tremal-Naik."

"We'll see him again in Sarawak."

Dawn broke as they were talking, bathing the clouds in a warm pink light. Sandokan and Yanez quickly turned about to assess their situation.

The old frigate had smashed into a group of reefs and islands ringing a small lake. A tortuous canal lined with coral shoals led to the sea.

Chance had driven the frigate into that basin, smashing her opposite a small, cone-shaped island covered with thick vegetation that towered more than two hundred meters above the sea.

"We may be able to spot the coast from up there," said Sandokan, directing Yanez's gaze towards the island. "Once the waves settle, we'll make our way there and climb to the top."

They returned to the ship as the sun broke past the horizon, the waters shimmering gold in the morning light.

Having weathered the storm, the convicts had set to work, knowing full well they would have to build a raft to survive. Skilled in such tasks, the Welshman had taken command, directing the demolition work and trying to salvage as much wood as possible. Sandokan, Yanez, Tanauduriam and Sambigliong went below to search for food, hoping that a few supplies had somehow escaped the celebration feast.

Their search yielded moderate results. Even though the galley and the lower deck had been almost entirely destroyed, they managed to find several cases of biscuits in the crew's common room and various barrels of salt pork that had miraculously escaped the fire. Unfortunately, the hold lay underwater and any provisions stored there had probably been swept away through the breach in the hull.

"We've got barely enough for a meal," said Yanez. "If those rascals hadn't gorged themselves, we could've survived for several days."

"There' nothing we can do about that now, Yanez," observed Sandokan. "No matter, we'll be on land by tomorrow."

Towards noon, the waves in that basin had settled and the two captains, Tanauduriam and Sambigliong, embarked in the small launch, planning to land on the island opposite the ship. They were certain of sighting the shores of Borneo from the summit of the cone, for its green slopes towered above the reefs to the east of them.

Despite the rough waters, it took them only a few minutes to cross the basin and land upon the gently sloping beach. At the sight of those intruders, pratincoles, petrels, and aluste flew off, filling the air with their cries. With a quick shot, Yanez knocked down a magnificent pelargopsis.

"It'll make a magnificent lunch," said the Portuguese.

Once they had moored the small launch and collected the bird, Sandokan and his companions headed into the brushwood and began their ascent.

They marched through luxuriant vegetation: casuarinas, arboreal ferns, cycas plants, palm trees and masses of gambirs bristling with thorns, but unfortunately, not a one bore edible fruit. Lizards appeared among the vines from time to time, hissing menacingly as they scurried off to find new shelter.

Advancing slowly through the thick foliage, a half hour later, Sandokan and his friends reached the summit of the cone and found it barren of even the smallest blade of grass. Having reached the top, they cast their gaze towards the horizon and spotted a long, low-lying shore defended by numerous small islands.

"It's only twenty miles from here," said Sandokan. "We'll be there by tomorrow."

"That point stretching towards the north must be Cape Sirik," said Yanez.

"I think you're right," replied Sandokan.

They remained there for a few more minutes, scanning the sea in hope of sighting a prahu, then went back down the hill and got into the launch, taking their large bird with them.

Back aboard the frigate, they found the convicts still occupied in demolishing the vessel.

Once enough lumber had been gathered at the stern, Sandokan, Yanez and the Welshman began to direct the raft's construction. It had to be solid enough to withstand the waves, which were especially violent in that area bristling with coral, rocks and sandbanks.

They threw the yards and foremast beams into the water to form a skeleton; four small rafts immediately moved toward it, manned by the most capable men the Welshman could find.

The waves had settled and construction proceeded quickly. The yards and mast beams were bound together tightly in a parallelogram; several empty barrels and kegs taken from the crews' common room were fastened to the corners.

Lumber from the hull, planks from the deck, and the remains of the bulwarks were quickly thrown into the water, and the convicts, under the direction of the Welshman and the two captains from Mompracem, began to construct the base.

They had found the carpenters box, which had escaped the fire; it contained numerous woodcutting tools and a good supply of nails. The remainder of the work was quickly executed and the raft was ready to receive the castaways before sunset.

They installed a long oar at the stern to serve as a rudder; raised a small mast, constructed from a yardarm and the bowsprit, in the center of the raft then hoisted a sail.

At eight that evening, as a blood-red moon appeared above the horizon, the convicts embarked, supplied with two cases of biscuits, a bit of salt pork, several barrels of fresh water, forty axes, and twenty rifles with three or four hundred cartridges. The small launch had also been placed on the raft, for it could render precious service during their journey. At nine o'clock, the raft, propelled by two-dozen oars, abandoned the remnants of the frigate and slowly made its way forward among the reefs.

Sandokan had taken the rudder; Yanez, Sambigliong, Tanauduriam and the Welshman stood watch at the bow, eyes peeled for signs of any upcoming reefs. Crossing the canal was a lot easier then the two captains had predicted, and a half hour later, the large raft, its sail stretched taut by the wind, was sailing slowly towards the Bornean coast, pitching heavily upon the large waves.

"If this breeze holds, we'll reach land by tomorrow morning," Sandokan told Yanez, who had joined him on the stern.

"I've got a bad feeling about this," replied the Portuguese.

"What troubles you, my friend?"

"I keep thinking about the crew in those launches."

"They're probably a good way off by now."

"What if they're searching for us? What if they've set up an ambush ashore?"

"They're probably in Sarawak or Sedang by now."

"That would be worse, Sandokan. If James Brooke learns of our escape, he'll set sail in that damned schooner of his and come hunt us down."

"He'd be too late, my friend."

"Do you plan to part company with these convicts any time soon?"

"Tomorrow night, we'll escape while they're asleep."

"How?"

"We'll take the launch."

"Hmm, a long trip fraught with its own dangers. We're a good distance from Mompracem, little brother."

"Once we reach Uri, we'll find a prahu that'll take us to the Romades."

"Is the Welshman coming with us? He'd be a precious addition to our crew, Sandokan."

"He's promised to join us. He prefers our company."

In the meantime, the raft, driven by a light irregular breeze, continued to advance eastward, heading towards the shore that Sandokan and Yanez had spotted from the peak of the small island.

Though the sea was still choppy, the enormous raft held well. From time to time, a wave would crash upon its planks, drenching the convicts gathered round the mast; but the raft had been solidly constructed and it resisted tenaciously to every knock and bump. Towards midnight, the breeze faded, stopping the raft's advance; the waves, however, continued to rise, shaking it violently. When the sun rose on the horizon, the shore was still about fifteen miles away, but there was not so much as a breath of wind to fill the sail.

The sea was deserted. Not a single ship was visible on the horizon, nor any black dots to indicate the presence of a launch. A few frigate birds soared aloft as flocks of gulls wheeled above the waters.

Numerous diodon swam about them, dragged there by the waves. Bodies bristling with white thorn-like spines, these balloonfish when threatened, undergo a remarkable transformation. By swallowing water and air, a diodon can swell to three times its normal size and become a rigid, near-perfect sphere covered in spiky armour. Though not the

225

most edible of fish, the convicts quickly gathered the few harpoons they had salvaged and began thrusting them into the water, hoping to supplement their meagre supplies.

Towards three in the afternoon, the breeze returned, and after lying becalmed for several hours, the raft resumed its march once again, loudly slashing through the waves that attacked its bow.

As they drew nearer the shore, its vague outline quickly transformed into a long arc stretching from north to south, covered in thick vegetation. A range of mountains towered against the bright horizon; perhaps a branch of the Crisallos, the principal backbone of the Sultanate of Varauni.

Numerous rocks protected the beach, making the approach difficult, even dangerous, especially for a raft that did not obey every pull of its rudder.

"Stand ready to lower the sails, we don't want to smash the raft," Sandokan shouted.

The noise was deafening. The waves, driven by the wind, rushed at the shore in a heavy crash of surf and spray. Obstructed by the rocks, the counters bounced back with great violence, shaking the raft incessantly.

Clutching the long oar that served as a rudder, Sandokan and Yanez worked desperately to keep the raft on the right course, but sandbanks lay hidden beyond the reef and each passing moment brought new obstacles. The convicts had all jumped to their feet, ready to plunge into the water. Many had grabbed weapons or provisions, precious commodities they did not want to lose.

The jolts grew more violent. The waves tossed the raft about so violently, the men were unable to stand. Despite that, they had arrived to within three hundred meters of the shore, thanks to the ability of Sandokan and Yanez.

At one point, however, a wave, larger than the others, grabbed the raft and violently hurled it forward, almost standing it on end.

A moment later, there was a terrible jolt. With one blow, the bow smashed beneath the convict's feet, the planks gave way and swept against the reefs.

"Every man for himself!" yelled the Welshman.

The hundred and thirty men dove into the water. Fortunately, they were surrounded by reefs. Hurled forward by the waves, minutes later, the convicts stood reunited upon the shore, where they had been preceded by Sandokan, Yanez, the Welshman and the two Tigers of Mompracem.

Chapter 20
The Convicts Are Slaughtered

The shore was deserted. The island gave no sign of habitation. The beach was lined by a feathery row of casuarinas, their roots partially submerged among the waves. Behind it, a tangled jungle filled with an infinite variety of vegetation: rubber trees mixed with mangosteens, pombos, rambutan and bread trees laden with fruit. Several pairs of *budeng*,[5] beautiful monkeys with glossy black fur, frisked among the branches, performing all sorts of acrobatics as they played with their offspring.

The sun was hot, and after having issued orders for the convicts to build shelter, Sandokan, Yanez, the Welshman, Sambigliong and Tanauduriam grabbed their rifles and headed into the forest.

They wanted to ensure the area was indeed deserted, so as not to expose the convicts to a sudden attack by the native Dyaks, audacious cannibals that abounded in the western forests of Borneo.

They scouted until sunset but did not find a single village or a trace of inhabitants. Certain the island concealed no dangers, the small party returned to camp. It had been raised on the outskirts of the forest in a small clearing that stretched to the shore.

While their leaders had been off exploring, the convicts had constructed several huts out of large banana leaves, raided the nearby trees and made an abundant harvest of assorted fruit. Others had scoured the reefs and returned with several large oysters, cephalopods, and halioti, magnificent shells of enormous size considered a delicacy among the

---

[5] Ebony Leaf Monkey

Chinese. They had even caught a large pair of sea turtles, surprising their prey while they were digging in the sand to bury their eggs.

An abundant dinner was assured; there was no need to touch their meagre stores, which was fortunate, for most of the supplies had been swept away when the raft had smashed. However, when the convicts went to prepare the fire, they quickly learned they did not have so much as a match or lighter among them.

As it was absolutely necessary to light a fire, if for no other reason than to keep the animals in the forest at bay, Sandokan and Yanez asked Sambigliong and Tanauduriam to do the honours.

It was not as difficult as the convicts had thought. As can be imagined, not all cultures have matches and lighters, yet they manage equally well to build a fire for cooking and keeping warm during cold, damp nights.

The Malays have developed a quick and ingenious method for creating a fire in less than a minute. A section of bamboo is split lengthwise, and a notch is cut across the back of one piece. Bark, twigs, grass or other tinder is placed below this opening and then the thin edge of the second piece is rubbed against the notch, the sawing becoming more rapid with every stroke. Soon, enough heat is generated to set the tinder afire, the whole operation needing less than sixty strokes.

After several fires had been lit, the convicts dined happily then stretched out beneath their shelters, overcome by exhaustion. Despite the repeated councils of Sandokan, Yanez and the Welshman, not a single man could be persuaded to guard the camp's perimeter.

"If you're afraid, stand watch," they replied and promptly went off to sleep.

"Leave them be, Sandokan," said Yanez. "If they're attacked, they'll get out of it as best they can."

"I knew we'd lose our clout once these wretches were out of danger. Come tomorrow, they'll no longer obey us; in two days, they'll knife us."

"That's true, Señor Yanez," said the Welshman. "Now that they're safe, they no longer have any need of us."

"All the worse for them," replied Sandokan. "We have no further business here."

"Are we leaving, Sandokan?" asked Yanez.

"As soon as they're asleep. Where's the launch?"

"I pulled it ashore just as the waves were about to sweep it away," said the Welshman.

"Do we have any ammunition?"

"About forty cartridges, sir."

"Should be enough to get us to Uri," said the Tiger of Malaysia. "We'll stretch out as well and pretend to sleep. If they think we're planning to escape, they may try to kill us."

"Or skin us alive, sir," said the Welshman. "We're dealing with the dregs of the British colonies."

The five men lay down beneath a giant durian tree three hundred paces from the shore and pretended to sleep.

Some convicts were still awake, sitting around a fire, telling tales, however, it would not be long before exhaustion took its toll and sent them off to sleep.

By eleven o'clock, everyone in the small camp had fallen asleep. The fires, left untended, were slowly beginning to die.

Not wanting to risk discovery, Sandokan waited until midnight, then shook his companions and said, "It's time."

"Are you sure everyone's asleep?" asked Yanez.

"There's no one about the campfires; hear those snores?"

"Yes; if they dare stop us from leaving, we'll introduce them to our rifles," added Yanez.

The Welshman had crawled behind a large tree and carefully scanned the area. Not a single man stood guard around the dying fires; the outskirts of the camp were deserted. The convicts were snoring quietly beneath their shelters, as if they were still in their bunks on the lower deck of the frigate, certain they were finally out of danger

"Time to go, gentlemen," said the giant, grabbing his rifle.

The two captains, Sambigliong and Tanauduriam quickly got to their feet. They looked about the camp one last time, then, led by the Welshman, headed silently towards the shore.

They found the small launch sheltered between two rocks. The Welshman had installed a small mast, a sail, a pair of oars, and as a precaution, had added a small barrel of fresh water. He had not provided any food, planning to coast near the shore and draw sustenance from the forest as the need arose.

"All aboard," said Sandokan.

He was about to take a seat at the stern when a sharp whistle reached his ears.

"What was that?" he asked, coming to a halt.

"Some kind of signal?" said Yanez.

"All the more reason to hurry," replied the Welshman.

"Perhaps a convict was keeping an eye on us and has sounded the alarm."

"Man the oars!" commanded Sandokan.

Sambigliong and Tanauduriam grabbed the oars and began to row vigorously, while Sandokan, Yanez and the Welshman quickly loaded their rifles and readied for an attack. Contrary to their fears, however, not a single convict rushed towards the shore.

Rapidly driven forward, the launch soon reached the reef that had destroyed the raft then headed towards a promontory off to the north. They had sailed about a half-mile when frightening cries suddenly erupted from the beach.

Sandokan, Yanez, and the Welshman froze.

Several bright points, torches perhaps, raced along the outskirts of the forest, while flashes, followed by loud detonations, thundered about the clearing. Ferocious cries and desperate invocations echoed with an ever-increasing crescendo. It sounded as if the camp had suddenly come under attack and the unfortunate convicts were being massacred beneath their very shelters.

"The convicts have been attacked!" yelled the Tiger of Malaysia.

"They may just be fighting amongst themselves," said Yanez.

"No, hear that? Those are Dyak war cries. We've got to go back!"

"Let them fight it out, Sandokan."

"No, Yanez. We're warriors; we can't just sit back impassively and let them get slaughtered."

"Fine, fine. We'll go back. We'll probably be too late."

With the Welshman's help, Sambigliong and Tanauduriam brought the launch about, rowing with all their might.

It appeared as if the camp had indeed been attacked by a horde of those formidable warriors that inhabit the western shores of Borneo. Deafening, savage cries echoed throughout the inlet, drowning out the rifle blasts.

The slaughter was merciless, and at times, through the clamour, came the sound of the convicts shrieking in pain. The bravest among them had attempted to organize a resistance; flashes of light appeared at one end of the camp now and again, accompanied by volleys of gunfire.

The small launch passed the reef and came within a cable length of the camp. Only then were Sandokan and his men capable of determining the severity of the situation.

The beach was swarming with cannibals armed with spears and wide bladed parangs. Several hundred of them had completely surrounded the camp, attempting to disperse the squads of convicts with furious attacks.

Decimated, the former prisoners had gathered around a grove of trees and were attempting to put up a desperate resistance with the few weapons at their disposal. Shots thundered from time to time, but only a cannon could have dispersed that horde of ferocious men.

Taking advantage of the moment in which the cries had diminished, the Tiger of Malaysia yelled out, "Hold tight! We're coming to help!"

Four shots were fired, knocking as many cannibals to the ground.

The launch was about to land.

At the sound of those shots, the Dyaks quickly retreated. Spotting the launch, thirty or forty cannibals rushed towards the shore to fend off the new attack.

"Stop, Sambigliong!" commanded Sandokan. "Keep away from the shore. If they get too close, we're done for."

"Fire without mercy," said the Welshman. "We may be too late to save those wretches, but we can sure try to avenge them!"

Crouching behind the rowboat's sides to avoid being struck by the spears raining down upon them from all directions, Sandokan and his companions opened fire, pointing their weapons into the thick of the attackers.

"Fire!" yelled Sandokan. "We'll land once they've retreated."

Despite the large holes the musketry fire created among their ranks, the savages held their ground. While their companions slew the remaining convicts, the Dyaks along the shore resolutely rushed into the water to attack the small launch.

To escape that dangerous boarding, Sambigliong and Tanauduriam were forced to abandon their rifles and pick up their oars once again, rowing to safety, as Yanez, Sandokan and the Welshman fired their muskets at the oncoming swimmers.

Realizing that their efforts were in vain, the savages, after one final attempt, retreated towards the shore, yelling ferociously.

The battle in the camp had ended and the horde was quickly withdrawing into the dark forest, carrying with them the weapons and the heads of the vanquished, for the Dyaks were great collectors of human skulls. Once the last bands had disappeared beneath the trees, Sandokan and his men came ashore. A deadly silence reigned over the camp.

Mounds of corpses lay among the huts, mutilated by the heavy axes and parangs wielded by the attackers. Every man had been stripped of his clothing and possessions; not a single head had been left behind.

"What a horrible massacre!" exclaimed the Welshman.

"I doubt there were any survivors," said Yanez. "We were lucky we left. An hour later and our heads would have gone to adorn the huts of those abominable cannibals. Let's go, Sandokan; there's nothing more we can do here."

"Not so fast, Yanez," replied the Tiger.

"What now?"

"Some men could have escaped the massacre and be hiding in the forest."

"You want to explore the forest? Now!?! For all we know a few Dyaks could still be hiding in there."

"We'll remain here, near the launch, ready to row to safety at the first sign of danger. If some convict has managed to escape the slaughter, he'll undoubtedly return to camp in the hopes of finding a companion or some weapons."

"That's true, sir," said the Welshman. "Do you think the Dyaks could have taken any prisoners?"

"Unlikely," replied Sandokan.

"Why would they slaughter a bunch of men that had never done them any harm?"

"To take their weapons and harvest their flesh. Dyaks are worse than animals, they never pass up the opportunity for a surprise attack. They believe a skull taken in battle is a sign of bravery, the more a man has, the greater his honour and rank."

"Like the natives of the northern United States."

"There's a slight difference, those natives scalp their victims, these savages take the entire head," added Yanez.

"Do you think they'll return?"

"It wouldn't surprise me, John," said Sandokan. "There are still a lot of bodies lying around, enough for several big meals. Once the Dyaks have devoured the carcasses they dragged off, they'll come back and make a new harvest."

"The wretches!" the Welshman exclaimed, "If we had had the frigate's two cannons, we'd have taught them a hard lesson."

"They would have been of no use," said Yanez. "The crew spiked them before they left the ship. Hey!"

"What's the matter, Yanez?" asked Sandokan.

"I just spotted something moving on the water," said the Portuguese. "Look over there!"

Sandokan and the Welshman turned about quickly and fixed their eyes upon the waters. Two dim shadows, two launches or perhaps two canoes had suddenly appeared at the tip of the promontory towards the south.

"Must be two boats," said Sandokan.

"Could the Dyaks be planning to attack from the sea?" asked Yanez. "That would mean there are still a few enemies hiding among the trees."

"They may be spying on us at this very moment," the Welshman added nervously.

"Yes, they're two launches," confirmed Sambigliong and Tanauduriam, who had rushed towards the shore.

"Sandokan, let's get out of here," said Yanez. "The savages in the forest may be preparing to attack as well. We'll be caught between two fronts."

"Those two launches will give chase, Yanez," replied Sandokan. "Once they caught us, we wouldn't stand a chance."

"What are we going to do then?"

"We'll set up on one of those reefs and fire off the remainder of our cartridges."

"We only have about a dozen shots left, sir," said the Welshman.

"Then we'll defend ourselves with our axes and the butts of our rifles," replied Sandokan. "Quickly, into the rowboat!"

They were about to rush towards the shore, when Tanauduriam, who had already embarked in the craft, yelled out, "Those aren't Dyaks! They've got rifles!"

"Castaways?" asked Yanez, coming to a halt.

"Ready your weapons. Let's see who they are," said Sandokan.

The two rapidly advancing launches had already arrived to within two or three hundred paces from the shore. They were manned by two dozen sailors armed with rifles and axes. Sandokan quickly leaned toward Sambigliong and said, "Don't leave the launch, no matter what happens."

The pirate jumped into the small boat and hid from view.

At that moment, a voice from the first launch yelled out in English, "Who goes there?"

"Castaways, sir," Sandokan readily replied.

"Were you attacked by savages? We heard shots and cries."

"Yes, they surprised us while we were sleeping; all our companions have been massacred."

"Have the savages escaped?"

"Yes, they retreated into the forest," replied Sandokan.

"Do you wish to come aboard?" asked the man in the launch.

"We ask nothing better. Do you only have the two launches?"

"We have a jong a short distance from here."

"If you take us aboard, we'll pay for our transport."

The two launches had by then reached the shore. The twenty-four men that manned them disembarked, grabbed their weapons, and headed towards the group comprised of Sandokan, Yanez, Tanauduriam and the Welshman.

"Let's go meet them," said Sandokan, turning towards his companions.

Without warning, the twenty-four men rushed towards the three pirates and the Welshman, and pointed their rifles at them as a menacing voice cried out, "Surrender or you're dead!"

Surprised by that sudden attack, Sandokan froze. A cry from the Welshman warned him of the grave danger before them.

"The crew!"

Sandokan let out a howl of fury and rushed at those men, clutching his rifle by the barrel, planning to use it like a club. Ten arms immediately grabbed hold of him, knocked him down and tore the weapon from his hands.

The Welshman had raised his axe, ready to strike, but Yanez, as quick as a flash, stayed his arm.

"Do you want to get yourself killed?" he whispered.

The sailors had already trained several rifles on the giant's chest and were on the verge of firing.

"We surrender, gentlemen," said the Portuguese, who had not lost so much as an atom of his usual cool. "Good Lord! Allow me to congratulate you on this cleverly executed surprise! Well done!"

A man came forward, removed his hat, and addressing Yanez said, "Good to see you again, sir!"

"Great heavens! Lieutenant!"

"In the flesh, Señor Yanez," said the officer with a laugh. "I was certain I'd find you on some nearby shore, the frigate could not have remained afloat much longer."

"You have excellent instincts, sir."

"And also a bit of luck. Were all the convicts killed?"

"We're not certain. You can check the forest for Dyaks if you like, we'll wait hear," Yanez said ironically.

"My mission was to recapture you, the others matter not. We'll leave them to the savages."

"Ah! You came after us! How flattering! Well, now that you have us, what are your plans?"

"We'll take you back to Sarawak and arrange for another ship."

"In those launches?"

"No, we were rescued by a jong. I can assure you, you won't find anyone aboard to help you escape."

"Fortunately, we have allies everywhere," Yanez looked about, then, raising his voice so as to be heard by Sambigliong, who had not left the small launch, laughed and said, "Who knows? We may run across Pangeran Macota or that cunning pirate Sambigliong." Noting that the lieutenant was looking at him with amazement, he added: "A little joke, sir; let's go pay another visit to James Brooke. He may be happy to see us."

He let himself be led to the larger of the two launches and took his place beside Sandokan, Tanauduriam and the Welshman.

Chapter 21
Lord James' Yacht

The two launches had not gone more than three hundred meters when Sambigliong's head emerged from the water behind the bow of the row-boat, which still lay at anchor between two rocks.

Taking advantage of the moment in which the crews of the two crafts were rushing upon Sandokan, Yanez, the Welshman and Tanauduriam, the clever pirate had slipped into the water and hidden behind the reef. Realizing he would have been of greater service to his captains as a free man, he had silently moved away from the shore instead of rushing to their defence.

The reef was forty paces from the beach and he had heard Yanez' last words quite clearly.

"Pangeran Macota," he murmured.

He fully understood what Señor Yanez had meant. The Tiger had been planning to ask Muda Hassim's nephew for help. Sambigliong would relay the message.

He rushed back into the camp and searched the huts and battle grounds, threw anything useful he could find into the small boat, took up the oars and rowed off at full strength.

His plan was simple. He would get a look at the enemy ship, set sail for Mompracem, gather the Tigers, rally Pangeran Macota and his followers, and descend upon Sarawak.

The two launches had already sailed past the southern promontory and were moving away with ever-increasing speed. Sambigliong was quick to follow, maintaining a great distance so as not to be spotted, even though the darkness made it unlikely. It was not long before the pirate spotted two bright points moving south; moments later, he sighted the dim silhouette of a small sailing ship. It must have been the jong that had picked up the frigate's crew. Sambigliong took in his oars and waited, fixing his eyes upon the small ship.

A short while later, two launches drew up beneath the jong's side. Once they were brought aboard, the ship raised anchor and hoisted sail.

"She's heading south," murmured the pirate. "They must be taking the Tiger and Señor Yanez to see the rajah."

Once the ship had set off towards Sarawak, Sambigliong began to row with all his might, heading north. It was not far to Uri, he would reach the island the following night. Once there, he would find a prahu to the Romades or Labuan. If all went well, the Tigers of Mompracem would be battling James Brooke within two weeks.

Sambigliong rowed throughout the night, taking only short rests; by dawn he had reached Cape Sirik, a large promontory at the far end of the vast Bay of Sarawak.

Exhausted by that long exertion, he was about to head towards one of the islands north of the promontory to search for food and a place to rest, when he sighted a beautiful sailboat attempting to round the cape.

"Who could that be?" murmured Sambigliong. "She appears to be coming from Sarawak."

He studied her more closely, attempting to take in every detail, until suddenly, a cry escaped his lips.

"It's a yacht!" he blurted. "Could it be... is it possible!... It would be an incredible stroke of luck!"

He grabbed the oars and began to row with renewed vigour, desperately attempting to cut the vessel's path.

"Yes, it is Lord Guillonk's yacht!" he exclaimed as joy emanated from his eyes. "Perhaps Ada and Kammamuri are aboard. What an unexpected bit of luck! The Tiger of Malaysia and Señor Yanez still have a chance!"

He rowed with fury, summoning all his strength. The small rowboat flew over the large waves.

The yacht rounded the promontory with a second tack and was about to head north. Fearing he would not reach her in time, Sambigliong drew in his oars, quickly armed his rifle and fired a shot into the air.

Several men immediately appeared on the quarterdeck and began to scan the waters with their binoculars. He reloaded his rifle and fired a second shot, then, removed his loincloth, tied it to the barrel and waved it desperately in the air.

There could be no mistaking that signal for help.

The yacht's two mainsails were braced round and the small ship began to move rapidly towards the rowboat. When it was only a hundred meters away, a voice yelled out, "Is that you, Sambigliong?"

"It's me, Kammamuri!" howled the pirate.

"Great Shiva! Sambigliong!"

Lord James and Ada rushed to the railing.

A rope was immediately lowered over the port side.

"How did you get here, alone in that rowboat?" asked Lord James and Kammamuri in unison.

"What happened to Sandokan?" asked Ada.

"And Señor Yanez?" asked Kammamuri.

"They're heading back to Sarawak, sir," said Sambigliong.

"Back to Sarawak!" they exclaimed.

"They were recaptured last night, just as they were about to set sail for Mompracem."

"We heard they were being taken to Norfolk aboard a convict ship," said Lord James. "I knew they would escape. No prison has ever held the Tiger for long. It's only a matter of time before he's back on Mompracem. Tell us everything, Sambigliong."

With a few words, the pirate narrated all that had happened to them aboard the frigate. When Ada and Kammamuri learned that their brave rescuers were to be imprisoned in the rajah's capital until another transport ship arrived, a cry escaped their lips, "We have to free them."

"Let's not rush things, my friends," said Lord James. "Brooke will be on his guard, he won't be fooled so easily."

"Milord," said Sambigliong, "The Tiger of Malaysia had planned to return to Sarawak with the Tigers of Mompracem, join forces with Pangeran Macota and tear the rajah from his throne. The Malays are still loyal to the Sultan's true heir."

"I know."

"Well then, let's put Sandokan's plan into effect," said Ada. "That brave man restored my reason and reunited me with Tremal-Naik; we'll do whatever is necessary to free him and his companions."

"Yes, we'll do whatever has to be done," said Kammamuri.

"We won't be able to do much without the pirates of Mompracem," observed Lord James.

"I'll take care of that," said Sambigliong. "Lend me one of your launches and a few sailors, I'll set sail for Mompracem, gather the pirates and conduct them to Pangeran Macota."

"I have a steam launch; it's at your disposal."

"I'll set off immediately, Milord."

"What about us, what shall we do?" asked Ada.

"We'll go back to Sarawak."

"A word, Milord," said Kammamuri.

"By all means."

"Won't the rajah become suspicious if we return to Sarawak? It would be better if he believed we were still on our way to India."

"That's true," said his lordship, struck by that thought. "He could suspect we were planning to free Sandokan and Yanez."

"Milord," said Sambigliong. "Have you learned where they're keeping Pangeran Macota?"

"Yes, he's in Sedang."

"Imprisoned?"

"Well guarded, under unofficial house arrest."

"If I'm not mistaken, Sedang is near a river of the same name."

"Yes."

"Go and drop anchor at the mouth of that river, within two weeks I'll join you with a fleet from Mompracem. In the meantime, try to approach Pangeran Macota and inform him of our plans."

"Harry," yelled Lord James.

The second in command, a tall handsome man with lightly tanned skin, came forward.

"At your orders, Milord."

"Have the steam launch readied, stock it with provisions, weapons, and enough coal for five days."

The order was executed immediately. Minutes later, four men and a stoker descended into the launch and fired up the engine.

"Any last instructions, Milord?" asked Sambigliong, grabbing onto the ladder.

"Gather your fleet. Rest assured; we'll be waiting for you at the mouth of the Sedang. How many men will you have at your disposal?"

"Two hundred, Milord."

"Do you have enough prahus?"

"We have thirty, armed with forty cannons and sixty firelocks."

"Try to avoid the rajah's fleet."

"We'll be careful."

"Excellent! Best you set sail immediately, time is precious. The launch can reach a speed of ten knots an hour; you should reach Mompracem within two days."

"Good-bye, Milord. See you soon."

Sambigliong climbed down into the launch and gave the command to set sail. A quarter of an hour later, the rapid vessel was no more than a black dot barely visible upon the azure surface of the sea. The yacht had resumed her course eastward, keeping well away from the mouth of the Sarawak to avoid the rajah's coast guard. His lordship did not want anyone to know of his trip to Sedang.

During the night, the rapid ship rounded the cape at the far end of the bay and began her advance towards the coast. The next day, at seven in the evening, she reached the mouth of the Sedang River and dropped anchor in a small basin shaded by tall durian trees and splendid sago palms.

"Do you see anyone, uncle?" asked Ada, who had just come up on deck.

"The mouth of the river is deserted," replied his lordship. "Not many people visit Sedang."

"When do you intend to visit Pangeran Macota?"

"Tomorrow, but we'll need a disguise."

"What do you mean?"

"We'll stand out among the locals. It wouldn't be long before the rajah was informed that some Europeans had arrived in Sedang."

"What shall we do then?"

"Apply a little make up and dress like the natives."

"I'll do whatever's necessary to save Sandokan and his brave friends, uncle."

"Sleep well, Ada. Tomorrow will be quite eventful."

Chapter 22
The Governor of Sedang

Twelve hours later, a launch manned by six Bugi crewmen, his lordship, Ada and Kammamuri was making its way up the river towards Sedang. The sailors had donned their traditional costumes, multicoloured skirts and small turbans; his lordship and Ada, their skin having been dyed a charming bronze, had wrapped themselves in rich, brightly coloured clothing, cinched at the waist by wide sashes of red silk, giving them the appearance of Indian royalty on a pleasure cruise.

Only Kammamuri had retained his Maratha's costume, for it could not have aroused any suspicion. The narrow, muddy river was almost deserted. From time to time, a large Dyak hut appeared on the shore, resting upon rows of posts that towered fifteen or twenty feet above the ground.

Large forests stretched out along the course of water, teeming with luxuriant vegetation. Giunta wan rubber trees, banana trees, gluga trees, areca trees, and immense camphor trees arched and interlaced over piper nigrum plants covered with red berries. Hanging creepers and rotang vines wreathed many a tree, swaying slightly as proboscis monkeys swung among the branches. Giant calaos fluttered about, while flocks of magnificent arguses, black cockatoos and kulang bats made brief appearances among the foliage.

By midday, the launch had made its way up the river, reached Sedang and dropped anchor on the outskirts of the hamlet.

Though Sedang appears on all maps as a city, it is little more than a village about the size of Kuching, the second most important city in the kingdom of Sarawak. At that time, it was comprised of about a hundred huts inhabited by Dyak-lants[6], several small houses with arched roofs that belonged to Chinese merchants, and two villas built of wood. One belonged to the governor, a man absolutely devoted to the rajah, the other to Pangeran Macota, a man determined to retake the throne.

It would not be easy to visit Muda Hassim's nephew, for he was kept under constant surveillance by twenty armed Indian guards. Soldiers patrolled the streets, ready to report any suspicious arrivals.

Since there was not so much as a modest inn in all of Sedang, his lordship bought one of the nicest Chinese homes at the northern end of the city, led Ada and Kammamuri there, then turned to his niece and said, "This is as far as I can take you. I've done everything I could do without compromising my honour as a British officer and one of James Brooke's fellow countrymen. I cannot participate in the revolt that you and the pirates plan to incite, even though I cannot condone the excessive severity used against Tremal-Naik. The state of Sarawak may be completely independent, but it does have ties with England. I remain your uncle and guardian, but as an Englishman, I must remain neutral."

"You're leaving?" Ada asked sadly.

"I must. I'm going back to my yacht; we'll sail to the mouth of the river. We'll remain there until hostilities have begun, on the off chance you may need my help. From what I've seen, you're quite able to act on your own."

"Thank you, uncle!"

"I've assigned four men to assist you. They'll obey you as they do me; they're men of proven courage and unquestionable loyalty. Good-bye, then! Should you find yourselves in danger, send one of them to me. My yacht will immediately make her way up river."

They embraced at length then his lordship got into the boat and headed down the river. Rooted to the shore, the young woman watched him sail off towards the horizon, unaware that one of the rajah's guards had been studying her with great interest and was now slowly advancing towards her.

"Who are you?" asked the guard, drawing up beside her.

---

[6] Coastal Dyaks

The young woman started then cast a sharp and haughty look upon the Indian.

"What do you want?" she asked.

"To know who you are," replied the Indian.

"That's none of your concern."

"Those are my orders; you are not from here."

"Whose orders?"

"The governor's."

"I've never met him."

"Nevertheless, he must be informed of all those that visit Sedang."

"And why is that?"

"Pangeran Macota is here."

"Who would that be?"

"The nephew of the former Sultan of Sarawak."

"I've never had the pleasure of meeting the Sultan or his nephew."

"It does not matter; I have to know who you are."

"I am an Indian princess."

"From the proud tribes of the Marathas," said Kammamuri, who had silently made his way towards them.

"A Maratha princess!" exclaimed the Indian with a start. "I'm a Maratha."

"No, you are a traitor," said Kammamuri. "If you were a true Maratha, you would be as free as I am, not a slave to one of our British oppressors."

For an instant, anger flashed in the soldier's eyes then he bowed his head and murmured, "You're right."

"Go," said Kammamuri. "Free Marathas despise all traitors."

The Indian started then raised his head; his eyes were wet with tears.

"No," he said sadly, "I have not forgotten my country; I have not abandoned my tribe. I'll always be ready to fight against India's oppressors, I'm still a Maratha."

"Give me some proof!" said Kammamuri with even more disdain.

"You need but ask."

"Very well, my mistress is a princess from one of our bravest tribes. If you are indeed a true Maratha, swear obedience to her as do all the free sons of our mountains!"

The Indian rapidly scanned the surrounding area to ensure that no one was watching, then fell to Ada's feet, put his forehead to the ground and said, "I am yours to command. I swear by Shiva, Vishnu and Brahma, divine protectors of India, that I will obey your every word."

"I recognize you as a brother," said Kammamuri. "Come!"

They returned to the house; four sailors guarded the door, hands resting on the butts of their pistols, ready to defend their commander's niece at the first sign of attack. Once inside, they entered a room furnished with bamboo chairs and papered with a Fung floral print. Teapots and small porcelain cups cluttered several small tables.

"I await your orders," repeated the Indian, prostrating himself before Ada once again.

The young woman studied him for awhile, as if attempting to read into the depths of his soul.

"I hate the rajah," she said, after a brief silence.

"What!" exclaimed the Indian, raising his head and looking at her in amazement.

"Yes," the young woman said energetically.

"Has he harmed you?"

"No, I hate him because he is British, I hate him because I am a Maratha and his people are oppressing our nation, I hate him because he was once part of the army that destroyed our rajah's freedom. Those of us that remain free have pledged eternal hatred against all Europeans."

"Are you powerful?" asked the Indian, his amazement increasing.

"I have brave men, ships and cannons at my command."

"Have you come to declare war?"

"Yes, Rajah Brooke's reign must come to an end."

"Who's going to assist you in this undertaking?"

"Pangeran Macota."

"What!"

"Yes."

"But he's still a prisoner!"

"We'll free him."

"Does he know of your plans?"

"Not yet, but I'll inform him."

"He's well guarded."

"We'll get around the guards."

"How?"

"You'll find a way."

"Me!"

"That will be your test, if you wish to prove to me that you truly are a Maratha."

"I've sworn to obey you and Bangawadi will not go back on his word," said the Indian solemnly.

"Listen," said Kammamuri, who until then had remained silent. "How many men guard Macota?"

"Four."

"Night and day?"

"Always."

"He's never alone?"

"Never."

"Are there any Marathas among those Indians?"

"No, they're all Gujaratis."

"All loyal to the Governor?"

"Incorruptible."

Kammamuri gestured angrily, fell silent and immersed himself in thought. A moment later, he thrust his hand into the large sash fastened about his waist and drew out a diamond as large as a hazelnut.

"Go to the governor," he said, turning towards the Indian, "And tell him that Princess Raibh offers him this gift and begs to have an audience with him."

"What are you up to, Kammamuri?" asked Ada.

"I'll tell you in a moment, Mistress. Bangawadi, we're counting on your pledge."

The Indian took the diamond, prostrated himself before the young woman one last time and quickly left the room.

Kammamuri watched him disappear down the street then turned towards Ada.

"So far so good," he said.

"What are you up to, Kammamuri?" repeated Ada

Instead of replying, the Maratha drew a small box from the folds of his sash and opened it. It contained several tiny pills.

"Señor Yanez gave them to me," he said, "Slip one into a glass of water, wine or tea and even the strongest person will fall asleep."

"How do you plan to use them?" asked the young woman, amazed.

"We'll drug the governor and Macota's guards."

"I don't follow you."

"Once he's received the gift, the governor will undoubtedly invite us to lunch. I'll make sure he drinks the narcotic, then once he's asleep, we'll go visit Macota and play the same trick on his guards."

"Do you think the guards will allow us to visit the prisoner?"

"Bangawadi will introduce us, claiming that the visit has been authorized by the governor."

"Where will we take the prisoner?"

"Wherever he wishes to go; wherever his supporters are. I'll have our men buy a few horses."

He was about to leave when he spotted Bangawadi making his way back towards the house, smiling happily.

"The governor wishes to receive you," he said, upon entering.

"So he liked the gift?" asked Kammamuri.

"I've never seen him happier."

"Well then, best not to keep him waiting," said the Maratha.

They left, the guard leading the way. The four sailors accompanied them, having been ordered not to leave Ada's side. A few minutes later, they arrived at the residence of the Governor of Sedang.

That building, pompously called a palace by the city's inhabitants, was a modest two-story wooden house, its roof covered with the blue tiles common among the buildings in the Chinese quarter of Sarawak. It was defended by a palisade and two rusty pieces of artillery, kept there mainly for show, for they could not have fired more than two successive rounds without exploding. A dozen barefoot Indians dressed like Bengali Sepoys, in red jackets, white pants, and turbans, were stationed in front of the enclosure and presented arms at the sight of the Maratha Princess. The governor had come to greet the young woman at the foot of the stairs, a sure sign that the expensive gift had made a favourable impression.

Sir Hunton, the Governor of Sedang, was an Anglo-Indian that had been the quartermaster aboard the *Royalist* during the bloody expedition against the pirates of Borneo. He was forty years old, but seemed older, the tough tropical climate having aged him beyond his years. He was tall and muscular, with light bronze skin, dark black eyes, and a thick grizzled beard. Having shown great courage and loyalty, he was given command of Sedang and entrusted with keeping Pangeran Macota under constant surveillance. James Brooke was well aware that Muda Hassim's nephew was a powerful, dangerous rival.

At the sight of the Indian princess, Sir Hunton, removed his hat, bowed, then gallantly offered his arm and led her into a parlour furnished with elegant European furniture.

"To what good fortunate do I owe the honour of your visit, Highness?" he asked, sitting down opposite the young woman. "Our small city seldom plays host to such distinguished visitors."

"I'm on a pleasure cruise, visiting the islands of the Sunda, sir. I've been told there were Dyak headhunters living in Sedang. I was hoping to catch a glimpse of them."

"You came here out of curiosity? I thought perhaps you had another reason."

"What would that be?"

"To see Pangeran Macota."

"Who is that?"

"One of Rajah Brooke's rivals; he passes his time dreaming about conspiracies."

"Sounds like an interesting man."

"Most assuredly."

"With your permission I would like to visit him."

"If it were any other person I would not allow it. But for you, Highness, seeing as you're from India and merely seek to satisfy your traveler's curiosity, I will most certainly oblige."

"Thank you, sir."

"Are you going to remain here long?"

"Several days, as long as it takes my crew to make repairs aboard my yacht."

"And then you'll set sail for Sarawak?"

"Certainly; I wish to see the rajah. He's quite legendary and I am one of his most ardent admirers."

"Yes, Rajah Brooke is a brave man! Are you going back to your yacht this evening?"

"No, I've rented a small house."

"Then I hope you will give me the honour of accepting my hospitality. It's the best in Sedang."

"Thank you, sir, that's very generous, but I must decline."

"I hope you will at least spend the day with me then."

"I could not refuse such courtesy. Can we visit your royal prisoner as well?" asked Ada.

"We'll have tea with Macota after dinner, Highness."

"Is he a gentleman or a savage warrior?"

"He's a clever, educated man. We will be well received."

"I'm looking forward to it, sir. I'll dine with you this evening."

She had gotten up at a sign from Kammamuri, who had kept to a corner of the room throughout the conversation. The governor did so as well and escorted her to the gate, where the Indian guard saluted her with the honours due an Indian princess.

She returned to her house escorted, as always, by Kammamuri and the four Indians from the yacht. The Indian Bangawadi sat waiting by her door.

"You again?" asked the young woman.

"Yes, Mistress," he replied.

"Any news?"

"I've talked with Macota."

"When?"

"A few minutes ago."

"What did you tell him?"

"That we're going to help him escape."

"What did he reply?"

"He'll be ready."

"You're a good man, Bangawadi."

"We'll be even more grateful if you go back to him with a message," added Kammamuri.

"I'm at your disposal."

"Tell him that the Princess Raibh will pay him a visit tonight. She'll be accompanied by the governor and her secretary. He must ensure the three of us are alone and arrange it so that I can prepare the tea for the governor."

Then taking a small diamond from his belt, he gave it to him and added, "This is for you, buy drinks for the sentries guarding Macota's home. Later tonight, I'll treat them to another round!"

Chapter 23
Pangeran Macota Escapes

Believing he was in the company of an authentic Indian princess, Sir Hunton played host with the greatest courtesy, sparing no expense, wanting to show his gratitude for the diamond she had given him.

The lunch offered the princess could not have been better. The cook had raided the pantry, the Dyaks' chicken coops and all the fish hatcheries. The Governor had even supplied authentic bottles of Spanish wine, gifts from a friend in the Philippines he had been preserving for a special occasion. It was a pleasant meal and lasted several hours, the guests finishing their pudding shortly after sunset.

"Has Pangeran Macota been informed of our visit?" asked Ada.

"He's expecting us for tea, Highness," replied Sir Hunton.

"Then we shouldn't keep him waiting," observed Ada, casting a glance outdoors. "It's getting dark, Governor."

"As you wish."

"It looks like a lovely evening, let's walk along the shore."

She got up and draped a silk mantilla over her head to defend her from the damp night air. Kammamuri, who had also taken part in the meal in his capacity as secretary to the lovely princess, had already left. Two sailors from the yacht were waiting for him by the river.

"Has everything been prepared?" he asked.

"Yes," they replied.

"How many horses have you bought?"

"Eight."

"Where are they?"

"On the outskirts of the forest."

"Well done, go and join the others"

253

Ada came out of the building on the governor's arm. Kammamuri drew up beside her and quickly gestured that all was ready.

The night was magnificent. In the east, a pink cloud marked the place where the sun had set. The sky was quickly filling with stars, their soft light reflecting against the placid waters of the river.

Giant bats flitted through the air as small Draco lizards wandered among the foliage. To-chi lizards emerged from their hiding places, heralding the night with cries of To-chi! To-chi!

On the river, a few boatmen sang their monotonous tunes, as Chinese junks came alight in the glow of their large, paper lanterns.

A thousand fragrances wafted in from the nearby forest; camphor trees, walnut trees, carnation plants and mangosteens filled the air with their exotic perfumes.

Ada remained silent, trying as best she could to quicken their pace, but the governor had drunk a bit too much and staggered slowly as he took in deep breaths of the night air.

Fortunately, they did not have far to travel. A few minutes later, they found themselves before the palace that belonged to the Sultan's heir: a modest abode, a simple two-story cottage with a verandah. Four armed Indian soldiers stood guard.

After having himself announced, the governor led the princess into a small parlour furnished with old divans and threadbare carpets. Several mirrors hung from the wall, a large table stood in the centre, cluttered with cups, teapots, and Chinese knickknacks.

Pangeran Macota was seated upon an old battered chair, crowned by a small gilded gavial[7], the emblem of the Sultans of Sarawak.

James Brooke's rival was thirty years old. He was tall and of noble bearing, with lightly tanned skin, long dark hair, intense, intelligent eyes and a handsome face framed by a magnificent black beard.

He wore the green turban of the Sultans of Borneo and was dressed in long robes of white silk. Two krises, standard among great leaders, peered from the folds of the red silk sash round his waist; a golok, a long, sharp, heavy, Malay sabre of iron, hung from his side.

---

[7] A type of crocodile commonly found in the rivers of Borneo.

At the sight of the governor, the Pangeran stood up and bowed courteously, then fixed his eyes upon the young woman and said, "Welcome to my home."

"The Princess Raibh expressed her desire to meet you; I thought a visit might amuse you," replied the governor.

"I thank you for the courtesy, sir. The distractions in this city are so rare, visits even more so! Rajah Brooke's precautions have left me quite isolated."

"You know the rajah does not trust you."

"His fears are unfounded; I no longer have any supporters. Rajah Brooke's wise administration has taken them all from me."

"The Dyaks yes, but the Malays..."

"They have abandoned me as well, Sir Hunton, but enough talk of politics, allow me to offer you some refreshments."

"I've heard tell you have some excellent tea in your possession," the governor said with a laugh.

"Real flower tea from China. My friend Tai-Sin always brings me some when he comes to Sedang."

"I'm looking forward to tasting it," replied Sir Hunton.

The Sultan's nephew clapped his hands and instantly the sound of clinking teacups emanated from the adjoining room. Kammamuri quickly slipped through the door. Moments later, he reappeared with a short Malay servant carrying a tea service upon a silver tray.

The clever Maratha poured the delicious beverage, slipping a pill into the cup destined for the governor. It dissolved almost immediately. He offered the first cup to his mistress, the second to Sir Hunton and the third to the Sultan's nephew then returned to the adjoining room. He quickly filled four more, dissolved as many pills then turned to the Malay and said, "Come with me, bring the tray."

"Are there other guests, sir?" asked the servant.

"Yes," replied the Maratha, smiling mysteriously. "Is there another way out of here that does not lead through the parlour?"

"Yes."

"Lead the way."

255

The Malay led him through a third small room and out a door that let out onto the street. The four guards stood a few paces from them.

"Gentleman," said the Maratha, moving towards them. "My mistress, Princess Raibh, offers you some of Macota's tea. Drink to her health, and please accept these rupees with her compliments."

The four Indians did not wait to be asked twice. They quickly pocketed the rupees, toasted the health of the munificent princess and gulped down the tea in one shot.

"Good evening, gentlemen," said Kammamuri, as a smile spread across his lips.

He went back to the drawing room, arriving just as the governor, overpowered by the powerful narcotic, rolled out of his chair and crashed heavily onto the carpet.

"Sleep well," said the Maratha.

Ada and Macota got up.

"Dead?" asked the Pangeran, an almost savage tone in his voice.

"No, just asleep," replied Ada.

"So he could awaken?"

"The effects last for twenty-four hours. We'll be quite far from here by then."

"Then it's true you've come to free me?"

"Yes."

"And help me reclaim my ancestral throne?"

"Also true!"

"But why? What do you expect in return?"

"We'll discuss it later; it's time to escape."

"I'm ready, just give the orders."

"Do you have any supporters?"

"All Malays are with me!"

"What about the Dyaks?"

"They'll fight for Rajah Brooke."

"Do you know a safe place where we can await the arrival of your men?"

"Yes, my friend Orang Tuah has a kampong. We'll be safe there."

"Is it far?"

"It's near the mouth of the river."

"Excellent. Time to go; we've arranged for some horses."

"What about the guards?"

"They're asleep," said Kammamuri.

"Let's go," repeated Ada.

The Pangeran gathered some gems from a small coffer, removed a rifle from the wall, cast a last glance upon the governor then went off with Ada and Kammamuri.

The four Indians were lying in front of the door, one atop the other, fast asleep. Kammamuri relieved them of their carbines and cartridges then let out a sharp whistle.

Bangawadi and the four sailors from the yacht emerged from the nearby forest, leading eight horses. Kammamuri helped his mistress mount one of the fastest, then nimbly hopped onto another and said, "Let's go!"

Led by the Pangeran, the squad left at a gallop, following the river along the edge of the forest. The group had arrived at the outskirts of the city, when suddenly a voice cried out from the opposite shore.

"Who goes there?"

"No one answer," said the Pangeran.

"Who goes there?" the voice repeated menacingly.

Not receiving a reply, the guard, who despite the darkness must have spotted that group on horseback, fired and shouted, "To arms!"

The bullet whistled over the riders and disappeared into the nearby trees.

The response was immediate. Alerted by the rifle blast, the sentries guarding the governor's palace raised the alarm, filling the air with cries of, "To arms! To arms!"

"Full speed!" yelled Kammamuri.

The horses bolted forward and the band of riders raced up the shore. When they had gone a mile, they forded the river and took a road that led to the coast.

"Do you think they're following?" Ada asked the Pangeran.

"I'm afraid so, Miss," replied Macota. "By now they'll have found the governor and learned of my escape. They'll be after us before long."

"But there are only twenty of them."

"Sixteen, Miss, four are asleep."

"So much the better. It should be easy to fend them off."

"They'll summon reinforcements from the Dyak village and within twelve hours we'll have two or three hundred armed men at our heels."

"How long before we reach the kampong?"

"We'll be there within two hours; it's well defended and can easily hold off an attack. Within two days I'll have gathered five or six thousand Malays and about a hundred prahus."

"Are the prahus armed with cannons?"

"Some of them are; they should suffice to attack Brooke's fleet."

"With any luck, you'll receive a good supply of artillery within four or five days."

"Artillery?" the Pangeran exclaimed, amazed.

"Yes, a present from the most formidable pirates in all of Borneo."

"From who?"

"The pirates of Mompracem."

"Mompracem!?! The Tiger of Malaysia is coming to my aid?"

"Not in person, but his men are sailing towards the Bay of Sarawak as we speak."

"But where is Sandokan?"

"In the rajah's hands."

"He's been imprisoned? Impossible!"

"His forces were outnumbered. He was taken prisoner after a terrible battle, along with a few of his men and my fiancé. I helped you escape so you could help me rescue them."

"Where are they now?"

"Sarawak."

"We'll free them, Miss, I promise. Once the Malays learn the pirates of Mompracem have joined the battle, they'll flock to my banner. James Brooke's days are numbered."

"Halt!" yelled a voice at that moment.

The Pangeran reigned in his horse, quickly positioned himself in front of the young woman and unsheathed his golok.

"Who goes there?" he yelled.

"The warriors of Orang Tuah."

"Tell your leader that Pangeran Macota requests the pleasure of his hospitality."

He turned to Ada and pointed to a dark mass at the edge of the forest.

"There's the kampong!" he said, "We're safe!"

Chapter 24
The Defeat of James Brooke

Orang Tuah's kampong was a large Malay village comprised of three hundred wooden huts with thatched roofs of nipa leaves. It was defended by tall, thick palisades and dense thickets of thorny bamboo, insuperable obstacles for the barefooted warriors of the native tribes. Those defences were common among the villages of Borneo, subject to constant raids by the inland people and endless wars with the Dyak tribes. In addition, the inhabitants could also count upon a half dozen prahus equipped with firelocks anchored in a small lake that communicated with the sea by way of the canal.

Orang Tuah, a well-built, dark-skinned Malay with almond-shaped eyes and prominent cheekbones, had scoured the seas in the days before James Brooke's bloody campaign. Promptly informed of the Pangeran's arrival, he rushed to meet him, accompanied by a large number of torchbearers.

The small squad was enthusiastically received. The entire population, awakened by the tom-toms, ran en masse to celebrate the arrival of the future sovereign of Sarawak. Orang Tuah led his guests into the best part of the village. Informed that the governor's guards were in pursuit, he immediately sent fifty men armed with rifles into the nearby forests to await the first attack.

Those measures having been taken, he summoned his lieutenants and advisors and ordered them to gather a large body of soldiers and begin the insurrection in the Malay villages, before the news of the Pangeran's escape could reach Sarawak.

That same night forty emissaries left for the interior and three prahus set sail to spread word to the Malays along the coast that a great battle was brewing; two other ships were sent to patrol Cape Sirik to lead the pirates of Mompracem to the kampong.

In the meantime, Ada had dispatched one of the sailors to the yacht anchored at the mouth of the river to warn Lord James of the upcoming battle.

The next day the first reinforcements arrived in the kampong. Bands of Malays, armed with rifles, sabres and krises had flocked from all over to fight beneath the Pangeran's banner. An endless procession of prahus sailed in from the sea, manned by large crews and equipped with artillery.

Three days later, seven thousand Malays were camped around the kampong, awaiting the arrival of the pirates of Mompracem to begin their march toward Sarawak.

All paths into the interior had been blocked to prevent the Dyaks from carrying news of the impending insurrection to the rajah. Security had been so tight it was unlikely that Brooke even knew of his adversary's escape.

On the fifth day, the fleet from Mompracem dropped anchor before the shores of the kampong. It consisted of twenty-four large prahus armed with forty cannons and sixty firelocks. Two hundred battle-hardened warriors manned the decks, each pirate worth five men in courage and experience.

As soon as he disembarked, Sambigliong went to report to Ada; she had been given lodgings in Orang Tuah's hut.

"Miss," he said, "The Tigers of Mompracem are ready to descend upon Sarawak. They have sworn to free Sandokan and his friends or die in the attempt."

"The Malays were only waiting for your arrival to begin the insurrection," replied the young woman. "However, before you set off, promise me that you will not harm James Brooke and that, if you do defeat him, you'll set him free."

"It shall be done. You speak for our captain, your word is law."

Two hours later, the Malay army, led by the future Sultan, left the kampong, taking the road along the shore, while the fleet from Mompracem, which had taken aboard Ada and Kammamuri, sailed off, leading a squadron of another hundred prahus drawn from the villages along the vast Bay of Sarawak.

All measures had been taken for a surprise attack upon the rajah's capital and plans had been set for a simultaneous strike from land and sea.

The fleet was sailing slowly to give the troops the time to advance and get into position, at night it gathered off the coast to wait for Macota's messengers. As they drew close to their destination, Sambigliong took great pains to restrain the impatient Tigers of Mompracem who burned with the desire to avenge their captain's defeat.

Four days later, toward sunset, the flotilla arrived at the mouth of the river. That same night, Macota's troops were to move on the capital.

Sambigliong, in command of the Tigers of Mompracem, ordered the prahu transporting Ada to remain hidden in a small inlet by the mouth of the river, so as not to expose the young woman to the dangers of battle; Kammamuri climbed aboard the captain's vessel, not wanting to remain inactive now that the battle was at hand.

"Bring me back Tremal-Naik," said Ada before he departed.

"I'll make sure the master is safe, even if it costs me my life," replied the brave Maratha. "Once we land, I'll take some men and surround the rajah's palace, I'm certain the prisoners are being kept there."

"Go, my brave friend. May God protect you!"

Sambigliong issued the final orders. Armed with cannons and manned by the bravest pirates of Mompracem, the largest prahus were sent to lead the squadron.

At ten that night, the flotilla was rapidly making its way up the river. All sails had been lowered and the small ships advanced under the power of their oars.

The river appeared deserted; not a single soldier patrolling the forest, not a single enemy vessel along either shore.

However, that silence did not reassure Sambigliong. The insurgency had been sweeping across the kingdom for the last five days and it was highly unlikely that no news of it had reached the capital. The rajah, an audacious man, faithfully served by the Dyaks and his Indian guard, would not let himself be caught by surprise. He feared a trap somewhere near the city and kept his eyes open, listening for the slightest suspicious sound. By midnight, the flotilla was only a half-mile from Sarawak and the first houses began to appear against the dark horizon.

"Do you hear anything?" Sambigliong asked Kammamuri who was standing at his side.

"Nothing," replied the Maratha.

"The silence is disturbing. Macota should have arrived by now and started the attack."

"He may be waiting to hear our cannons."

"Ah!"

"What is it?"

"The fleet!"

The rajah's ships had appeared just past the river bend, waiting in battle formation, ready to attack.

Twenty flashes of light suddenly tore through the darkness, followed by a thunderous explosion. Brooke's fleet had unleashed an infernal fire against the pirate squadron.

A thunderous cry erupted along the river, "Long live Mompracem! Long live Macota!"

Almost simultaneously, a furious discharge of musket fire emanated from the north of the city. Macota's troops were attacking the capital.

"Attack, Tigers of Mompracem!" thundered Sambigliong. "Long live the Tiger of Malaysia!"

The prahus rushed towards the rajah's ships, ignoring the grapeshot sweeping their decks and slicing their rigging. Nothing could withstand the onslaught of Sandokan's men. In a flash, the numerous vessels manned by the intrepid pirates of Malaysia surrounded the enemy. Tigers and Malays climbed up the sides of the ships, jumped over the bulwarks, and stormed the decks. Unable to fend off such a furious attack, the crews were quickly surrounded, disarmed and forced into the holds and battery decks. The rajah's colors were taken down and replaced by the standard of Mompracem: a red flag emblazoned with the head of a tiger.

"To Sarawak!" thundered Kammamuri and Sambigliong.

The prahus set off to attack the city. In the meantime, the battle undertaken by the Malay troops raged relentlessly in the streets of the capital.

Musketry thundered throughout the canals and districts. Howls filled the air as the Malays advanced towards the rajah's palace.

Several houses blazed throughout the city, bathing the streets in a crimson light as clouds of sparks wafted over the countryside.

Sambigliong and Kammamuri landed upon the quay at the head of four hundred men and invaded the Chinese district where the inhabitants had also begun to fight. A squadron of Indian guards tried to repel them with two volleys, but the Tigers of Mompracem, clutching their scimitars, rushed forward and scattered them with their first attack.

"To the palace!" howled Kammamuri.

Leading those formidable men forward, he reached the great square. A fist full of guards had remained to defend the rajah's palace but quickly dispersed after a brief resistance.

"Long live the Tiger of Malaysia!" thundered the pirates of Mompracem.

A voice, as clear as a trumpet, replied from inside the palace: "Long live Mompracem!"

It was Sandokan.

The Tigers recognized it immediately. They burst up the stairs, smashing through doors and barricades, frenziedly searching for their friends, until finally, in a cell defended by thick iron bars; they found Sandokan, Yanez, Tremal-Naik and Tanauduriam.

They did not give them the time to speak. Immediately freed, the four were carried triumphantly into the square to the sound of deafening cries. At that exact moment, a wave of fleeing Indians, routed by Macota's troops, poured into the plaza. Sandokan grabbed a scimitar from one of his men and rushed in among the escapees, followed by Yanez, Tremal-Naik and twenty other men. Though the Indians scattered, one man held his ground, James Brooke, his clothing torn, his eyes threatening, still clutching his blood-soaked sabre.

"You're mine!" shouted Sandokan.

"You!" the rajah exclaimed darkly. "You again!"

"I had a score to settle, Excellency."

"Excellency! That title means nothing now. Macota has taken Sarawak; he'll take me prisoner and seek swift vengeance."

"No, James Brooke, you are free to go," said Sandokan, clearing a path for him. "Sambigliong! Take His Excellency to the mouth of the river. Guard him with your life."

The former-rajah looked at Sandokan in amazement, then, spotting a band of Macota's Malays charging into the square shouting cries of 'Death to the Rajah', he quickly went off with Sambigliong and an escort of thirty men.

"And so ends the reign of Rajah James Brooke!" said Sandokan. "He'll never return to these shores." [8]

Conclusion

The next day, Pangeran Macota entered James Brooke's palace with great pomp, taking his place in the ancient seat of the Sultans of Sarawak. The entire population of the city who had never forgiven the former rajah his European ancestry, despite the great improvements introduced by that wise, brave, energetic man, mixed with the insurrectionist troops. The new sultan was not ungrateful towards his allies: he offered Sandokan, Yanez and Tremal-Naik honours and riches, and begged them to remain in his kingdom, but all politely refused.

Two days later, Tremal-Naik and Ada, happily married, along with Kammamuri, embarked upon Lord James' yacht and set sail for India, taking with them several valuable presents. Sandokan and Yanez had

---

[8] Sandokan's words proved prophetic: James Brooke never returned to Sarawak. Weakened by fever, stricken with paralysis, and deprived of means, he retired to England where he would have died in poverty had it not been for a public subscription that provided him with several thousands of pounds. He died in 1868, in Devon almost forgotten, after having made the entire world speak of him during his reign.

come to see them off before joining their men and returning to Mompracem.

"When shall we meet again?" Ada, Tremal-Naik and Lord James asked the Tiger of Malaysia, as they were about to part.

"Who knows!" replied Sandokan, embracing them all in turn. "India is very tempting, perhaps one day the Tiger of Malaysia and the Tiger of the Sundarbans will cross blades among the deserted islands of the Ganges. Suyodhana! There's a man I wish to lay eyes upon. Farewell, my friends. Until we meet again, may good fortune greet you at every corner."

The Next Title

The Two Tigers

Just when Tremal-Naik's life was getting back to normal, the Thugs of the Kali cult return to exact their revenge by kidnapping his daughter Darma. Summoned by Kammamuri, Sandokan and Yanez immediately set sail for India to help their loyal friend. But the evil sect knows of their arrival and thwarts them at every turn. Have our heroes finally met their match? It's the Tiger of Malaysia versus the Tiger of India in a fight to the death!

The first two titles

The Mystery of the Black Jungle

An apparition has been haunting Tremal-Naik, the renowned Hunter of the Black Jungle. Try as he may, he cannot shake the hold it has over him. But when one of his hunters is mysteriously murdered, Tremal-Naik must put his feelings aside and obtain vengeance. Accompanied by his faithful servant Kammamuri, he heads deep into the jungles of the Sundarbans and discovers an evil sect that threatens all of British India.

The Tigers of Mompracem

The Tigers of Mompracem are a band of rebel pirates fighting for the defence of tiny native kingdoms against the colonial powers of the Dutch and British empires. They are lead by Sandokan, the indomitable "Tiger of Malaysia", and his faithful friend Yanez De Gomera, a Portuguese wanderer and adventurer. Orphaned when the British murdered his family and stole his throne, Sandokan has been mercilessly leading his men in vengeance. But when the pirate learns of the extraordinary "Pearl of Labuan" his fortunes begin to change...perhaps forever....

For more information contact: info@rohpress.com

LaVergne, TN USA
04 December 2010
207391LV00004B/116/A